THE LOCKET

The Locket

Lisa Arnold

Copyright © 2020 by Lisa Arnold.

Library of Congress Control Number:		2020913195
ISBN:	Hardcover	978-1-6641-2021-1
	Softcover	978-1-6641-2020-4
	eBook	978-1-6641-2019-8

All rights reserved. No part of this book may be reproduced or transmitted in any form or by any means, electronic or mechanical, including photocopying, recording, or by any information storage and retrieval system, without permission in writing from the copyright owner.

This is a work of fiction. All of the characters, names, incidents, organizations, and dialogue in this novel are either the products of the author's imagination or are used fictitiously.

Any people depicted in stock imagery provided by Getty Images are models, and such images are being used for illustrative purposes only. Certain stock imagery © Getty Images.

Print information available on the last page.

Rev. date: 09/09/2020

To order additional copies of this book, contact:
Xlibris
844-714-8691
www.Xlibris.com
Orders@Xlibris.com
812826

Chapter 1

August 1944

    The day was hot in Barnesville, Georgia, as Margaret drove her light blue Ford down the longest dirt road in Lamar County. Margaret's father owned the local Ford dealership and had selected the sleek vehicle for his youngest daughter the last time Henry was home from the war. Margaret recalled telling Henry that a car was a necessity for her while he was overseas. Relying on her parents for transportation was becoming such an imposition. Besides, everyone in the county expected Charles Harris's daughter to have a car. But Henry was too proud to take his father-in-law's handout. Henry's wife would not own a car until he could afford to place it in the driveway, and that had been made clear to his new in-laws.

    Margaret looked down at her swollen belly raking against the bottom of the steering wheel and felt happy and content but a bit uncomfortable. Even with the windows down and the breeze whipping through the automobile, beads of sweat rolled down her temples. The pregnancy had been hard with Henry away from home, and the entire town was awaiting the birth of Margaret's first child. The due date was a week away, and all details had been completed for the new arrival.

    "Now you jes git yosef down dat Old Mt. Zion road and drive a lil' fast," Mattie told Margaret early that morning. "Make show ya hit a few holes too," she continued. "If'n you want dat baby ta come any time soon." Mattie's eyes flashed black as coal, and the wrinkles deepened in the dark skin of her forehead as she imparted her good southern wisdom. Mattie had worked for the Harris family going on thirty years and had raised both Margaret and her sister, Anne.

"Now I can always give ya a good dose o' castor oil," Mattie shouted as Margaret slammed the screen door behind her.

"I think the dirt road will suit me just fine," Margaret yelled as she walked to the Ford. Margaret smiled now, remembering the exchange with her dear Mattie and thinking about what a help she would be when the baby arrived.

The day was hotter than usual, even for August. There was something comforting about the heat and the abundant crepe myrtles blooming by the side of the road. Margaret pulled off the road, feeling that she had sustained enough high-speed dirt road bumping for any pregnant woman in her ninth month. She walked beneath a large crepe myrtle tree and pulled some blossoms from the heavy branches. The blossoms were a fiery fuchsia color; she tucked them behind one ear to mix and mingle with her shiny black curls. She sat down in the shade under a tree by a small brook and pitched some of the blossoms into the water. It made her feel girlish again to watch the blossoms float by on the surface of the water while she remembered childhood picnics in that very field.

Her girlish days would be over soon. The arrival of a baby heralded the beginning of true womanhood for a young southern lady living in Barnesville. The little town had organized several baby showers, and Margaret's nursery was now complete. All that was left to do was the waiting. Of course, Margaret had lots of sympathetic souls to give her advice on how to deal with these last few weeks of confinement, as they termed it. Not that Margaret would always take their advice. There was a lot of talk when she had insisted on working at her teaching position at the local high school through the middle part of June. Margaret's mother, Joan, had endured countless catty remarks from gossipmongers over at the beauty parlor.

Margaret pulled Henry's letter from her pocket as she dangled her feet into the cool water of the brook. She had received the letter that morning and was anxious to read it in private. His letters usually brought tears to her eyes, and today would be no different. The last two years had been difficult, and Margaret yearned for the day when the war was over and Henry would be home for good. Though they had been married for several years, the war had separated them and forced them to marry in a scandalous fashion, according to Margaret's mother. A hurried civil marriage ceremony conducted by a justice of the peace was followed by Henry's return to duty in the Army Corps of Engineers. A larger Barnesville wedding took place a year later to calm the wagging tongues of the county and improve Joan's social reputation.

Margaret could still remember her mother admonishing her. "A civil ceremony is just so common," Joan raved. "Your father and I do not like this man being ten years older than you, and we have kept our mouths shut about that. I simply refuse to allow all of these old bitties around here to discuss this for the next year. You will have a church wedding just like your sister, Anne, and I will announce plans for this wedding at my bridge club meeting tomorrow."

There would be no stopping Joan when her mind was made up, and Margaret knew not to waste time arguing. Margaret knew when she and Henry chose to live in this small town that they would be bound by old southern traditions and the Harris family name. The yolk often chafed.

Margaret gazed at the return address of the letter in her hand, reading the name Lt. Colonel Henry Montgomery with pride. Henry had been promoted quickly during wartime from captain in 1941 to lieutenant colonel during the summer of 1944. He was now stationed deep in the Far East. Margaret read each line of the letter carefully, and as she hungered for Henry's touch, tears sprang to her eyes. She brushed the tears away, fighting her private anger with the war for cheating her of this time with Henry.

She released a heavy sigh while getting up from the bank of the brook to walk back to her car. The blue Ford had been purchased from her father's car lot last year. Henry had been a bit reluctant to buy a used automobile, but the war had forced Ford to cease manufacturing new cars for the time being. Margaret felt a twinge of guilt for using up all of her gas rations riding up and down the Old Mt. Zion road.

"Mattie is so full of foolishness," Margaret thought aloud. "My gasoline is almost gone, and I bet this baby won't come for another two weeks." Not knowing how true her prophecy would be, she drove the car back to her childhood home.

When Margaret turned the blue Ford into the driveway, she spied Granny Harris rocking slowly in one of the old cane rockers on the front porch. Granny was in her early seventies now and had moved in with Joan and Charles about two years ago after falling in her own home. Her body was becoming feeble, but her mind was as quick as ever. Granny was portly and cinched in all of her excess flesh with an expanse of girdle and a long-line brassiere. Margaret had always chuckled whenever she witnessed all of the tugging and huffing required to squeeze Granny into what she considered to be the latest youthful fashion.

"And this old white hair is starting to look just like cotton again," Granny would exclaim. "Joan, you simply must take me to the beauty parlor a little early this week. Marie needs to put on another application of that sweet silver rinse." Granny wanted her hair to have a glorious silver sheen. But Marie always seemed to apply so much sweet silver rinse that Granny's hair had a permanent blue hue. Her white comb was forever tinged blue, and rivulets of blue sweat poured from her temples on a hot summer day.

"Oh, Granny." Margaret sighed. "How can you stand sitting out here in this unbearable heat? It's making you sweat something horrible." The blue rivers of perspiration were flowing.

"Don't forget, Margaret-child," Granny said. "Horses sweat, men perspire, and women just feel the heat." They both laughed.

"Well, I think we're both feeling the heat something awful today."

"Where have you been, child?"

"Oh, I believed Mattie's foolish advice about riding fast down a bumpy dirt road to bring the baby on sooner," Margaret responded. "And I used up all of my gas rations doing it."

"Don't fret too much," Granny said. "That baby will come when it's good and ready and not a day before. I just wish this silly old war wasn't keeping Henry from being with you when your baby's about to be born."

"I know, Granny," Margaret said. "The war has kept us apart since the day we were married, and his leave time is always so short. But I did get a letter today, and he hopes to be home for Christmas."

"When the war is over, you'll end up having to get to know each other again," Granny responded.

Margaret looked a little uneasy as she said, "That's what scares me the most. They tell me a man can change after something like this. What if Henry becomes a stranger in my eyes?"

"I'm not going to lie to you, Margaret," Granny said. "You know that's not my way. It could happen. Shell shock isn't pleasant to watch. After the First World War, I saw a few young marriages change. Comfort yourself with the fact that Henry is a sensible and mentally strong man. And whatever happens, the Lord has promised us that He will never give us more than we can bear."

Granny's religious faith was strong, and her spiritual life had taken her through the death of a son and husband when she was a very young woman—before her marriage to Margaret's grandfather. Granddaddy Harris's death had been difficult but not unexpected. Margaret watched Granny now as her eyelids became heavy and her head began to nod in the rocking chair.

It was late afternoon, and the temperature had dropped a few degrees, so Margaret walked into the backyard. Hawk, the yardman, was stooped over, tending the vegetables in their victory garden. Ever patriotic, Charles had insisted that Hawk grow and cultivate an array of vegetables. Hawk was getting old, and he looked frail today after toiling in the August heat. Margaret smelled Mattie's cooking, so she went through the back screen door to inquire about the evening meal.

"We havin' country ham, cord on da cob, green beans, slice tomatoes, butter beans, and cracklin' corn bread," Mattie announced.

Margaret smiled as she said, "It sounds and smells delicious. Let me fix a plate for Hawk. He looks so tired today. I wish Daddy didn't make him work so hard in that garden."

Margaret assembled a plate piled high with food and poured iced tea in an old jelly jar. She walked out to the edge of the garden and called after Hawk. He looked up from the field peas with a weary smile.

"Thank ya kin'ly, Miss Margaret," Hawk said with appreciation. "You sho is good to ole Hawk." He smiled a broader, toothless grin. "I'll jes set right down here on da back stoop 'fore I goes home."

"Go right ahead, Hawk. I hope you enjoy it," Margaret said.

Margaret was always amazed at how Hawk could gum his food, as only one or two badly decayed teeth were left in his mouth. Margaret felt strange making Hawk eat on the back stoop. Joan never liked for the colored help to eat in the house, not even in the kitchen. She made an exception for Mattie since she was a housemaid and wore uniforms. Hawk and his younger helper, Pierce, were given the chipped plates and the jelly jars with the back stoop or the screened porch as a dining room. Colored and white, separate but equal, permeated the South, and Barnesville always followed those defined lines. Margaret witnessed the separate part, but the equal part was a farce. The situation nagged at deep-seated feelings within her, and she touched her belly to feel her unborn child move. Margaret wondered if her son or daughter would witness a societal change that was hard to imagine in a static place like Barnesville.

Margaret heard her father's car in the driveway, so she walked back to the front yard.

"How is my little pumpkin today?" Charles grinned.

"Well, Daddy, your little pumpkin is not so little anymore," Margaret responded as she patted her swollen abdomen. "It has to be a boy. I never imagined I would get so huge. I guess it's good Henry isn't here to witness the transformation." They laughed.

"I can smell Mattie's dinner," Charles said. "Let's go sit down with your mother and have some of that good food."

They walked into the house together to join Joan and Granny for the evening meal as Mattie left for home.

Suppertime in the Harris household was enjoyed by all.

The Locket

Everyone was able to catch up on the day's events, and Joan always finalized pertinent social plans around the dinner table. The social calendar updates were usually rather boring to Margaret, as most of Barnesville's high society seemed so trite to her. So, rather than listen to that portion of the conversation, Margaret concentrated on the food.

"Margaret," Joan began, "I've told you to watch what you eat. Those helpings are way too big. Anything over twenty pounds will stay on your waistline after the baby comes. Dr. Bartholomew won't be happy when we go to see him Friday."

"Leave her alone, Joan," Charles admonished. "She's got to feed that baby boy so we can have the next star quarterback at Gordon Military Academy."

"Charles," Joan said, "I think Margaret and I should go on and check in at the Winecoff Hotel on Friday when we go to Atlanta for her doctor's appointment. In fact, we could drive both cars, and you could stay the weekend with us and come back home Sunday night to be here for work next week. I just won't feel good until we're at a hotel near St. Joseph's Infirmary. The baby could come any time now."

They all agreed that the plan was a good one as they topped off the meal with Mattie's pound cake and coffee. Charles lit his pipe after dinner and sat down in his armchair to read the paper. Margaret enjoyed the familiar aroma of her father's tobacco burning. Joan used this time to call friends and cancel social engagements scheduled during the coming weeks, in preparation for the birth of her grandchild. Granny went back to her rocking chair on the front porch to enjoy a cooler evening breeze. Margaret wondered how her life would change after the baby came. Comfort was drawn from the constancy in her life, but she knew a metamorphosis was about to begin within her as she prepared for motherhood. She was engulfed with feelings of uncertainty about her new role and whether she could do more than just play the part.

Margaret went to bed a bit confused and perplexed about her conflicting emotions. She resolved to go visit Miss Winnie the next day to gain a different perspective on her situation.

Chapter 2

The day dawned dark and dreary with the rain pelting against the house, forcing Margaret to close her bedroom window. Her sleep had been fitful. She never seemed to be able to find a comfortable position. Her dreams had been full of worry over Henry away at war and the new baby coming. Margaret's greatest fear was that Henry might be killed and never come home to get to know his child, to enjoy a real marriage, and to grow old alongside her. A shiver ran over her body, and she wondered why her thoughts were so disturbing.

Margaret heard Mattie clinking dishes downstairs in the kitchen. When she looked at the clock, she was shocked to discover that it was already nine. The fitful night and rainy morning had caused her to sleep later than usual.

Margaret took off her nightgown and caught a glimpse of her form in the mirror. Her breasts were heavy above her belly, but her legs and arms were long and slender. She stood tall for a woman. Her hair was black and curly and bobbed right below her jawline. Henry had always admired her figure with full breasts, slim hips, and long legs. She giggled a bit as she mentally likened herself to a potato with toothpick legs and arms. Her hips had widened a bit, and her father had joked about her not so elegant pregnant-style walk that began this month. Margaret dressed quickly to avoid further views of those now shocking curves.

She remembered her bedtime decision to spend some time with Miss Winnie today. Winifred and Robert Mitchell lived next door and had assumed the role of second parents to Margaret throughout her life. Margaret had been born four months after the marriage of the Mitchell's only daughter and had easily become their substitute daughter who just happened to live next door. Margaret often sought Miss Winnie's advice, and her home had sometimes been a haven during troubling times. Winifred had suffered many losses in her life, producing a special kind of wisdom that Margaret respected. Robert, too, was a dear, trusted friend and had enjoyed watching Margaret grow and mature over the years.

Margaret remembered a day several years ago when she witnessed Robert talking to a six- or seven-year-old dark-haired little girl selling cookies door-to-door. Robert had melted under the child's charm, and after he bought several boxes of cookies, she heard him say, "There used to be two little girls living next door to me who looked just like you. But now they're all grown-up." Tears had come to Margaret's eyes from the realization that being grown-up meant her relationship would change with Winifred and Robert.

The entire town had taken to calling Winifred *Miss Winnie*. Winnie had been used by Margaret as a toddler when she began struggling to say her first words because the entire name, Winifred, had been too difficult to say. Joan had added the *miss* to it due to the fact that a nice little southern lady should never address an adult by their first name only. Winifred had not insisted on the *miss* part but knew she could not change Joan's way of thinking. Winifred loved the nickname and considered it to be a term of endearment. Margaret remembered a day when she was sixteen, and she attempted to begin calling Winifred by her given name. Winifred's response had been, "I don't answer to anything but Miss Winnie." And so the nickname had stayed.

Margaret descended the stairs and followed the scent of bacon and coffee. Coffee had been nauseating to her throughout the pregnancy, so she made a cup of tea and ate some bacon and buttered toast. Mattie was shuffling around the kitchen, clearing plates, as everyone had eaten in shifts that morning. Charles had already gone to work.

Joan was in town taking care of some errands before their trip to Atlanta later that day.

"Where ya goin' dis mornin', Miss Margaret?" Mattie inquired.

"I thought I would spend some time with Miss Winnie and Robert. I won't have much time after the baby is born," Margaret responded.

"Ya sho is right 'bout dat," Mattie said. "But everythin' gonna be jes fine wi' me here an' all. Ya know Miss Winnie'll wanna babysit all da time too."

"Where is Granny this morning?" Margaret asked.

"She went inta town wi' ya mama to git dat hair done agin. Ah swear to da Good Lord, she got 'nuff sweet silver rinse on dat dere hair dat her brain got to be blue."

They laughed. Margaret collected her rain jacket and umbrella and headed out the front door. On the porch, she reached down and petted their basset hound, Pierre. "I guess you won't be getting any meat scraps from behind the butcher shop today," Margaret said to Pierre as she watched the steady rain falling on the front yard. "I'll tell Mattie to get you some extra food later."

Margaret held the umbrella above her head and walked between the two houses. She knocked on the front door, and within a few moments, Robert appeared.

"Good morning, little one," Robert said. He always enjoyed teasing Margaret about her expanding waistline.

"What is Miss Winnie up to today?" Margaret asked.

"Cleaning closets. You know when she gets a hankering to do something, there's no stopping her. She's been trying to get me to help, but closet cleaning isn't my idea of fun." Winifred appeared following that remark. She came over and gave Margaret a quick hug.

"I was hoping you would come by today," Winifred began. "Isn't today the day y'all leave for Atlanta to stay until the baby comes?"

"Yes, today is the day. But I don't think the baby knows that. I certainly don't feel like I'm about to deliver any time soon."

Winifred and Margaret walked back to the spare bedroom where she had been organizing the closet. Boxes, books, and old clothes were strewn all over the room.

Margaret quietly gasped at the enormous mess and said, "Now I see why Robert didn't want to help you with this. Maybe I'll just head on back home," she teased.

Winifred laughed and said, "Oh, this won't take long, and you can talk to me while I organize it all. You might like looking through some of these things."

Margaret picked up old newspaper clippings and scrapbooks and began browsing through them. She smiled while looking at wedding pictures from the marriage ceremony of their only daughter, Barbara. They joked about the outdated fashions. Margaret found some of her childish artwork and creative writing assignments from school and said, "I can't believe you kept all of this." Hours passed by, and they were both shocked to discover that it was nearly time for Margaret to leave with her family for Atlanta.

Margaret looked up at Winifred and watched as she opened an old family Bible. A haunted look came over Winifred's face as she said, "Margaret, I had five babies, and only one of them lived." Margaret shuddered when she heard the pronouncement in the quiet bedroom. "Oh, I'm sorry, dear. I shouldn't have said that. You don't need to listen to my sad stories when you're about to have a baby of your own."

"No, it's all right," Margaret said. "In fact, I've been thinking about you a lot lately. I don't know how you made it through with your babies."

"It was terrible," Winifred said quietly.

They continued to clean up in silence as Margaret remembered the stories she had always been told about Miss Winnie and Robert and their failed attempts to complete their family. Their first child, Barbara, had been born at home in the usual manner as it was in those days. She grew and matured as any normal baby would, and Winifred became pregnant again when Barbara was only a year old. They looked forward to the birth of their second child, and she arrived seemingly healthy. This baby, named Mary, began displaying developmental delays at the age of five or six months. Her mobility was impaired, she never learned to sit alone, she developed respiratory problems, and she was found lifeless in her crib one afternoon.

Those events were quite distressing to Winifred and Robert, but infant deaths weren't uncommon. They resolved to continue trying to expand their family, and a third pregnancy came soon enough. The result of this pregnancy was a stillborn baby boy that was another stinging blow to the couple. Still, they always had Barbara, who continued to thrive and had grown to be a playful preschooler.

When Barbara was seven years old, Winifred became pregnant again for the fourth time. This pregnancy was difficult from the beginning, and Winifred was confined to her bed during the last months. However, the birth was uneventful, and they had another girl they named Caroline. The baby was thin and weak and failed to thrive from the beginning. Her cry was a mournful wail similar to that of a small, wounded animal. She did not take her bottle well and had to be held almost constantly. Most of the time, Winifred had to sleep in a chair, holding the sick infant. Caroline was hospitalized at nine months old with symptoms similar to Winifred's second child and died several days thereafter. A cursory autopsy revealed internal organs that were spongy and like those of an old woman, but no real conclusions regarding the exact cause of death were ever made.

Ten years elapsed before Winifred became pregnant for the fifth time. At this point, Winifred was in her late thirties, and she and Robert felt ill prepared for more heartache. When the pregnancy was confirmed, several doctors from the area discussed terminating the small life growing inside of Winifred, but since she had delivered a normal child in the past, they felt that the possibility of a good outcome still existed. The pregnancy continued, and a baby girl named Alice was born. Both Winifred and Robert insisted that the physicians conduct thorough examinations of the infant because of their past history. The doctors assured them that this little girl was completely healthy in every way.

The doctors were wrong. When Alice was five months old, the familiar symptoms began surfacing, and her development did not

The Locket

progress. She never learned to sit alone, she began developing the same respiratory problems, and her tongue became swollen and protruded from her mouth as she struggled to breathe. Alice died at home in her mother's arms at the age of thirteen months. Mercifully, this was the last baby born to Winifred and Robert.

Now Margaret and Winifred looked at each other in knowing silence, not wanting to speak of those babies. Winifred then smiled while she gazed at a photograph of Barbara and her three grandchildren. Winifred had been a devoted mother to Barbara and had lavished love and attention on Margaret when her duties as a mother were all but gone, following Barbara's marriage and subsequent move to North Carolina.

"I feel confused right now," Margaret began. "I don't know if I'll ever be a good mother. What does it take to be a really good mother?"

"It's hard to put it in so many words," Winifred responded. "I think finding that middle ground is the key. You can't be too selfless or too selfish. You shouldn't be too overprotective or too permissive. You don't want to give the child too much attention or too little attention. I could go on and on. Motherhood is a balancing act, and sometimes you fall off the high wire. Don't fret too much about it when you do."

Her words made sense, and Margaret thanked her for the advice. Winifred and Robert embraced and kissed Margaret when she left. They knew that when she returned to Barnesville, there would be a new baby in her arms.

The rain had ceased, and Margaret walked back home to find her parents loading their suitcases into separate cars. Margaret had packed most of her things several days ago, always worried that the baby might come a few days ahead of schedule. Before long, Margaret and her mother were headed down the steamy highway toward Atlanta, with Joan chattering on about various planned activities to distract Margaret during this waiting period. Charles followed behind in his car, with plans to go directly to the Winecoff Hotel and check in for his family. Joan and Margaret had to drive sixty miles to the downtown office of the Bartholomew Group, a well-known obstetrical practice that was thriving in Atlanta.

Joan insisted on entering the examining room with Margaret when the nurse called her name. Margaret felt a bit embarrassed about this but allowed her mother to accompany her rather than cause a scene. Joan had to be in control and wanted to know every detail about every situation. Dr. Bartholomew knew her well and seemed to deal with her interference in a jovial manner.

The examination was finished quickly enough. Dr. Bartholomew stated that he had heard a strong heartbeat. Joan was pleased.

"Your weight gain has been a bit excessive," Dr. Bartholomew commented.

Joan nodded, and after a knowing look directed toward the doctor, she told Margaret, "I've been telling you that all along. You'll be as big as the side of a house soon. What in the world will Henry think when he returns from overseas?"

"The only problem I see now is that the baby is breech," stated Dr. Bartholomew. Joan began to look very concerned as Margaret felt the baby give a giant kick. "We will just have to deal with that a little closer to time for the birth. There are ways of turning a baby, and of course, I will try my best. You are delivering at a good hospital, so don't worry." He patted Margaret on the hand and Joan on the shoulder. "Leave the worrying to me. I'm the doctor."

Margaret and her mother left the doctor's office and drove to the Winecoff Hotel. Charles had taken care of all necessary details to secure the two adjoining hotel rooms. After noticing the late hour, everyone decided to dress for dinner. They departed soon thereafter to fill their rumbling stomachs.

Over the next few days, Joan attempted to distract Margaret from the endless waiting by keeping her as busy as possible with trips shopping at the downtown Rich's department store, walks in Piedmont Park, and visits to the Atlanta Museum. Joan kept up the busy schedule on into the next week because Charles had to return to Barnesville for work. Margaret's head was spinning from the hectic pace her mother had set.

Again, it was Friday and time for another doctor's visit. Margaret had passed her due date on the Saturday before and was now feeling disheartened. Dr. Bartholomew sensed her worry and unrest and attempted to lift her spirits with some good news.

"Well, looks like we won't have to turn that baby after all," Dr. Bartholomew pronounced. "The head is now down and in a good position for birth. I know you're past your due date now, but it looks like you may have to wait a little longer. I don't think you have dropped at all. You'll know it when the baby drops, and then it won't be very long. Try not to get all worked up. The baby will be here when it's good and ready and not a day before."

Joan interjected, "You took the words right out of my mouth, Doctor." With a wink to the physician, she added in a whisper, "I'm keeping her real busy, so the time will go by faster."

Margaret left Dr. Bartholomew's office with a disheartened feeling surrounding her. Joan tried to lighten her daughter's mood, but her attempts were futile. In the car while riding back to the hotel, Joan caught a glimpse of a large, salty tear falling into Margaret's lap.

"Why are you crying?" Joan queried.

"To be quite honest, I really don't know," Margaret responded. "I'm grateful to you and Daddy for watching over me so closely during this pregnancy with Henry away and all. But I feel so alone, and this waiting is terrible. You and Daddy have been great company, but you can't take the place of my husband. This damn war is wrecking our lives. I don't want to wait until my life is over before I know a true sense of togetherness and family unity with the man I married."

More tears fell as Margaret sobbed. Joan pulled the car over and held her daughter close as the flood of tears mounted. Margaret felt her mother's touch and realized it had been weeks or even months since another individual had held her or left any sort of lingering caress upon her skin. The sobs wracked her body, and Joan continued to hold her tight in the necessary silence.

When the sobs subsided, Joan checked her watch and noticed they had been sitting in the car beside the road for thirty minutes. It was now very late in the afternoon. The dinner hour was approaching. She started the car and drove back to the Winecoff Hotel.

At the hotel, Margaret stated in a firm voice that she would be having supper alone in her room. Joan nodded, understanding her daughter's wish for solitude following the emotional flood that had just occurred. They each headed for their respective rooms.

Margaret sat down in a large wing-backed chair near the window in her room and numbly watched the commonplace activities in motion outside of the glass. Long shadows began to appear as the day changed into dusk and then night. After the room had become cloaked in total darkness for some time, Margaret arose and removed her street attire to slip naked between the sheets of the large, empty bed.

She slept a deep, dream-laden slumber filled with images of Henry. Margaret saw Henry standing tall and tan alone on a beach. She felt the sand between her toes and warm water splashing on her legs. As she turned to walk toward her husband in response to his adoring look, she caught a glimpse of a slender Asian woman. The woman's hair was long, dark, and shiny, and her skin was tawny and flawless. Henry folded the small woman into his arms in a knowing embrace. A wounded, sobbing sound began to arise in Margaret's throat that caused her to awake with a start.

With her heart racing, Margaret felt a sharp pain course through her body. She sensed a warm wetness beneath her. After turning on the bedside lamp, she yanked back the sheet to reveal a large area of saturation with smears of bloody show. It was now two thirty in the morning as she pounded on the door to her mother's adjoining bedroom. A disheveled Joan opened the door and was not surprised to witness the evidence of Margaret's broken water.

They dressed to take the short drive to St. Joseph's Infirmary. Margaret was stunned to realize the significant intensity of pain she had to endure with each contraction. Each pain shot through her body in a wave of rising momentum, causing her belly to harden with radiating pain to the upper part of her legs.

The Locket

Holding onto Margaret, Joan helped her through the door of the hospital's main entrance. The attendant in the lobby of the hospital read the nonverbal signs of an expectant mother in labor and offered Margaret a wheelchair ride to her awaiting room. Joan followed behind but was told at the nurse's station that she would have to wait in the family waiting room until Margaret's labor and delivery were complete.

Margaret flashed her mother a frightened look, and Joan's face became firm and calm as she said, "You're going to be fine. You know we all love you, and soon you'll have a beautiful baby in your arms as a reward for all of this pain." She kissed her daughter before the nurse whisked her away. One small tear slipped down Margaret's cheek as she realized she would be doing this alone, without Henry.

Within a few moments, Margaret was in her hospital room, while nurses scurried in and out going about their usual tasks. From time to time, a nurse would make a remark regarding the progress of her labor. Margaret's eyes darted back and forth from nurse to nurse, searching for a comforting look, but none was found. More pain gripped her body, and an unrecognizable scream arose from her throat. A red-haired nurse rushed over to her bedside following the primal sound and acknowledged Margaret's fright and shock mixed with a host of other emotions.

Margaret stared at the nurse's name tag and made out the name, Betty Weaver. Betty grabbed Margaret's hand and said, "This is your first, isn't it?" Margaret nodded, looking like a frightened doe. "It helps," she went on, "to think of something besides the pain. Let your mind play tricks on you. Imagine all sorts of things except this hellacious pain. This shot should help. Dr. Bartholomew will be here any minute now, and we can begin the delivery. You won't feel any pain then."

Margaret gave Nurse Weaver a weak, grateful smile. As promised, Dr. Bartholomew entered the room within moments. He made a quick examination of Margaret, pronounced her ready for the delivery room, and patted her hand. The nurses began pushing her gurney down a long hallway toward a set of swinging doors. Margaret's last memory was that of a black mask coming down over her nose and mouth, filled with a strange-smelling substance that made the room spin. The pain had ended for now.

Chapter 3

"Wake up, Mrs. Montgomery. Wake up." Nurse Weaver was shaking Margaret's arm, attempting to arouse her from a deep slumber. Her vision was a bit blurry when she opened her eyes to encounter Nurse Weaver's face and flaming red hair near her cheek.

"Is my baby all right?" Margaret queried.

"It's not just one baby, Mrs. Montgomery." Margaret's eyes began to widen. "Look over here, my dear," Nurse Weaver continued with a knowing smile. "You just gave birth to two healthy boys."

Margaret's mouth opened, and she released a gasp of shock as she turned her head toward two hospital bassinets to the left of her bed. Each bassinet had a small blue card stating, "Baby Boy Montgomery."

"Two babies?" Margaret asked with a weak smile.

"Oh yes," Nurse Weaver responded with a small giggle. "Fraternal twins. Forgive me for the laughter, but I always enjoy breaking the news of a multiple birth to my new mothers. The shocking look is priceless, and it never gets old to me. I actually had one father who fainted when I told him he had triplets."

Margaret's shocked look continued. Nurse Weaver patted her on the shoulder. "The babies are fine and healthy, but one is a little on the scrawny side. Come on, you need to get to know them."

Nurse Weaver picked up one infant who was totally bald and enjoying a very deep sleep. She placed the baby in Margaret's outstretched arms and stated, "Now this one is sweet as sugar and loves to snuggle up." Margaret watched as the baby curled closely inside the crook of her arm. He was bundled with a lightweight receiving blanket. Margaret opened the blanket to count all the fingers and toes. He was long and quite thin. A look of concern crossed Margaret's face.

"Don't worry," Nurse Weaver said. "I know he looks like skin stretched over bone, but he's had to share his space with his brother over here." As Nurse Weaver chattered on, Margaret pulled down the baby's diaper to check the remaining anatomy and was pleased to discover that nothing was amiss. Nurse Weaver collected the long, lanky infant and then placed him back in his bassinet. "Now let's take a look at his chubby brother," she continued.

In silence, Margaret accepted the second baby. She was amazed to encounter a baby boy with a full head of thick, dark hair that stood on end. The baby was awake and searched his mother's face up and down several times. He wriggled in Margaret's arms, seeming to find his blanket confining. Margaret opened up the blanket to see an infant weighing at least eight pounds with all of the required fingers and toes. She again unfastened the diaper to complete her examination. The baby urinated a tall golden stream that reached up to Margaret's right cheek.

"Well, he just taught you a lesson, didn't he?" Nurse Weaver laughed.

Margaret remained silent, still thinking about how she was now responsible for two new lives. Nurse Weaver sensed the overwhelmed look that had fallen over her patient's face. "Let me take these two back to the nursery," she said. "You need your rest. You also need to get used to the idea that your one baby is now twins." Nurse Weaver rattled on. Margaret's head was spinning. Tears sprang to her eyes when she watched the babies being wheeled from the room. She missed Henry. Her eyes became heavy again, and she fell into a deep sleep.

Margaret awoke a few hours later to discover her mother and father sitting near her bed. Joan could not contain her mirth at the unexpected surprise of twins. Charles beamed down at his youngest daughter, and Margaret began to see him now as a grandfather.

The Locket

Margaret smelled the heady perfume of at least a half dozen large floral arrangements already in the hospital room.

Joan smiled as she said, "How are you feeling, dear?"

"Not so wonderful right now," Margaret said in a slurred tone induced by pain medication. "It's just so shocking to find out that I now have two babies in my life. If only I could see Henry's face when he hears the news."

"Well, I had your father send him a telegram. So he'll know soon enough." Joan gave her daughter a reassuring smile. "Charles and I are going to head back to the hotel to get some rest. We'll be back tomorrow morning to visit before we go home for a few days to make all the arrangements for the babies." Joan gathered her purse and added, "Now don't you fret over anything. Mattie and Miss Winnie will all pitch in to help for the first few weeks at home until we get a routine set up. You rest now."

Margaret watched as her parents left the hospital room. She felt numb, but her thoughts were still racing. She attempted to process the inevitable changes that would soon occur and how they might affect her fledgling marriage, a marriage that had been interrupted by the war. For the first time since entering the hospital, her mind was drawn toward the disturbing dream she had experienced just prior to the onset of her labor. Margaret had felt occasional twinges of worry about Henry's fidelity during the long separations forced upon them by his military service, but she had pushed those unsettling thoughts aside. Dwelling on such things could only breed mistrust, so again she chose to dismiss them.

At that moment, the shrill ring of the telephone on her bedside table interrupted her dark thoughts. She picked up the receiver and said, "Hello."

"Well, hello, doll," a male voice responded. "I just had to call with my congratulations. Boy, I bet Henry will be surprised to discover that his wife had a litter of chillun."

Margaret laughed and said, "Only James Walsh would describe my two beautiful babies as a litter of chillun."

"As their new godfather," James said, "I'm entitled to certain liberties, and I intend to take them. Seriously, Margaret. Are you fine?"

"My body is mending nicely," Margaret replied. "At least that's what the nurses have told me. My heart just aches to have gone through all of this without Henry. It's strange to feel so alone when you're almost always around people who are showering you with attention."

"You know Henry asked me to watch over you and check up on you periodically while he was away. Will he be home for Christmas?"

"He plans to be here for the holidays. I miss him so, and I hope nothing happens to prevent his leave," Margaret said.

"If Henry can't come home for Christmas," James went on, "then I insist that you and your entire family spend Christmas up here in Connecticut with me."

"That would be far too much of an imposition on you," Margaret replied.

"That is utter nonsense, and you know it," James said. "You get some rest now. Those two boys will keep you hopping at home. Talk to you soon."

Margaret told James goodbye in a soft, pensive voice. James was such a dear and trusted friend who had been a close confidant of Henry's since early in their college days. James was one of those unassuming, seemingly ordinary souls with an extraordinary life. His father had amassed a fortune in the construction business. Henry and James had developed a fast friendship during college as they both studied to become civil engineers. James's jovial manner had always been infectious, and with no cash flow problems, he was known for throwing the most memorable parties during those carefree college days.

A near fatal bout with polio as a young boy had sentenced James to a life spent within the confines of a wheelchair. The physical suffering he endured had produced a serious side to him that few individuals ever witnessed during his time at Georgia Tech. It had made James a shrewd businessman who had certainly doubled, even tripled his father's fortune by now.

The Locket

Since the world was not an easy place for the disabled, Henry took on the responsibility of aiding James in any manner during those college years. James had a regular driver who also doubled as an all-purpose manservant in the rather large apartment he rented in Atlanta while attending Tech. However, James preferred to leave the hired help at home and relied on Henry to assist him when navigating any physical hurdles within the community.

James was an excellent judge of character and could observe people, situations, and relationships with a discerning eye. He possessed an uncanny talent for unearthing the truth. Henry always commented that James should have studied criminal law. James would reply, "Lawyers are crooks only looking to line their pockets while they speak loudly for a cause they rarely believe in. I see the truth too clearly to fight a battle in court for some deadbeat who chooses to violate the law. I also see the truth too clearly to put up with the bullshit politics involved in becoming a judge."

Still, Henry relied upon James's final judgment where Margaret was concerned. Henry had been eager to introduce the two before he contemplated any permanence to their courtship. After the three had enjoyed dinner in Connecticut one crisp autumn night, James pronounced that Margaret was an interesting addition to their circle of friends. Henry was pleased at James's approval. Soon they were engaged.

Again, Margaret's eyelids grew heavy, and another deep sleep overcame her. She slept a long, dreamless, healing sleep that was difficult to awake from when a new nurse entered the room and began to shake her arm. Margaret opened her eyes to encounter a short, stout, and stern nurse saying in a gruff voice, "Rise and shine, sleeping beauty. It's time for a feeding."

Margaret glanced over beside her bed to see her chubby infant boy as he wriggled and fussed in his bassinet. She looked up at the nurse and asked, "Where is my other baby?"

"Oh, we left him in the nursery. Two babies at once would be too much for you right now. If you'll just slip out of your gown, I'll bind you up."

"Bind me up?" Margaret asked.

"Of course," the nurse responded. "You have no need to breastfeed. Bottle feeding is the best thing for your babies. If we don't bind you up real soon, you'll become engorged, and your bosom will be hard as a rock. Even with this binding, it will be uncomfortable. It's the only way to dry up the milk."

Margaret felt uncomfortable with this strange binding ritual the nurse had just described, but she was too exhausted to argue the point. Tears again sprang to her eyes at the thought of not enjoying the act of bringing her infants to her breast to strengthen their bond. Margaret's cheeks were stained red in embarrassment while the nurse wrapped four cloth diapers securely across her chest and around her back, fastening them tightly with four large safety pins.

When the binding was complete, the nurse handed Margaret the fussy infant, who howled from hunger. She thrust a large, warm bottle into Margaret's right hand, and Margaret placed the nipple into her son's rooting, open mouth. He sucked with his eyes wide open for quite some time as Margaret enjoyed the heady perfume of his newborn skin. The nurse watched for a while and then commented, "It looks like he's gonna take five ounces at his first feeding. Watch out for this one. He's tough."

The nurse left the room. The baby finished the bottle of formula but continued to whimper and wriggled in Margaret's arms. In a moment, he released a robust cry, and it then occurred to Margaret that she needed to burp her newborn son. She placed him high on her left shoulder. A large belch slipped out and was ended with a contented sigh. Margaret smiled to watch her thick-haired son drift into slumber.

The stout nurse again entered the room with the second bassinet. She collected the chubby, sleeping infant from Margaret's arms and replaced him with the thin, bald baby boy who had joined his brother in a long nap. "We'll have to wake this one up," the nurse said. "He's too skinny to sleep through a feeding." The nurse opened up his receiving blanket and began thumping the baby on the pads of his feet. This caused him to whimper and raise his sleep-laden eyelids.

The Locket

The nurse again handed Margaret a warm bottle that contained very little formula.

"I'm sure this won't be enough," Margaret announced as she held up the puny bottle.

"We'll be lucky if he takes half of that two-ounce bottle," the nurse said.

A look of concern crossed the new mother's face. She placed the nipple between her infant's parted lips. He sucked weakly three or four times and then seemed to fall asleep again. The nurse thumped his feet again to jolt him from the illegal nap. She then said, "You'll have to keep this up so he'll stay awake long enough to eat. He only weighs four pounds, and the scrawny ones are always a bit sluggish at first. They lollygag around while you do all the work."

Again, the nurse left the room, and Margaret tried to coax the smallest infant into taking more formula. When the nurse returned, Margaret gave her a weak, exhausted look. She held up the small bottle and said in a strained tone, "Look, I've been working with him for an hour, and he has only taken about one half of an ounce."

"Like I told you," the nurse reiterated, "you have to be tough with the scrawny ones to get them to gain weight. We'll do the next few feedings in the nursery to give you some rest. He'll have to be fed every two to two and a half hours, while his brother will be able to wait four hours between meals."

The nurse gathered up the tiny infant, placed him back in his bassinet, and pushed him out the door for a ride back to the nursery. Margaret sat and stared out the window of her room to discover that it had grown dark outside. She was shocked at the sheer exhaustion that gripped her body.

Again, she fell asleep only to awaken moments later, it seemed, when Dr. Bartholomew entered the room. Margaret glanced at her bedside clock and realized she had slept for nine hours.

"Well, little lady," Dr. Bartholomew began, "you certainly gave us all a shock by delivering *two* babies."

"No one was more shocked than me," Margaret said with a yawn.

Dr. Bartholomew examined his patient and then stated, "You're coming along just fine. Our new mothers typically stay in the hospital ten to twelve days." Margaret flashed him a worried look at that comment. "However," the doctor continued, "I usually want a mother who has twins to spend roughly twelve to fourteen days with us. It's a tough adjustment dealing with twins."

At that moment, Joan and Charles knocked softly on the door and entered the hospital room.

"And here are the proud grandparents," the doctor pronounced as he shook Charles's hand and kissed Joan on the cheek.

The three began to discuss Margaret's medical progress as if she were not present in the room, which served to set her teeth on edge. Joan noted the angry flash in her daughter's eyes, and she ushered the two men together out into the hallway to complete the discussion. Within a few minutes, Joan and Charles returned to Margaret's bedside.

Charles leaned down and kissed his daughter on the forehead and said, "We're planning to drive back home this morning, sweetie. I hate to leave you here alone like this, but it's a bad time for me to be away from work. I hope you understand."

"Of course I do," Margaret replied. In fact, she welcomed the solitude to deal with the new changes occurring in her life, mind, and body.

"Your mother has loads of work to do," Charles commented.

"Mama, we'll have to go out and buy two of everything," Margaret began.

"I'll take care of it all," Joan said. "I'm certain Mattie and Miss Winnie will lend a hand too. Don't fret over anything. Now, we simply have to get going." She gave Margaret a quick hug and a kiss on the cheek. "I'll be calling you every day until it's time for you to come home. Oh, I almost forgot. The nurse gave me this telegram from Henry for you."

Margaret's heart leapt at the prospect of a few words from Henry, but she held the telegram in her hand and waited until she was alone in the room to read it. She opened the light yellow paper to read:

The Locket

> Twins. Stop. What a shock. Stop. I'm aching inside not to be there. Stop. I love you. Stop. Give the boys loads of kisses and hugs for me. Stop.

Instead of the usual tears, a rush of white-hot anger began to fill Margaret. Her anger was directed toward the circumstances that had taken Henry away. Birth was such an incredible event in her young married life to be missed by the man she loved. It dealt a stinging blow to Margaret, serving to harden her to a degree. She knew, in the deepest recesses of her heart, that there would be no more babies for her and Henry. Her husband's words rang a hollow chord.

~ ~ ~ ~ ~

At that moment, in a small thatched hut in East Asia, a waiflike Vietnamese woman was lying on a pallet prepared for her on the mat-covered floor. Her abdomen was swollen and hardened with each painful contraction. She released a piercing scream with each new contraction, and her eyes were wild with pain. An older woman tended to her and spoke rapidly in a foreign tongue. There would be no pain relief for the small, laboring young woman. Henry Montgomery knelt beside his lover, holding her hand and whispering words into her ear.

"I love you, Ma Le," he said in a low voice.

Another primal scream came from deep inside the woman. Henry watched the act of birth with a sinking feeling in his gut. He felt no embarrassment at the animalistic nature of what he witnessed. A rush of exhilaration overcame him as he heard the cry of his infant daughter. Henry reached down to hold Ma Le and the helpless new baby moving in her arms. His wedding ring glistened in the dim light of the hut, a sober reminder of his commitments at home. Henry pushed aside any further thoughts of Margaret.

Chapter 4

The morning dawned bright in the small thatched hut outside of Jakarta, Indonesia. Ma Le awoke to the fussing and whimpering of her infant daughter wriggling on the pallet beside her. Ma Le heard the early-morning rustling sounds of her mother, Madam Ky, on the other side of the hut. To calm the fussy baby, May Le brought her newborn child to her breast. The baby suckled, and Ma Le groaned to feel the pain of vigorous contractions deep in her belly. Those pains were serving to restore her young body back to its former state.

A pensive look crossed Ma Le's tawny, unlined face as she remembered the events of the previous year. It was the early fall of 1943 that found Ma Le working as a hostess in an upscale restaurant called the White Dragon. The owner, Ben Tre, a shrewd Vietnamese businessman, had chuckled at his good fortune to find a stunning young Asian woman, who had a good command of the English language, to engage and entice the wealthy American Army officers into numerous repeat visits.

Henry entered the White Dragon with two other officers around nine o'clock one Saturday evening. Ben Tre flashed Ma Le a knowing look, and she arose on cue to greet the Americans. Her thin, reed-like form was nestled comfortably into a red satin dress embossed with intricate embroidery depicting exotic birds and flowers. There was a deep slit on the left side of her straight skirt that revealed regular glimpses of her slender leg. Her long ebony tresses were pulled back at the nape of her neck with an unusual red and gold clasp. The contours and lines of her face were flawless, and her lips were full and inviting as she greeted the men with a well-rehearsed, "Good evening, gentlemen."

The three men were captivated, but Ma Le's eyes rested upon the tall, handsome form of Henry Montgomery. He entered the restaurant in his dress uniform, and he possessed the body language of a high-ranking officer. His hair was dark and wavy, and his cool green eyes raked over her body. Ma Le accepted the unspoken compliment with a slow nod of her head.

Ma Le seated the men at one of the best tables in the establishment, near the dance floor and the stage where the band was preparing to play. Ben Tre expected her to care for every need of these Americans. She took their drink orders and walked slowly toward the bar. Their eyes followed each movement she made.

Bob Reeves, a fellow officer of Henry's, whistled and said, "What a bombshell." He continued to ogle her from across the room. "A real long roll in the hay with that one could keep me singing through the rest of the war."

Jerry Miller, seated on Henry's left, chimed in, "Keep on dreaming, old buddy. She's been batting those eyelashes at lover boy Henry over here ever since we walked in."

Henry displayed a fake look of surprise. "Who, me?" Henry asked.

"Yep," Jerry went on. "They can smell out a senior officer a mile away. Don't think it's your charm, friend. She expects a good time and some money to be spent. Old fatso over there"—he pointed to Ben Tre—"knew what he was doing when he hired her. I bet every soldier in this room comes here all the time hoping to climb into her drawers when the place closes."

The men laughed and then watched as Ma Le turned from the bar to walk toward them with the drinks. She placed the drinks in front of the three officers, then Jerry grabbed her hand and kissed it. Ma Le feigned surprise. "Do you think your boss would let you dance the night away with an army officer like me?" Jerry queried as he puffed out his chest.

Ma Le responded, "Boss let me dance with biggest officer in place. I think that he bigger officer than you." Bob let out a hoot of laughter because Ma Le had pointed directly at Henry.

The band began to play a slow love song at that moment, and Bob said with laughter still in his voice, "Give the lady a thrill, Mr. Biggest Officer in the Place."

Henry looked nervous as he gulped down his entire glass of whiskey and stood to take Ma Le's soft, small hand. They walked out onto the dance floor, and Ma Le molded her body to his in a more intimate than expected embrace. Henry was aware that numerous soldiers in the room were watching each move. He was well known to all of them. He circled his right hand around Ma Le's tiny waist, while his left hand held her manicured fingers. She placed her temple against his cheek, and Henry smelled her intoxicating scent. He began to feel the old familiar ache of desire starting in the pit of his stomach and moving into intense warmth as they danced in a slow, fluid, rhythmic manner. No one had affected him in this manner since Margaret, and he was shocked at the boiling-hot desire that gripped him. He wanted to taste the fruit of this woman. Ma Le's sensuous being had revealed the pent-up forces locked away deep inside Henry. He could think of nothing else but possessing her.

"You, I like," Ma Le whispered in Henry's ear. "Maybe we go out on date sometime. You come to White Dragon with no friends. I show you good time after work. Work over for me at eleven."

Henry was surprised to find himself saying, "I would like that." He darted a look around the place to see if other soldiers could read his planned betrayal.

Ma Le understood the meaning behind his nervous look and reassured him with, "You no worry. Ma Le keep secret. You come late tomorrow. Meet me outside White Dragon. Go to back of White Dragon. I be there."

Henry and Ma Le continued to circle the floor dancing while other couples began to join them on the hardwood. They danced as if their movements had been well rehearsed. They were a handsome couple, and Henry's friends found it difficult not to watch their artistry. The music soon ended, to be replaced with a fast-paced melody, and Henry and Ma Le left the dance floor. Ma Le caught a look from Ben Tre, whispered something in Henry's ear, and joined her employer in response to his commanding glance.

When Henry joined his friends, he knew he was in for more ribbing. Jerry chuckled and said, "Well, what's the little woman at home gonna think when she finds out about your little gook girlfriend?"

Henry flashed him a piercing, cool green look and said in a chilling voice, "It was just a dance. No more. Let's talk about all the little gook girls you've nailed down. What's the grand total of half-breed brats running now?"

Henry had touched a nerve, but Jerry laughed it off. "Touché, old buddy. Can I help it if I'm the great white stud?"

The three men laughed. A new, less attractive waitress came up to their table and took orders for another round of drinks. The officers enjoyed their evening for several more hours. The whiskey kept flowing while Bob and Jerry became quite drunk. Henry decided to put his glass down. It was becoming difficult to hide the burning light of desire that sprang to his dark eyes whenever Ma Le crossed the room. When Henry had taken all that he could bear of his drunken buddies and the sexual frustration produced by Ma Le's provocative looks and graceful movements, he bustled Jerry and Bob out the door to the awaiting jeep to take the short drive back to their hotel.

Henry had arrived in Jakarta a month ago, along with numerous other army officers and enlisted men. As part of the Army Corps of Engineers, he had been deployed to coordinate anti-Japanese activity in the now Japanese-occupied Indonesia. His chief objective was to plan and build an airfield that would aid in air support against the Japanese in Southeast Asia.

Henry parked the jeep in front of the hotel and then glanced in the rearview mirror to catch a glimpse of his two cohorts sleeping in the back seat. Jerry's boyish head had slumped to his right and rested on Bob's left shoulder. Henry wished he had a camera to capture the drunken buddies. He chuckled a bit to himself and decided to leave the two there to sleep it off in the jeep. He entered the hotel lobby and went straight to his room. Henry undressed and stretched out in the inviting bed. In spite of the fact that he had consumed enough liquor to forget his dreams, the thought of Ma Le burned up and down his spine. Henry's sleep was fitful as images of Ma Le flashed on and off. He awoke early Sunday morning with a stiff erection from searing thoughts of his ultimate possession of the Asian beauty. He resolved to accept Ma Le's whispered proposition from the previous evening. No thoughts of Margaret entered his musings.

Henry left his room to encounter his very hungover friends climbing the stairs to their respective rooms.

"Hey, chump," Bob called out to Henry. "The payback for my night spent in a jeep is gonna be hell."

"You said it, buddy," Jerry chimed after him. "I thought my head was resting on the bosom of some Oriental cutie like the one we met last night. Instead, I was huggin' this ugly bastard. And the weird thing is he didn't look so ugly to me."

"Go sleep it off, you two," Henry responded. "I've got some ground inspections I want to do today to get a jump start on next week. I may not make it back until morning."

Henry finished a large breakfast at the hotel and then made good on his promise to his fellow officers by loading survey equipment into the back of his jeep and heading for the outskirts of town to a predetermined site his task force had discussed last week. He spent the entire day practicing his craft as an engineer and attempting to push thoughts of Ma Le to the back of his mind. His efforts were futile. As the sun started to set, he packed up his equipment and headed back into Jakarta. Once inside the city, he found a public bathhouse where he spent an hour washing up and relaxing his tired muscles. Henry chose a restaurant three blocks away from the White Dragon to quiet the hunger he felt in his stomach. The other primal hunger he felt was yet to be satisfied.

Henry took time enjoying his meal. He completed some necessary paperwork and did some reading following dinner to distract himself from the burning thoughts of Ma Le. Near eleven o'clock, he gathered his notes and books, deposited them in the jeep, and walked the three short blocks to the White Dragon. Henry went down the alley beside the restaurant to wait in front of a small door he discovered located on the back of the building. He checked his watch to see that the hands read exactly eleven. Within seconds, the small door opened, and Ma Le stepped out into the dimly lit alley.

Ma Le caught her breath to see Henry, and a small fire leapt into her eyes. She looked down to cover her telling gaze but not before Henry had caught sight of the desire raging in her. Ma Le was, once again, stunning in a white satin gown that rose high to encircle her slim neck like a choker. The back of the dress, however, was bare and revealed her flawless skin as the opening came to a point in the small of her back.

"You are so beautiful, Ma Le," Henry commented in a low voice.

"Thank you," she replied.

"I'm glad you came to meet me. I was afraid you wouldn't be here."

"What make you think that?" Ma Le asked.

"I'm sure all of the GIs try to take you out every night," Henry stated.

"You right, but I no go out with all GIs."

Henry smiled at her last comment and noticed that she shivered in the chill of the night air.

"Here, take my coat." He draped his jacket around her delicate shoulders and then said, "It's late. Most places will be closed. Would you like to just take a walk?"

"That be fine," Ma Le replied.

They walked down the alley and onto the sidewalk in silence. Ma Le reached out to slip her small right hand into his large, callused left hand. Henry smiled into her ravishing face. Ma Le's blue-black hair was pulled back at the nape of her neck into a chignon, which made her look more elegant and exotic than ever.

The two continued to walk in silence for three blocks, and then Ma Le said, "My house right here." She pointed above a storefront to the top of a building. Henry noticed a staircase beside the store that most likely led up to the apartment. "You come up. Have drink." Henry allowed her to lead the way up the dark staircase. Ma Le opened the door at the top of the stairs to reveal a small, dingy apartment. It was one room with a couch, two chairs, a bed, and a small kitchen area. Ma Le said in a low voice, "I get that drink for you."

Henry sat down on the couch and stared at Ma Le as she moved about the kitchen area filling two small glasses with whiskey. She walked her slow, provocative stride back over to the couch and placed a drink in Henry's hand. Ma Le placed her own drink to her lips and swallowed the amber liquid without sipping. Henry followed suit.

As the spirits began to take effect, Henry touched Ma Le's hand and brought her soft fingers to his lips. He drew her into a feverish embrace and placed his lips against her full, moist mouth in an endless kiss. Her taste, her touch, and her smell were much more intoxicating than the whiskey.

For a small moment, Henry felt the entire scene should be stopped, and he drew back only to find Ma Le's arms touching his shoulders, beckoning him forward into the intense pleasure that was waiting.

Henry picked up Ma Le's small form and walked over to the bed. He placed her on the bed, and she watched as he removed his shirt to reveal a muscled, tan expanse of chest. She caught her breath as this first glimpse of his maleness began to arouse an intense fire in her stomach. In a moment, he was fully naked, glistening in the dim light. He reached down and unsnapped the high collar of her satin gown to reveal her flawless, feminine form. He pulled the clasp from her hair to allow the black tresses to cascade past her shoulders. Her breasts were firm and taut, asking to be touched and loved. Henry pulled the gown down farther so nothing could occlude his view of this Asian goddess.

Henry's erection was pulsing and hard. But he waited, wanting to lie beside Ma Le to touch and tease her body. His hands raked over her body in a slow, reverent manner and then moved down to pull her legs apart. He admired the exquisite flower that was the core of her sex. Henry moved his head closer to smell the heady scent and taste its erotic juices. He pushed her legs wider apart and began to lick in a slow, rhythmic movement. This brought Ma Le into a frenzy of desire, and she reached down and pulled Henry's head up to kiss his lips. She tasted herself during the hungry, lingering kiss.

Henry could wait no longer. He entered her soft, wet recesses and groaned from deep inside himself. Henry had never felt such ecstasy. Ma Le was a willing, eager partner who matched the fevered pitch of his lovemaking. Henry knew she was very experienced as her sensuous form moved against him. Her breasts against his chest caused him to release a sigh of pleasure. They writhed against each other until the heady climax was reached, leaving them both spent and breathless.

Henry stayed the night, and twice more their lovemaking ignited to leave them satiated for a bit but soon hungering for more. In the early dawn, Henry placed a soft kiss on Ma Le's full, inviting lips. He looked at her lying there naked and knew that image would stay in his mind forever. He dressed and whispered in her ear, "I'll be waiting for you again tonight." Ma Le nodded her agreement with a knowing smile.

And so it was that fall of 1943. Ma Le and Henry were together almost every night but were careful not to be seen together. Many times, Henry would tell his buddies he was retiring for the night, and then he spent several hours reading in his hotel room, only to sneak away to Ma Le's apartment.

Ma Le remembered it as a heady time as they experimented with reckless abandon in their lovemaking over and over. Henry opened up to Ma Le about his marriage and that his love for her could not change the fact that he had a wife waiting for him at home. Ma Le understood but could not help feeling resentment for this faceless woman living across the sea and sharing her lover's name. She told Henry about her childhood in the fields of Vietnam, how she had learned English from a missionary, how Ben Tre had found her at the age of fourteen and had taken her along with her mother to Jakarta for a better life. Ma Le had carved out a career of sorts based upon her exotic looks. Ben Tre profited from her presence, gave her a small salary, and rented the apartment for her. He had also provided a small thatched hut residence for Ma Le's mother, Madam Ky, about ten miles outside of Jakarta. Ma Le visited her mother as much as she could and always brought monetary support she had earned from her salary or from men she had entertained. It had become a satisfying arrangement for all concerned.

Satisfying until now, Ma Le thought as she looked down into her daughter's newborn eyes. She had lost her job with Ben Tre along with the apartment when the pregnancy could no longer be hidden. She spent the last few months of her pregnancy with her mother in the hut, with Henry visiting as much as possible, always bearing necessities for living along with a small amount of money. The baby wriggled in Ma Le's arms again. She had named the infant Susan because of her American heritage and after an American actress she had seen in a movie that year.

Again, Ma Le recalled how Henry had left for Jakarta on leave to visit his wife during the Thanksgiving holiday of 1943. They both ached inside at the separation, but Ma Le knew better than to display the emotions she felt regarding the holiday with his awaiting wife. Upon Henry's return in mid-December though, the fires of passion again ignited, and their regular tryst resumed.

One evening, Henry knocked softly on Ma Le's apartment door. He held a letter in his hand, and a tortured look was on his face.

Ma Le ushered him into the apartment and said, "What wrong?"

"It's Margaret. She's pregnant." The words hung in the air like a black cloud. Henry was shaken, accepted a drink of whiskey, and did not stay that evening. For several weeks, his visits were sporadic, and Ma Le was aware of his suffering. He was torn between the wife waiting in the States and the erotic temptress he had forged a deep bond with in Jakarta. In his mind, he loved them both. They complemented each other well. But in his mind, the adulterous behavior was beginning to rip him apart.

Within a few weeks of Henry's return to Jakarta, Ma Le informed him of the new life growing inside of her. Oddly, the news did not appear to disturb him more. In a way, it now gave a strange balance to the triangular love relationship he had created.

Now, Ma Le looked down at the perfect body of her new baby girl, the fruit and ultimate expression of her love for Henry. She smiled, knowing that Henry would not forget his duty to her or their daughter. She looked up at her mother on the opposite side of the hut and released a sigh. Ma Le would deliver them all from this war-torn region.

Chapter 5

Margaret sat in a wheelchair watching the hospital door open and close while she waited in the lobby on her parents to bring around the car for the ride back to Barnesville. Nurse Weaver asked, "Do you think you can hold both of them for a minute?" Margaret nodded. Nurse Weaver picked up the chubby infant first and said, "Here is big Matthew." She placed him in the crook of Margaret's right arm. "He goes on your strongest arm since he's so fat." They laughed. "And here is his little brother, Aaron." Aaron's thin form was placed in the crook of Margaret's left arm. Margaret glanced back and forth between the two babies with a smile. They had both thrived during her two-week hospitalization.

Nurse Weaver pushed Margaret's wheelchair out the door into the warm September day. She leaned down and whispered in Margaret's ear, "Now you're leaving the hospital as a totally different woman. Never again will you think of yourself first."

Margaret soaked in the sobering truth in silence. The largest infant, Matthew, was given to Joan for her to hold in the front seat of the car. Margaret was bustled into the back seat with the smallest infant, newly named Aaron.

Before long, Charles had navigated the car onto the highway, and they were heading home. Margaret had not realized how stifling her hospital confinement had become until she began watching the scenery whipping by outside her window. This simple ride in the car was exhilarating, and it caused her to release a small giggle.

The Locket

"Margaret," Joan said, "Anne is waiting at home. She was so sweet to come and help us for the first few days while we're all getting used to things."

Margaret was surprised to hear that her older sister was lending a hand. Anne had married well into a wealthy family eight years ago. She then moved to the much larger city of Griffin that was about fifteen miles north of Barnesville. Anne had spent years attempting to conceive a child with no success. She spent her days shopping for expensive antiques, had numerous social engagements, and enjoyed membership in the country club, the garden club, the bridge club, and the like. Anne, who at one time had been interested in children, had abandoned any further musings about starting a family several years ago. Margaret and Joan had witnessed her disturbing transformation. Anne had become nervous and jumpy, and people around her had to pick their words carefully. To further aid herself in dealing with her personal disappointment, Anne had limited contact with any friend or relative who was pregnant or had small children. Telephone calls and letters from Anne had been sparse during Margaret's pregnancy.

"Do you think it's wise for her to be with us during this time?" Margaret asked Joan in an uneasy tone.

Joan flashed a worried look that was soon masked and then said, "There was nothing I could say or do. She called up and offered to help, and I had to let her come. Daniel is away on business for the next two weeks."

Anne and Daniel's marriage had also become strained. His business trips had become more lengthy and frequent over the past two years.

"How long is she staying?" Margaret asked, hoping the visit would be brief.

"She said she would stay with us for at least a week, or maybe the whole two weeks, if we need her," Joan replied. "You know, Margaret, she has to get bored from time to time with Daniel away so much. This will probably be good for her."

Margaret gazed down into tiny Aaron's sleeping face as the car continued to whiz down the road to her hometown. She was amazed that the two babies already displayed very distinct and different personality traits. Thin and frail Aaron seemed pensive and quiet and had a somewhat weak, mournful cry that pulled at her heart. He only cried when something was significantly amiss. Aaron was also quite loving and would burrow deep into the soft, fragrant skin of his mother's neck. Margaret found herself always longing to hold the infants in spite of Joan's warnings that she would spoil the newborns.

Matthew had a strong, demanding cry that could not be ignored. He cried for even the smallest of reasons. A loud sound could startle him and set off ceaseless crying for a full ten minutes or more. Matthew craved attention and distraction and was always aware of his surroundings. He was chubby but active and enjoyed kicking his legs or looking at his flailing fists. Matthew did not always enjoy being held but displayed a great need for adult attention and amusement.

Before long, the car pulled into the driveway of the Harris family home. Large blue bows adorned the mailbox and the front door, announcing the twin male births to everyone. Granny Harris, Anne, and Miss Winnie were all waiting on the edge of their front porch rockers to see the new babies. Mattie came out the front door with a wide smile on her face. "Y'all git on in here. Jesus done bless us wi' two fine boys." She hustled her heavy frame toward the car and reached Margaret's door before anyone. Mattie opened up the car door and said to Margaret, "Now you gimme dat young'un an git yosef in da house. You'll be havin' da vapors in dis Georgia heat out here." Margaret smiled and surrendered Aaron. "Mattie gonna fatten up dis one. I already got my baby scales ready so we's be weighin' him 'bout two or three time a week."

Anne rushed up next and claimed chunky Matthew from Joan. A hungry look came into her eyes as she gazed at him, and he let out a loud howl to announce the wetness of his diaper. Anne's beautiful auburn hair glistened in the September sun as it curled under to sweep along her shoulder. She was a bit awkward, not knowing how the baby should be held. Granny Harris adjusted her granddaughter's hands to give Matthew the proper support, and Anne gave her a grateful smile. It was strange seeing Anne holding a baby, something very foreign to the life she had sculpted. Her expensive suit, high-heeled pumps, made-up face, and manicured fingernails contrasted against the newborn trappings.

"Oh, Margaret," Anne said in an awestruck tone. "He is just beautiful. And what a head full of hair! I think he looks like Henry."

Anne continued to rattle on about Matthew, and Margaret smiled at her sister. It had been many years since she had felt this close to Anne. Glimpses of the girl Margaret had grown up with were emerging on this joyous day, and it was comforting to see those subtle changes in Anne. The instances were many in which Margaret had hoped, wished, and prayed that Anne would find contentment and peace in her marriage. A child with Daniel would have helped solidify their bond.

Miss Winnie rushed up and hugged Margaret and looked into her substitute daughter's eyes. Only Winifred sensed that a new mother needed additional time and attention to adjust to all of the new changes. "This is a tough time without Henry," Winifred stated. "Are you holding up all right?"

"I'm really emotional," Margaret replied. "I cry at any little thing, but I guess that's to be expected." Winifred nodded her agreement. "I'll be fine. I've got so much help from everyone."

They all walked into the house, and the parade continued upstairs to the spare room Mattie had converted into a nursery. Joan had selected two of everything. Two beautiful white organdy skirted bassinets were placed toward the right side of the room. To the left were two large baby cribs adorned with sleepy-eyed lambs and bearing each baby's name that had been painted on the respective headboards. A changing table located on the back wall was complete with shelves filled with diapers, diaper shirts, safety pins, various creams and powders, and other necessary implements. Shelves on the right wall were loaded with teddy bears, rattles, infant toiletry sets, and several empty picture frames waiting to be filled with photographs.

Joan had even adorned the walls with playful, childlike scenes to complete the nursery. Margaret was aghast and grateful to all involved for creating such a pleasing environment to welcome her babies. Tears sprang to her dark brown eyes, and she choked out the words, "Thank you all for this. Words aren't enough to show you how grateful I am." She walked over and gave each person a tight, meaningful hug. Her thoughts flew to Henry, and it took great will to hold back a flood of tears mourning her husband's loss of this treasured memory and her hatred for the war that had taken him away.

"Charles," Joan commanded, "please take the bassinets downstairs so the babies can rest in them while we're preparing supper."

Charles laughed and said, "I don't think those babies will be resting in the bassinets too much. Looks like Mattie and Anne won't be letting go of them any time soon."

Both Mattie and Anne looked up at the mention of their names and gave Charles a double dose of piercing looks.

"Now, Mr. Charles," Mattie began, "don't ya be killin' my joy at raisin' mo' chillun. Dese babies gonna warm our hearts and wake up our tired bones, an if'n us womenfolk want to hold 'em all day long, ya best not say one word." And with that, Mattie pranced out of the room to head downstairs with Aaron, her soft, fat flesh jiggling with the quick movements.

Anne giggled and said, "I guess she told you, Daddy. You remember how protective Mattie is with her babies. Just follow her child-rearing rules, and you can't go wrong. Margaret and I are great examples." Anne looked over at her younger sister with a knowing smile. Charles just scratched his head.

"All right, all right," Charles said. "Women have been running this household for years, but now I've got two healthy grandsons who will be ruling the roost, so to speak, before you know it."

The house was full of activity for several more hours as everyone rushed around tending to baby needs, helping Mattie with supper, unpacking suitcases, or completing routine chores. Just yesterday, this childhood home of Margaret's was quiet, as long years had silenced the girlish cries and giggles of the two Harris daughters. Margaret

The Locket

gazed over at Anne, who had been holding Matthew for hours, rocking him and talking to him when she could between hugs and kisses. For some reason, Anne had attached herself to Matthew and hardly seemed to notice Aaron. Margaret realized that Matthew's countenance was calmer than ever before during Anne's lingering attention. A twinge of guilt crossed Margaret's mind as she felt that perhaps her attention to Aaron in his thin, frail state had tipped the scales unfairly, causing her bond with the smallest infant to be greater.

In response to her disturbing thoughts, she walked over to Anne and said, "Let me hold Matthew for a while. It takes a lot of time for one mother to get to know two babies." Anne understood, relinquished Matthew, and placed him in Margaret's arms.

"Do you think I could hold Aaron?" Anne asked, also feeling that she had neglected half of the duo.

"Sure," Margaret replied. "And take that scared look off of your face. He may be small, but he won't break. Just make sure you support his head well like Granny showed you." The two sisters sat side by side on the couch, holding the two brothers.

Joan spied them and said, "I have to get a picture of this for their baby books." She retrieved the camera and took several pictures. "Now, as soon as Aaron fills out a little more, we'll take them both downtown to the photography studio for some posed pictures to frame. I don't want to miss a thing about my first grandchildren."

Anne took a nervous look around the room after her mother's comment. Margaret sensed her sister's unrest and opened her mouth to distract Anne in some way, but she was too late. Anne arose with a start, placed Aaron back in his bassinet, and excused herself to help Mattie in the kitchen. Margaret had seen so much of the old Anne this evening, and she wanted to see more. She vowed to continue to create an open environment for her sister over the next week. Perhaps the Anne of her youth would emerge for longer periods.

The Harris household found dinner to be somewhat disorganized that first evening home with the babies. Everyone took turns eating because both newborns proved to be fussy during the meal, requiring some comfort and walking the floor to ease a slight case of colic they had both developed. By the time the dishes were cleared away, Margaret's eyes were drooping, but she was determined not to give into the exhaustion. Margaret felt the uneasy gazes of her family as they wondered whether mothering would come easily for her or if she would need a great deal of guidance. She stepped into her role with determination and purpose, accepting only the least bit of help from Joan or Anne when feeding the babies and preparing them for bed. When both infants were asleep in their bassinets on each side of their mother's bed, Margaret walked down the hall to Anne's old bedroom and knocked on the door. When Anne opened the door, Margaret whispered in a weary tone, "I might need your help with the babies during the night."

A warm light glowed in Anne's eyes as she replied, "Don't worry. I'll be right there with you."

Four times that night, the sisters arose to the beckoning cries of the two baby boys. They worked together in unison, with Anne always reaching first for Matthew and Margaret always attending to Aaron's mournful cries. The tasks were menial and custodial in nature but fulfilling and comfortable. During the last feeding of the night, Joan looked into the nursery and watched her two daughters rocking the newborns back into slumber. Anne hummed a familiar lullaby while a hungry light continued to burn in her eyes. Joan whispered a short prayer of thanks to God for her healthy grandsons who were filling her home and heart with gladness.

~ ~ ~ ~ ~

The smell of strong coffee wafting upstairs awakened Margaret around nine o'clock. She arose, donned her cotton robe and slippers, peeked in to witness the babies sleeping, and padded downstairs for breakfast. Margaret was surprised to find Joan, Granny, and Anne dressed for the day and finishing the morning meal.

"Well, y'all are mighty chipper this morning," Margaret observed. This mothering business is making me a real sleepyhead. And how in the world"—Margaret turned to Anne—"can you look so good after the night we just had?"

Anne responded, "It probably has something to do with the fact that I didn't carry those two little ones for nine months. I think we would all agree that those darlings will be worth all of the sleepless nights and rough mornings." The women nodded their agreement.

Mattie placed a steaming cup of coffee into Margaret's grateful hands. Joan piped in with, "Besides, Margaret, we'll probably have several visitors today coming to see the babies. Some of the ladies at the beauty shop told me they would be dropping in, and Effie and Aubrey will definitely be coming by around eleven."

"Well, that's just my luck," Margaret said in a disappointed tone. "Our first visitors just had to be Effie and Aubrey. Mama, I don't know how you can stand to be in the same room with those two for more than five minutes. I've often felt you need your head examined for striking up a friendship with that woman and her weird son."

Mattie and Anne giggled at Margaret's last comment. "Now, Margaret," Joan chided, "I don't like to hear you speak badly about other people. Effie has had many hardships she's had to face over the years. The death of her husband just about killed her too, and that's why Aubrey turned out to be the way he is. You know Charles can't abide either one of them, so I had to schedule their visit when he was at work."

Anne said, "Maybe I'll just follow Daddy's lead and leave to run some errands before they get here." A broad smile crossed Anne's face.

"Oh no," Margaret replied. "You're staying right here. Effie and Aubrey will need another warm body to kiss on. Yuck!" Margaret wrinkled up her nose at her musings.

"Oh me, I forgot about the endless hugs and kisses," Anne stated, dreading the visit as much as Margaret.

"You'll have to help me keep the babies away from the shower of hugs and kisses," Margaret told Anne. "Let's think positively. We'll be getting the worst visit out of the way first. Anne, did you hear what Aubrey did in June?" Anne shook her head to indicate that she had not heard any of the gossip. "Remember how Effie's been bragging all over town about how Aubrey has been attending Emory University for the past four years, and he has done so well and all?" Anne nodded. "He was supposed to be getting some sort of fine arts degree. Well, come to find out, he's been duping us all by just driving to Atlanta every week, living with his aunt Cattie, and acting like he's going to school. He even fooled Effie and Cattie and then sent out invitations to commencement at Emory this past June when, over all of these years, he hadn't even registered at that highfaluting school. And to think that we all were about to start sending him graduation gifts. But Sadie Samuels called up a friend of her husband's who is a dean at Emory. He checked it all out and confirmed all of our suspicions. Of course, Sadie spread the embarrassing news all over town, and Effie has been sort of scared to show her face much over the summer. To tell you the truth, I kind of enjoyed that vacation from Effie and Aubrey."

Anne, Mattie, and Granny Harris let out a roar of laughter at the ridiculous story. Anne said through tears of laughter, "I'll have to tell Daniel all about it. He knows Effie well."

Joan gave both of her daughters a stern look and admonished them with, "I can't believe I raised two daughters who enjoy engaging in the worst kind of gossip. And as for you," she said, pointing to Mattie, "be nice to Effie and Aubrey, or I'll be sending you out to work in the garden with Hawk and Pierce."

Mattie stopped her chuckling and squared her shoulders a little straighter while she cleaned up the breakfast dishes.

Margaret left the kitchen and walked up the stairs to get dressed for the day. As she passed by the nursery, she heard some soft baby fussing that was about to escalate into crying. She walked into the room and noticed that Aaron had rooted around in his bassinet, and his body now was shoved deep into the side of the small bed. Matthew was in a deep sleep. Margaret picked up Aaron, and the fussing stopped, but he was wide awake. She took him with her to the bedroom and placed him on the bed so she could talk to him while she got ready for the day. Aaron watched her movements with his small blue eyes, which were about to turn brown.

Margaret selected a simple beige dress with an elastic waistline, as her figure wouldn't be back to normal for several more weeks. The small belt had to be fastened in a hole two points away from its usual location. Margaret sighed and looked at her reflection in the mirror. She hoped her figure would soon return to its former state before Henry came home on leave. Her thoughts flew to their lovemaking, and that familiar thrill of desire was felt in the pit of her stomach. She looked over at Aaron flailing about on the bed and smiled at the satisfaction of knowing that her babies were the ultimate expression of her love for Henry. It made her feel special to know that no other woman could share this bond with him. She yearned to hear from him. His letters had been somewhat infrequent of late.

Margaret heard a noise and pulled back the white eyelet curtain in her bedroom to see Effie and Aubrey Cunningham coming up the front walkway. She ran a comb through her shiny black curls, put red lipstick on her full lips, and placed some black pumps on her feet. Margaret then scooped up Aaron and took him downstairs to greet the guests.

Effie and Aubrey were waiting for Margaret at the bottom of the stairs. Both of them were overdressed for the outing, as was their custom. Effie had donned a flamboyant fuchsia suit with stiletto-heeled black pumps and seamed stockings. She was now in her midfifties but considered herself as young and attractive as ever. Effie was a small woman with a delicate build who flitted around a room. She was a big talker, had a short attention span, and had trouble holding a decent conversation because of her poor listening skills. She was dripping in diamonds acquired from her late husband's estate. Diamond earrings twinkled on her earlobes, a diamond watch adorned her wrist, a diamond pin was fastened to the left lapel of her suit, several diamond necklaces clinked around her neck, and more of the glistening jewels peeked up from most of her ten fingers. The sight was blinding.

Aubrey hovered behind his adopted mother with a wide, silly grin on his face. Effie had never conceived a child during her marriage but had been asked to raise Aubrey as her own when her cousin's wife died unexpectedly one winter. At the time, the boy was only two years old. Effie then launched into raising Aubrey in a manner that caused him to be an exact replica of Effie, only in a somewhat male form. Aubrey was dressed in his Sunday-best navy suit, resplendent with a diamond tie tack and chunky gold cuff links. As he waved his hands about in a girlish fashion, the diamonds from his two pinky rings flashed in the morning sunlight. He attempted, and had done so all of his life, to imitate Effie's every mannerism, gesture, and speech pattern. It seemed that he never had an original thought. In fact, Margaret had been surprised to hear of his devious plan to fake attend Emory University. The originality of his plot was a break from his usual traditions. Aubrey's only talent was the fact that he displayed some good taste in interior decorating, and Effie's home was a testimony to his gift. Margaret could see that Aubrey might have become an excellent interior decorator if only he had the guts to let go of his dear mama.

Margaret held Aaron directly in front of her, hoping that she could avoid one of the gushing embraces. Her plan was foiled when Effie rushed up from the left and Aubrey from the right to squeeze her from both sides and to plant wet, sloppy kisses on both of her cheeks. Margaret endured the unwanted attention and excused herself to the kitchen, where Mattie chuckled to watch her wipe the slobber from her cheeks with a napkin. Margaret then returned to the living room to endure the rest of the visit.

As Margaret sat down in a comfortable living room chair, Effie asked, "Joan, where is Charles on this fine day?"

"Oh, he asked me to tell you how sorry he was that he would have to miss your visit, but there was some pressing business to tend to down at the Ford dealership," Joan lied. "I'm just so glad you two could drop by and see the babies. You know, you're our first visitors."

"Well, I feel honored," Effie replied. "Don't you, Aubrey?"

"Oh yes, Mama"—Aubrey's favorite, overused reply.

Anne had taken Matthew out of his bassinet to join everyone in the living room. Effie observed the twin boys being held by Margaret and Anne. She then said, "Well, Margaret, these two hardly look like twins."

"That's because they're fraternal twins," Margaret responded with very little patience.

Effie and Aubrey then proceeded to walk over to each infant and evaluate every aspect of the newborns. It was as if no one else was in the room. Effie began with, "Now Aubrey, look at this fat one over here. Goodness, I guess he looks like Henry, but it's hard to tell."

"Oh yes, Mama. It must be Henry," Aubrey parroted back.

"That hair is going to be a problem though, sticking up like it does and all. But they sell that special pomade at Wally's Drugs and Soda Fountain that would slick that hair down just right."

Aubrey came back with, "You're right, Mama, but remember, I used that pomade on my cowlick, and it gave me that terrible case of dandruff. Thought I'd never get rid of it. Land sakes, it looked just like there'd been a snowstorm on my shoulders."

"Oh, I forgot about that, Aubrey. I guess they will have to just use petroleum jelly. Something has to be done because he's beginning to resemble a rooster, and I'm sure Henry wouldn't want that."

"Oh no, that would be terrible, Mama." Aubrey hung on every word that tumbled out of his mother's very large mouth. Margaret's face began to turn red, and she started to open her mouth with a heated retort when Joan touched her daughter's arm in a silent warning to keep her comments to herself. So Margaret continued to endure the torture.

After examining all of Matthew's attributes, Effie and Aubrey moved over to Aaron to pass further judgments on his physical features.

"Oh me," Effie began, "this one's skinny as a rail. Why, Aubrey, it looks like he just left one of those concentration camps overseas with the funny names. What was it now? Oh, I remember—Ashwootz. Wasn't that it?"

"You're right, Mama. He looks just like one of those poor Jew boys who have been suffering over there. I guess Margaret's going to have to work long and hard to fatten this one up. But he's cute in a funny sort of way. Kind of looks like our cat. Don't you think?"

"Aubrey," Effie said, "you always find the beauty in everything, honey. But I think he strikes a resemblance to my dear Pepper before his passing. Oh rest his sweet canine soul. I miss that pooch something terrible."

An offended look came over Margaret's face at the comparison of her dear Aaron to a ratty little Chihuahua Effie had at her home for years. He had passed away early in the summer after a chronic case of the runs.

Aubrey saw the offended look and attempted to rectify the situation with, "Oh, Margaret, that was a genuine compliment. You know we all loved Pepper. I think the whole town of Barnesville is still grieving since his unfortunate passing."

"Margaret," Effie began, "I almost forgot to give you the gift Aubrey and I picked out."

Effie handed Margaret a small jewelry box wrapped in paper with a baby motif. With her jaw clenched to bite back all of the heated retorts that came to mind, Margaret unwrapped the gift and opened the box to reveal two tiny gold pinky rings designed to be small enough for a toddler to wear.

"Now you train these boys right," Effie said, "and they won't put small things in their mouths. Why, I gave Aubrey his first pinky ring when I got him at age two, and he's been wearing them ever since." Aubrey proudly waved his elaborate pinky rings in the air to model his gaudy finery.

Joan said, "Oh my, Effie and Aubrey. How thoughtful of you. We'll just put these rings up there on a shelf with their silver baby cups. I'm sure Margaret will want a picture of them wearing these rings. We can have it done down at the photography studio."

"Yes, do make sure we get a copy of that picture," Effie replied.

Margaret choked out, "Thank you, Effie and Aubrey," but then noticed Sadie Samuels walking through the front gate. "Well, there is Sadie coming up the front walkway." Margaret noticed a nervous look come into Effie's eyes. Aubrey was so torn up at the prospect of encountering the woman who had exposed his sneaky little secret that he started to shake a bit. Margaret thought how much he looked like that nervous little dog named Pepper.

"Oh, Mama," he said. "We just have to get going. Maybe we could go out the back door and see that victory garden the whole town has been talking about."

Before Effie and Aubrey could make a speedy exit, Granny Harris was already ushering Sadie into the living room. Effie and Aubrey looked like scared cats, but Sadie had an evil sort of grin on her face when she encountered the two.

"How nice it is to see you, Effie and Aubrey," Sadie said. "I haven't seen much of y'all this summer."

"We've been busy," Effie replied.

"Busy doing what?" Sadie questioned them.

"Oh, this and that. Catching up on things," Effie responded, having been caught off guard without a rehearsed answer.

Sadie smiled again with a mischievous glint in her eyes and said, "Yes, I guess Aubrey has had a lot of extra time on his hands to catch up on things now that he's not up in Atlanta all week going to school and all. I bet your aunt Cattie is really missing your company now, Aubrey, since you've finished school and you won't be living with her anymore. We would all just love to hear your future plans now that you've got that degree behind you."

Effie and Aubrey squirmed under the close scrutiny and made quick excuses while Sadie followed them to the door with, "So long now, and don't be a stranger."

When Sadie returned to the living room, everyone was laughing. Joan could not hide the grin that appeared on her face as she said, "You're cruel, Sadie."

"I'm sorry," Sadie said through her laughter. "I just couldn't resist such a wonderful opportunity to make those two squirm. It's so entertaining."

Sadie plopped her full-figured form onto the couch with a sigh. She was an attractive woman who was now in her late fifties. Her hair was curly and styled so that the silver-gray strands framed her face.

Sadie's appearance was classic and understated in her navy blue suit, a sight that was in stark contrast to her forward, outspoken manner. She was a powerful woman in this tiny kingdom because she relished her role as the mayor's wife. Born into a humble household and raised in poverty, Sadie's quick mind and resourcefulness had landed her a good job as a milliner's assistant at Samuel's department store when she was a young woman. It was there that she caught young Thomas Samuels's eye. Their heated romance lead to marriage into the most prominent family in Barnesville. Sadie knew all of the town's gossip. Margaret had heard that Sadie had even taken to eavesdropping on local telephone calls when she filled in for the operators in an emergency. Margaret was glad that federal laws prohibited her from reading other residents' mail. However, even with certain restrictions on her nosiness, not one bit of gossip passed her by. Her memory was sharp. If you were Sadie's enemy, you were in hell.

Sadie stayed quite a while that afternoon and even joined them all for a light lunch. The Harris family had always gotten along well with Sadie and her husband, Tom. Joan, Anne, and Margaret were careful to filter their conversations so as not to reveal anything too personal, knowing that all of Barnesville would be privy to the information before nightfall. Just before Sadie's departure, the postman delivered the mail. Margaret retrieved it from the foyer floor, where it had fallen from the mail slot, while she walked Sadie to the door. Her heart started beating a bit faster when she noticed a letter from Henry. As was her usual custom, she folded the letter and placed it in her pocket to read alone, in a private moment, after dinner that night.

Margaret rushed through her usual tasks that evening and did not chat much during dinner, with the awaiting letter on her mind. Mercifully, the babies were not as fussy, seeming to fall asleep on cue at nine o'clock. When they were resting in the bassinets, Margaret stretched out over her bed to read the letter that had been beckoning all night. Her eyes raced back and forth, consuming each line of Henry's script, wishing he were lying beside her at that very moment. A rising feeling of disappointment overcame her. Tears welled up in

The Locket

her eyes, the letter fell from her trembling hands to float to the floor, and she buried her head into her folded arms as quiet sobs wracked her body.

Anne walked past her sister's open bedroom door to witness the disturbing scene. She entered the room and picked up the letter from the floor, the obvious catalyst for her younger sister's distress. Anne read only the last few lines of the letter that revealed the reason for Margaret's heartache. Henry would not be home for Christmas, and his words left little hope that there would be any change of plans.

Anne touched Margaret's arm, and it startled her a bit. She then folded Margaret into a tight embrace while the sobs escalated. Anne was uncertain of how to comfort Margaret because she had never allowed herself to feel this sort of loneliness and longing turned to disappointment. Motherhood was foreign to her, and her marriage lacked the depth of feeling she had stopped fantasizing about several years before. But she held tight to the distraught Margaret, and that served to bring some comfort to both of their bruised hearts.

After a long while, Anne said, "I don't know what to say except that I'm sorry." Anne looked down into Margaret's distressed face.

"And I don't know why," Margaret choked out, "I get my hopes up and start counting on something that I have absolutely no control over. When will I ever learn?"

"Learn," Anne repeated. "Learn to be numb like me and no longer feel anything?" Margaret looked up following those words. "You don't want that." Anne looked straight into Margaret's face as she spoke. "Do you know that I can't remember the last time I felt real joy, real hate, real loneliness, or real love? Maybe I've never felt it. I won't even let Daniel touch me anymore. We haven't slept in the same room in months, and Mama and Daddy wonder why he's always out of town on business trips. I know he has other women, but at least he's discreet about it. No, Margaret, you don't want to learn how not to feel anything. It's a horrible existence."

Margaret's tears had stopped as she listened to Anne's revelations. "Anne," she said, "I had no idea things were so bad."

"Of course you didn't. I've worked very hard to hide it all. You talk about control, and I guess we've both had an awful lot of control over our lives up until now. You can't control the war and the fact that it has taken Henry away from you, and I can't control the fact that I'll never conceive a child." Her words rang with a strange sort of finality.

"Anne," Margaret began, "you have been so distant over the past few years that I've been afraid to talk to you about all of this. Do you really feel that you won't ever have children?"

"That's what Dr. Bartholomew tells me. Daniel and I tried to conceive for two or three years, and it just never happened. Then one day Dr. Bartholomew examined me again, and he ran some additional tests. Then he told me that my female organs are not fully developed. He said I must not be releasing any eggs, so I'll never get pregnant. Daniel was so disappointed. I could tell. He has changed a lot since we found out that there won't be any children. And I really don't know what to do with myself. I had all of these ideas about what my life would be like. Never once did I imagine that motherhood would not be mine to experience. Count your blessings, Margaret. You have two beautiful sons and a husband who will be yours when the war is over."

Margaret's tears now seemed to be selfish ones in light of Anne's revealing words. "Have you thought about adoption?" Margaret asked the obvious question.

"Yes, we've discussed it. But you know how Daniel's family is about that sort of thing. His mother believes that we would surely get a child with bad blood coming from low-class stock. Even if Daniel and I went against his parents' wishes and adopted a child, I don't think the Cheavers would ever accept the child as a true member of the family." That hungry, haunted look entered Anne's eyes once again.

"You know I'll share my boys with you as much as possible," Margaret offered to her sister.

They walked into the nursery. Anne reached down and picked up Matthew to hold him close as he slept. The fragrant baby smell that no perfume manufacturer could imitate was heady. His skin was like velvet, his smell and lethargic movements were comforting, and his dark hair tickled her nose when she kissed his head.

"Just let me share in these special months you have here with your babies. I'll hold these memories close in my heart." Anne placed Matthew back in his bassinet just as his own mother would. She then said, "I'll help you with the feedings every night that I'm here. Don't take that away from me."

Margaret nodded her agreement to the shared relationship, and then Anne walked down the hall to her own bedroom. Feeling the need to make some immediate plans that she had total control over and ignoring the lateness of the hour, Margaret walked down the stairs to the telephone table located beside the staircase. She placed a call to James Walsh and heard his deep voice say, "Hello."

"James," Margaret began as he recognized her distinctive voice from the solitary spoken name, "I've decided to accept that offer of Christmas in Connecticut."

Chapter 6

Margaret stood in the middle of her bedroom surveying the three suitcases she had packed for the Christmas trip to Connecticut. Each case was overflowing with what she considered necessities. Margaret smiled, remembering how Henry had always teased her about what he termed her obsessive packing ritual. He loved watching her fret over everything placed in the suitcase. Margaret always felt quite certain that various items were required for the trip, and then Henry would note that the articles were never touched or that, even in the remotest sense, they could not be considered necessities. But Margaret knew one thing. If she didn't pack it, she would need it during the vacation. So a lot of things were packed.

Joan walked into her daughter's bedroom to say, "Margaret, I wish you would reconsider this trip and spend Christmas here with your family. It just kills me to think that I won't see my grandsons on Christmas morning." Joan picked up Aaron from his pallet on the floor to hold him high in the air and watch him giggle. His form had filled out now at nearly fourteen pounds. Mattie had known just how to fatten him up. She had added Karo syrup and cooking oil to each bottle of formula that produced a sweet and fattening concoction to round out his cheeks.

"Mama, the babies are so little that they will never remember this Christmas. Besides, they aren't even old enough to know or understand what's going on.

There will be plenty of other Christmases for us to share when

The Locket

the boys are older, and we can all enjoy their excitement. I need some time away. Sometimes Barnesville seems so stifling, and it's been a long time since I've seen James. You know he promised Henry he would look out for us. In his last letter, Henry seemed so pleased we were making the trip."

"I know," Joan replied. "It's just that you've never been away from home at Christmas." Joan looked at her youngest daughter with new eyes that cold December morning. Margaret had seemed so different over the past few months since the birth of her twins. She was much more opinionated and outspoken, to the point of offending others at times. Margaret had become very self-sufficient and needed little, if any, help caring for the two babies. Joan saw through the helpless façade Margaret had assumed when Anne came home to visit. It was an illusion created for the older sibling's benefit to allow her to share the boys and for Anne to feel needed and a part of everything.

Joan knew she could not argue the point further. Margaret had a stubborn streak, and it was now magnified. Joan helped her gather the suitcases and deposit them in the foyer.

Before long, Joan, Charles, the babies, Margaret, and the mountain of luggage were contained in the Harris family car to take the half-hour drive to a small airport located in Griffin. James was sending his private airplane, a small six-seater, to collect Margaret and her little ones. He had even promised to send a hired nanny to assist Margaret in caring for the infants during the trip. Every detail had been orchestrated by James, and no problems were anticipated, but Joan could not erase the lines of worry etched around her brow as she waved goodbye to her determined offspring. Joan and Charles stood by their car and watched the airplane wing its way north until only a small dot was visible in the sky.

Mrs. Oliver, the nanny promised by James, proved to be very competent. The middle-aged English woman described her qualifications and past employment history at length during the flight. She and Margaret then discussed personal issues in an easy manner so that by the conclusion of the journey, Margaret felt she was traveling with an old friend. Aaron slept on Mrs. Oliver's ample bosom, while Margaret gave Matthew a bottle. Just before landing at James's private airfield located at the edge of his massive estate, Margaret watched Mrs. Oliver's strong hands complete the quickest, most efficient diaper change she had ever witnessed. Now fully convinced that Mrs. Oliver was well qualified for her position and feeling that her newly acquired mothering skills were a bit lacking, Margaret gave a sigh of contentment, knowing the holiday would be a memorable one.

Margaret looked out of the airplane window to witness a huge expanse of snow glistening in the midday sun. She had never seen a white Christmas. This was a rare treat. The airplane landed on the shoveled runway as the Walsh family butler watched and waited beside a large, sleek black car. He ushered the group into the awaiting car for the drive to the main house located in the center of the one-hundred-plus-acre estate. Margaret was delighted to view the snow-covered terrain with its diamond-like brightness. She felt like a princess off on some mysterious adventure in a fierce but beautiful foreign land that was far removed from the last few months filled with midnight feedings and endless diaper changes.

Margaret glanced over to see that her babies were banging their favorite rattles while sitting on Mrs. Oliver's more than ample lap. When the car stopped at the bottom of the brick steps leading to the double front doors, Mrs. Oliver said, "Now you go ahead. I'll look after these two and get them set up in the nursery."

Margaret followed Mrs. Oliver's command and rushed up the brick front steps to be greeted by Leonard, James's personal manservant, who accompanied him during those college days back at Tech. Margaret gave him a warm, special greeting because of his importance to James and Henry now and in years past. Leonard was still looking fit, strong, and vital.

Leonard took Margaret's coat and ushered her into the formally appointed living room, complete with lavish antique furniture, deep-hued oriental rugs, ornate framed paintings, and the like. Margaret had always been a bit put off by the formal part of the Walsh family estate but knew that she would soon feel at ease in James's

The Locket

unassuming presence. Leonard had, of course, offered Margaret a seat, but she felt too excited to sit down. So she walked around the room, admiring various objects of art and surveying photographs of family and friends.

A smile came to her lips when she encountered a picture of her, Henry, and James around the time of her engagement. Margaret noted the handsome, rugged lines of James's face and remembered his sky-blue eyes fringed with heavy, dark lashes. In the picture, a curly blond lock of hair fell over his forehead. James would have been a tall man if polio had not claimed the use of his legs. But even at that, he was quite handsome, and his Scandinavian heritage had produced good looks that were not lost on Margaret. His torso was broad and powerful with overdeveloped muscle groups gleaned through many years of propelling his wheelchair and transferring his immobile lower body, giving him sculpted definition in the upper body.

The man of Margaret's musings wheeled his chair through the large, marble-floored foyer to see her lovely form while she was still unaware of his distant scrutiny. Ever practical, Margaret had chosen a camel-colored wool pantsuit in which to travel on this cold winter day. The rich camel color made her dark curls shine. Her skin was like fine porcelain. Margaret's dark eyebrows winged over her hooded, dark brown eyes, complete with the longest set of eyelashes that James had ever seen. When James first met Margaret, he had teased her by saying that she must certainly trip over those lashes while walking on a daily basis. The memory brought a soft smile to his face. At that very moment, the woman in front of him, who had claimed his thoughts for years, looked up from her distraction to gaze at him with a bright glimmer in her eyes.

Margaret ran to James's wheelchair, and he folded her into a deep, tight embrace that lingered longer than both of them expected. Margaret smelled his maleness, a scent that had eluded her for well over a year since Henry's last departure. James's strong arms were like a warm blanket that could forever protect her from the cold winter chill. An audible sigh was released from Margaret's lips just before James planted a quick kiss upon them. She was surprised to realize that a flash of desire arose in the pit of her stomach. It startled her and caused her to pull away quicker than James would have liked. He continued to hold fast to her small, soft hand.

"It's wonderful to have you here," James said. "I had forgotten how beautiful you are. You wear motherhood well."

A bit of a blush seeped into Margaret's cheeks. "You're too sweet. To tell you the truth, I had actually forgotten what it felt like to receive such a nice compliment from a man."

"That's a shame. You should be complimented often. But … then you might grow bored with it."

"Somehow," remarked Margaret, "I don't think I could ever grow tired of hearing it from the man I love. It's important to enjoy every aspect of being a woman and not to lose yourself in motherhood."

Silence ensued for a moment as both were a bit shocked at the instant intimacy of their words in Henry's absence. James changed the tone of his conversation. "Speaking of motherhood, where are those two little ones?"

"Mrs. Oliver took them on up to the nursery. By the way, she certainly is top-notch. That was so wonderful of you to secure her services during our holiday. How did you ever find her?"

"I can't take the credit for that. I found out about her through a friend who persuaded her to come out of retirement for this short assignment."

"Short but lucrative, I suppose," Margaret said.

"I must admit, I made it worth her while."

"Well, I can't thank you enough."

"It was nothing. I'm just glad to have you and the boys here. It's a special treat to be able to spend my holiday with a favorite friend. But I bet your dear mama was squawking when she discovered I had nabbed you for Christmas."

"You've got that right," Margaret said with laughter.

At that moment, Leonard entered the living room to inquire regarding their need for refreshment. James instructed him to bring coffee and sweets into the solarium. Just before Leonard walked out

The Locket

of the room, James added, "And have Mrs. Oliver bring the babies down so we can enjoy them for a while."

The large, airy solarium was one of Margaret's favorite rooms. She was surprised to hear that it was even in use during the winter. As they entered the room, Margaret gasped to behold the twelve-foot Christmas tree, resplendent with hundreds of gold balls and bows and numerous small, hand-crafted angels, all unique in some way. A mammoth fireplace at one end of the room crackled with a roaring fire. The outside wall of windows displayed the soft, fluffy snow scene Margaret had witnessed from the airplane and during the drive up to the main house.

Margaret inspected one of the angels and commented on their beauty.

"I'm glad you like them. When I found out you were coming for Christmas, I commissioned the artist to design one for you and one for each of your two new babies. It will be a keepsake to help you remember this holiday. Your angels are right there in the center of the tree."

Margaret looked to discover a beautiful, slender angel with dark, curly locks surrounded by cherubs. The angel's resemblance to Margaret was remarkable, and it caused her to ask, "How in the world could the artist have produced such a close likeness of me?"

"From the image that will always be etched in my mind and heart," James replied with a certain softness that had entered his eyes and the velvet, smooth tones of his voice.

Mrs. Oliver entered the room carrying both of the babies and said, "I won't be able to carry them both for too many more days. They are a wee bit on the heavy side."

"Don't I know it," responded Margaret. "I've developed a pretty strong back."

James piped in with, "I bet Mattie had a hand in fattening them up." He then took a long look at both infants and said, "Let me hold each one individually, and I bet I can guess what their personalities are like." Mrs. Oliver placed Aaron in his lap first. Aaron looked up into the stranger's face with curiosity and then responded to James's bright smile with a toothless grin. He snuggled close into James's warm chest to bury his face for an anticipated game of peek-a-boo. James let out a deep laugh that rang through to the rafters of the solarium. Margaret and Mrs. Oliver joined in the laughter, knowing that Aaron was asking for the game to begin as his eyes peeked back up.

"Aaron," James began, "I believe that you're good-natured and happy most of the time. You hardly ever cry unless something is seriously wrong. You are intelligent, and you will be quite articulate. You are your mother."

"I don't know about that last bit," Margaret stated, "but you were pretty accurate about everything else."

James then exchanged babies and attempted to hold Matthew. Matthew squirmed, not wanting to be held. "Woah, big fella," James said, but Matthew continued to squirm. "This one knows his own mind. He, too, is quite intelligent but stubborn. Matthew probably cries easily at the least little thing. He craves attention, but no matter how much you give him, it isn't enough." James's words were true and touched a guilt-ridden chord in Margaret, which caused her to lose interest in this little game.

Margaret gathered Matthew from James and held him up high to produce the desired giggle. James looked closely at the two, reading more about their relationship than Margaret wanted to reveal. She then deposited him in Leonard's waiting arms to be taken back to the nursery, along with Aaron, for the afternoon nap.

"I'll bet you're tired from the trip," James commented as he noticed a strained look around Margaret's dark eyes.

"I guess I am a bit tired."

"Leonard can show you to your room so you can rest before our Christmas Eve dinner. We'll be dining at seven o'clock tonight." Margaret nodded her agreement.

Margaret followed Leonard up the swirling staircase to one of the many guest rooms. Again, this room was lavish in its appointments and had a cheery air. The walls were painted sunshine yellow that served to lift anyone's spirits. There was a large canopy bed

The Locket

dressed with a yellow-and-white striped bedspread and canopy set. A cherrywood vanity had been placed on the left side of the large bedroom, complete with an antique sterling-silver comb and brush set and several bottles of expensive French perfume. Delicate chairs, upholstered in fabric to match the expansive bed, were scattered throughout the light, airy bedroom. A cream-colored chaise lounge added more opulence to the feminine room. Margaret opened a dresser drawer to find that all of her clothes had been unpacked and neatly folded in their appropriate places.

It then occurred to her that she should check on the twins, so she walked down a long hallway, hoping she would encounter the nursery. Margaret heard Mrs. Oliver's voice singing an old familiar lullaby, and she followed the melody. When she looked into the large nursery, only in use when guests arrived with children in tow, Margaret watched in silence as the nanny rocked Aaron to sleep. Matthew was already sleeping in his crib. Margaret whispered her intention to rest for a few hours to Mrs. Oliver. They agreed upon a time to bring the babies downstairs again to play by the Christmas tree, and then Margaret returned to her room.

It felt strange to be left alone like this without pressing tasks to be completed for Aaron and Matthew. Margaret slipped out of her traveling attire and wrapped a red satin robe around her tall, thin frame. She surveyed her appearance in a large mirror standing near the door to a private bath in her room. The scarlet, smooth satin skimmed over her form. She was proud that her figure had returned to normal by just watching her diet a bit. In fact, she had never looked better in her life, which seemed surprising because of the hard work involved in caring for twins. A sad light entered her eyes to know that the man she loved was not there to enjoy her body. "Things will be different when the war is over," she whispered aloud as she ran her right hand over her full breast and down to her hip.

Margaret turned to pick up a book she had been attempting to finish reading for weeks. It seemed that the birth of her two sons had bitten into her reading time. Normally, she could have finished the volume in two or three days. Constant interruptions and simple exhaustion had kept Margaret from reading more than ten pages at a time. She stretched her body out across the bed, covered her legs with a cream-colored, wool throw, and began reading the novel. As it had been over the past months, within minutes her eyelids began to droop, and she was forced to place the book on her bedside table as slumber overtook her.

Her sleep was warm and rejuvenating but difficult to awake from when she heard a soft knock on her door.

"Yes," she answered.

A young, uniform-clad maid opened the door a crack to say, "Mr. Walsh asked me to awaken you to dress for dinner."

"Thank you," Margaret said. She then glanced over to the clock. "Tell him I'll meet him in the solarium at six thirty."

"Yes, ma'am," the young woman answered.

Margaret arose from the warm bed to select an appropriate dress for Christmas Eve dinner. She opened the armoire to look through the line of dresses she had brought for the special holiday. She raked her hand over the dresses and stopped at a dark green velvet one Henry had admired during his last leave at the Thanksgiving holiday more than a year ago. Margaret looked over to discover a bottle of white wine chilled in an ice bucket, sitting atop a small table beside the chaise lounge. As she removed her robe, she decided to enjoy a glass of wine while she got ready for the evening.

Margaret uncorked the bottle as she stood naked beside the small table. The crisp, clear yellow liquid flowed into the crystal wine glass. She sampled the sweet, fruity vintage and released a small sigh. She then ran a hot bath and stepped into the steaming water with the wine glass still in her hand. The warm water coupled with the warmth of the wine coursing through her body was intensely relaxing. Thoughts of Henry began to emerge again while she ran her hands over her body in a cleansing ritual, but she pushed them away, not wanting to feel any sadness on this day.

She walked back into the bedroom to style her hair, apply some makeup, put on her jewelry, and indulge in one of the sweet-smelling French perfumes from the vanity table. The green velvet dress was classic in its design with a deep V-neck in the front and the back. It was fitted and had a straight skirt that stopped just past her knees, with a slit in the back. On her feet, she placed dark green suede pumps.

She checked the clock to discover that it was time to meet James. She walked down the long hallway and descended the curved staircase slowly while admiring small seasonal decorations she had not noticed before. When she entered the solarium, James was listening to holiday music and pouring two glasses of white wine. He looked up from his task as Margaret entered the room. His eyes devoured every inch of Margaret's quiet, seductive form moving closer and closer to him. Her presence alone made him catch his breath. Feeling that he might be revealing too much with his lingering gaze, he looked back down to the task at hand and picked up one of the wineglasses to place in Margaret's awaiting hand.

"You are, of course, lovely as ever this evening," James remarked.

Margaret murmured a quiet thank you and sipped a bit of the sparkling liquid that matched the vintage she had enjoyed with her bath.

Feeling a bit uneasy with the silence, Margaret said, "Tell me what has been happening in your life over the last few years. I miss seeing you since you left Atlanta. Do you think you'll ever be coming back?"

"I doubt it. My years in Atlanta were fun ones, but this is my home. The construction firm is running smoothly. I've even started doing some charity work."

"Tell me about the charity work."

"It's with the March of Dimes," James replied. "I've gotten involved with some public-speaking engagements, and I've started sending some of my executive officers over to the organization on three-month assignments. Those assignments always seem to change their perspectives on life. I get a kick out of watching the transformation."

"I'm sure you do," Margaret responded. "And I'm sure you pick your loaned executives wisely. I can just envision some greedy little backbiting ambitious type being sent over to the March of Dimes for an excellent adjustment in attitude. Have you ever had an executive to fail miserably at the charity work?"

"Now that you ask, yes I have."

"And what was his fate?"

"He was forced to leave the company," James stated with an ominous tone.

"Well, James, I do admire the fact that you consider this type of charity work to be so important."

"Since we're talking about it, I'm hosting a New Year's Eve charity ball for the March of Dimes. I would love for you to accompany me as my guest."

"It sounds wonderful," Margaret replied. "I would be honored to attend."

At that moment, Leonard entered the solarium to inform them that it was time for dinner. Margaret and James followed Leonard into the formal dining room, complete with a long, mahogany dining table that would easily seat twelve dinner guests in a comfortable fashion. This evening, only two place settings were present at the right end of the table, awaiting Margaret and James. Behind the table, another large fireplace crackled. Candles ensconced in elegant silver candlesticks burned on the table. The creamy china with golden edges was simple and classic. Leonard seated Margaret at her place on the right side of the table. The place settings were close and intimate, which made the cavernous room seem smaller.

"We're having duck tonight," James announced. "I thought you might enjoy something a little different since we'll be having the traditional turkey tomorrow."

"Duck is a favorite of mine that I haven't enjoyed in a long while."

The meal began with a soup course, then salad, the duck entrée with several side dishes, and then ended on a sweet note as Margaret savored every last morsel of a delicious piece of New York–style cheesecake. James laughed and teased Margaret regarding the amount of food she had consumed, likening her appetite to one belonging to a particular construction worker he employed. Their conversation had been light and funny over dinner while they brought out old memories and tried them on again. A bit of sadness had seeped into their voices, knowing they could never recapture those days.

James broke the sadness with a change in subject. "How are your parents doing?"

"Just fine, as always. Daddy still owns the Ford dealership, but wartime has been tough with no new cars being manufactured."

"Do they still have Mattie, Hawk, and Pierce?"

"Oh yes. They're like part of the family." Then Margaret thought a bit about her last words and added, "Well, not really part of the family, but you know what I mean."

"Yes," James stated flatly. "I do know what you mean. Colored people don't fare too well down south now, do they?" Margaret shook her head. "To be quite honest with you, Margaret, that's one of the reasons I will never return to live there." Margaret was surprised at that comment. "The Negroes have never been treated fairly in Georgia. In a few years, they will revolt. It won't be a pretty sight. Some of those die hard southerners who attended those clandestine Klan meetings will end up in jail. I do wish I could witness the incarceration of their ignorant asses."

"James, you've always been a progressive thinker, a visionary of sorts. You scare me when you talk like that. I agree with you that the colored folks haven't been treated well, but I have a hard time imagining any sort of change coming to Barnesville."

James replied, "It's because you grew up with it. I believe you when you say you don't agree with their oppression, but it's comfortable to you. You also have always looked upon people like Mattie, Hawk, and Pierce as a simple but happy folk, happy to settle for their current situation."

Margaret's brow furrowed at the truthfulness of his words. She remembered that day when she served Hawk his food on the old, chipped plate with his tea in a jelly glass and the back stoop for a dining room. Her, simple comfortable actions now seemed so wrong.

"What you say is true, James. I guess I've always been too close to it all to see their treatment as inhumane"

"It would be good," James went on, "if the Negroes had a leader, a leader to begin a movement for social change free of violence. But it's hard to imagine a change of this sort coming about without violence in the South. I'm afraid it is inevitable, my dear."

Leonard then entered the dining room to inform them that Mrs. Oliver had brought the babies down to the solarium. Leonard was a Negro. Margaret looked at him with new eyes that evening, following her conversation with James. A change was beginning to occur in Margaret, a change that might forever influence many aspects of her life, a change that would not be fully recognized for many more years to come.

Margaret and James joined Mrs. Oliver to enjoy the babies on that cold, winter evening. It was a time that warmed their hearts. Margaret was glad she had made the trip to Connecticut. It somehow eased the pain of a Christmas minus Henry. She had been surprised to discover how little Henry had entered her thoughts on that day.

The hour began to grow later as each infant nodded off. Mrs. Oliver and Leonard left the room to deposit the two sleeping babies into their cribs.

Margaret attempted to stifle a yawn but was unsuccessful. "Forgive me, James. I seem to fall asleep so easily these days. I should get to bed myself." She walked over to James and touched his shoulder. "Dinner was superb. I just can't thank you enough for having us here."

James touched the small hand on his shoulder and brought her outstretched palm to his lips for a lingering kiss. Her hand touched his cheek and strong jaw, feeling the slight stubble of his beard. A light shone in James's eyes, but he looked down to mask it when Margaret appeared to notice the telling look. He released her hand, and she let it trail down his powerful arm while she whispered her good night.

~ ~ ~ ~ ~

Margaret awoke the next morning feeling refreshed. She joined

The Locket

James in the dining room for a very light breakfast, anticipating the heavy Christmas Day luncheon to come.

"In a moment," James began, "we can open our presents in the solarium before the children arrive."

"Children?" Margaret questioned him.

"Oh, I forgot to tell you. Over the last several years, I've invited special children from my March of Dimes work to the estate for Christmas. I hope you don't mind sharing the table with them."

"Of course not. I look forward to it."

James smiled, knowing Margaret would enjoy the playful day ahead. They then entered the solarium to exchange gifts. Mrs. Oliver, Leonard, the babies, and all staff members present on that day opened their gifts with glee. Margaret noticed the pleasure James derived from this traditional custom. She was surprised at the extravagance of the gifts and laughed to see her two infant sons banging and chewing on the new toys they had been given.

Before long, everyone joined in to clean up the mounds of wrapping paper. Leonard commented that they shouldn't bother with the cleanup because the ritual would be repeated when the children arrived. A few moments later, when Margaret was standing alone by the tree, admiring more of the unique angel ornaments, James presented her with a small box wrapped in glistening gold foil paper. Margaret gave him a glance and said, "You didn't need to get me anything."

"Just open it, woman," James replied gruffly. She obeyed the command and opened the lid to a small jewelry box. Inside the box was a beautiful pair of earrings with dangling gold in the shape of ovals. The gold shimmered in the early-morning light.

Tears glistened in her large, dark eyes as she said, "Oh, James, this is just so beautiful. You shouldn't have been so extravagant, but I love the earrings. Thank you. Now it's time for yours."

Margaret reached for a small box that she had placed under the tree the night before and put it in James's lap. She then said, "It's not much, but you're difficult to buy for." He opened the package wrapped in paper with a silver hue to discover a set of gold and onyx cuff links.

"Actually, you must have read my mind," James responded. "I recently lost one of my favorite cuff links, and now I'll have this nice set to wear to the March of Dimes ball. You didn't need to get me a gift, but I'll cherish it for always. Thank you, Margaret." He reached over and brought her hand to his lips.

Margaret was again surprised by the unconscious flame of desire that arose in her each time she experienced James's touch. It was disconcerting and could not be ignored. She looked over at her host, now admiring the lines of his strong, masculine face framed by the wavy locks of blond hair. He was wearing a cream-colored turtleneck sweater made of cable knit wool, which accentuated his powerful muscles. Margaret imagined the look, the feel, of those powerful muscles rippling beneath the warm wool of his sweater. A blush warmed her cheeks in response to the intimate thoughts. James then looked up again into her glistening, dark eyes to read a bit too much from her telling gaze. Margaret slipped her hand from his grasp to move away and begin tidying up some of the numerous baby toys strewn throughout the solarium floor while she collected herself by pushing the disturbing thoughts aside.

A moment later, they heard the distinct ring of the front doorbell. The house was then alive with the voices and melodious laughter of ten little girls and boys who had all experienced the misfortune of the disease they shared with James. Margaret was certain that James knew each child by name and could probably relate extensive case histories or family stories. Some of the children were wheelchair bound, but most of them were maneuvering their paralyzed lower extremities with various crutches and adaptive equipment in the form of braces.

The children were aided by several adult volunteers assigned to them for the event by the March of Dimes. Margaret remembered when President Franklin Roosevelt had announced his establishment of a national foundation for infantile paralysis back in 1938. A comedian had coined the phrase "March of Dimes," which had become synonymous with the foundation. She had been unaware of the active role James had assumed in this charitable organization, but his interest and activities were understandable due to his personal experience battling poliomyelitis. A photographer, who seemed to annoy James, snapped photographs from time to time. Margaret helped distribute Christmas gifts to all of the children and then stood back to enjoy their excitement. The tender look that remained on James's face beckoned Margaret. She found it difficult to tear her gaze from his powerful form.

At that moment, James's resounding laughter was heard while he played with Aaron and Matthew, who were both sitting in his lap. Henry had never seen his twin sons. It was strange to witness another man taking his role on Christmas morning. The children warmed up to Margaret's sons and kept them entertained for quite some time.

The traditional Christmas Day luncheon, complete with turkey, stuffing, cranberry sauce, and the like, was delicious. The childish voices and laughter brought new life to the old Walsh family mansion. James was seated at his regular place on the right end of the enormous table. Margaret was at the opposite end, just as if she were the lady of the manor.

A small girl with shining blue eyes and very blond, angelic hair, seated to the left of Margaret, looked up into her mistaken hostess's eyes and asked, "Mrs. Walsh, could I have a little more of that sweet cranberry sauce?"

Margaret was surprised to realize the little girl had assumed that she was the wife of the powerful man seated at the other end of the table. In an instant, she responded with, "Oh, I'm not ..." but then her voice trailed off as she decided not to dispel the myth. She then replied, "Of course you can, darling," and passed the child the sauce she had requested.

Margaret then touched the beautiful golden earrings she now wore, James's thoughtful Christmas gift. She would cherish them always. The little girl's words rang again in Margaret's mind, causing her to imagine how different her life would have been if she had indeed become the wife of James Walsh. It would have been a life of incredible privilege. Margaret doubted that James's fortune was the source of his inner strength, wisdom, and courage. James appeared to view his wealth and power as merely an avenue that could lead him to greater and greater opportunities to complete work for these small, unfortunate souls, such as the blond girl sitting in the wheelchair to her left.

Oddly enough to Margaret, James never seemed to consider himself unfortunate, even though a puzzling disease had robbed him of the use of his legs. Margaret's mind again wandered to thoughts of James's masculinity. She had no knowledge of just how far his disability extended. Could he ever love a woman in the physical sense? Her intimate thoughts caused her to again survey James's handsome physical form while her cheeks displayed the warm glow of a blush, triggered by the primitive nature of her imaginings. James's gaze then met hers, and she looked away so as not to reveal the content of her musings to a man who possessed the uncanny ability to read much of her thoughts.

Following lunch, James commanded his staff members to set up various appropriate activities for the children in the dining room and solarium. The children became absorbed in board games, finger-painting, jigsaw puzzles, and various craft projects. Margaret participated in most of the playing with the exception of the finger-painting activity, which she allowed Leonard to supervise. Before the day was over, Leonard was covered with multicolored splotches of tempera paint. Margaret giggled to spy the disheveled employee whose personal hygiene had always been more than impeccable.

The hour began to grow late, and the adult volunteers returned to collect all of the children. Each child gave James and Margaret warm hugs and kisses full of gratitude for their special day. The small blond girl, who had remained close by Margaret for most of the day, gave her mistaken hostess a lingering hug and said, "You're so pretty, Mrs. Walsh. Do you think I will grow up to be as pretty as you are?"

Margaret smiled and touched the small child's face. She replied, "Of course you will. But the most important thing is to be pretty on the inside as well." It was obvious that Margaret's words had made an impression on the youngster.

James witnessed their exchange and wore a surprised look on his face. He then said, "So, Tammy thought you were my wife." Margaret nodded. "But you didn't correct her?" He questioned.

Margaret tried to sound flippant by saying, "Oh, it was just easier that way. She had gotten somewhat attached to me today, and I didn't want to spoil the mood by letting her know that I was just a guest myself and that she would probably never see me again." The finality of those last words smoked from Margaret's lips into the cold winter air of the open front door.

They both returned to the solarium to enjoy some cocktails before a very light dinner that was planned for later. It was strange, but Margaret sensed that after having spoken aloud little Tammy's assumptions about their fictitious marriage, both adults unconsciously began behaving somewhat as if they were husband and wife. The evening was then filled with easy banter, intimate conversations, and comfortable silences, reflecting an imaginary life they would steal from Henry over the next week.

Indeed, Margaret slipped into the role of lady of the manor, and James enjoyed the temporary pretense during the short vacation. Margaret was not planning to return to Barnesville until the second or third day of the new year. She and James filled their days with numerous planned engagements, including a visit to the museum, shopping excursions, box seats for a new theater production, and a dinner party given by friends. Margaret was not accustomed to the late nights and found that she would sometimes not awaken until ten o'clock most mornings. She finished reading the novel she had started months ago and was near the conclusion of a second novel that happened to be one of James's favorites. It felt wicked to enjoy all of the indulgences of this vacation, but Margaret found it easy to push that feeling aside in the wake of her host's attentiveness.

It was New Year's Eve as Margaret stood in front of the long mirror in her bedroom, taking care of a last-minute adjustment to an unruly curl in her dark tresses. James had purchased her new evening gown on one of their shopping trips that week. The gown was burgundy chiffon with a strapless, fitted bodice that gently hugged her provocative breasts. The skirt flowed in graceful, fluid lines with each movement of her long legs and delicate feet shod in burgundy pumps made of soft file. Her appearance was striking. Her eyes shone from the much-needed rest, and the burgundy color accentuated her tumbling, dark curls and creamy skin.

Margaret picked up her diminutive evening clutch purse and a black velvet cape and then left her room to meet James in the solarium. James was dressed in a tuxedo and was sitting in an easy chair reading a professional journal when Margaret arrived in the room. Her beauty made him catch his breath, and he felt the warmth of desire rising in his belly, a feeling he had encountered often over the last week. James propelled his lower body out of the easy chair and into his wheelchair with deft, lithe movements of his muscular arms.

He wheeled over to Margaret and said, "I have something I would like to give you tonight." He produced a black jewelry case and handed it to Margaret. She opened the case to catch her breath at the sight of a beautiful golden locket. Margaret opened the locket with trembling hands. Instead of the usual picture, the locket was engraved. The engraving read, "Eyes Opened by Truth. Pain Healed by Love."

"James," she said softly, "I've never worn anything so amazing. Of course, it goes perfectly with the earrings. All of the jewelry is just dazzling. The engraved message will be with me forever. Thank you so much."

"You are very welcome. A beautiful woman should wear beautiful things." James knew it would be difficult to tear his gaze away from her throughout the evening.

Before long, Margaret and James were heading toward a local hotel for the March of Dimes charity ball. Leonard drove at a rather fast pace, as the hour had crept upon them sooner than was expected. Upon their arrival, Leonard retrieved James's wheelchair from the trunk. Again, James effortlessly transferred himself into the awaiting chair. Margaret stepped from the car to encounter flashing lights coming from the cameras of some local reporters. They entered a grand ballroom containing at least fifty round dinner tables, fully set with white tablecloths, gleaming flatware and crystal, and small, glowing lanterns. That Cinderella feeling that had hardly left Margaret all week was reaching a climax this evening.

Margaret and her host were ushered to the head table. The evening began with a few opening remarks made by James, followed by a prayer delivered by a priest who had been active in the charitable organization. All of the guests then enjoyed dinner and stimulating conversations around each of the tables. Margaret could tell that the seating arrangements had been carefully planned to maximize the message James wished to impart. She recognized a few popular athletes and some minor movie stars who were present for the event.

Following the meal, James excused himself from the head table and wheeled his chair up to a small podium designed for him. He then delivered a heart-wrenching speech that moved many in the room to tears. James possessed a gift. He painted pictures with his words, pictures that would remain in the minds of those present that evening. Those mental pictures blazed with depth and were created without the help of photographs, slides, or a movie presentation. His words were compelling coming from one who had suffered the physical onslaught of polio, a disease without a cure or a vaccine. James's descriptions were graphic but not offensive, just moving. He ended his soliloquy by bringing two small children, themselves victims of the crippling polio, to the podium. One of the children, a boy named Benjamin, spoke of his experience in an iron lung. The little blond girl named Tammy, who Margaret remembered from Christmas Day, then related her story of permanent paralysis that sentenced her, like the handsome man beside her, to a life lived within the confines of a wheelchair. Tammy's sweet angelic presence, coupled with a disconcerting degree of maturity produced as the result of her suffering, brought the entire room to a standing ovation. Margaret looked around the room and smiled to know the men and women present that night would be contributing a significant amount of monetary support.

At that moment, James invited everyone to proceed to the adjoining ballroom for entertainment and dancing. He was quick to point out the location of volunteers seated at tables in the back of the ballroom for the purpose of accepting the anticipated donations. James and Margaret moved side by side into the ballroom. A raised stage area was located at one end of the room. It was filled with a band led by a tall, slender female singer. She began a slow ballad, and James reached out for Margaret's hand. She bent her head down very close to his, and he whispered, "It would please me to watch you dance. Bob, over here, is quite accomplished. Go on, enjoy yourself."

Margaret exchanged smiles with Bob Drake, the vice president of James's construction firm, who already knew his boss's plan. She then took Bob's hand as he led her out onto the dance floor. Bob was a tall man in his late thirties who possessed dark good looks that were a good match for Margaret's elegant silhouette. For quite a few minutes, they were the only couple on the dance floor. Many heads turned to view their fluid, swirling movements. James found it impossible to tear his eyes from Margaret's sensuous being. He gulped down the shot of whiskey a waiter had placed in his hand. Everything about Margaret appealed to him—her good looks, the smell of her skin when she sat near him, the sound of her quick steps on the marbled foyer, the feel of her soft hand in his. He longed to taste every inch of her and was amazed at the intensity of his emotions. James was also shocked at how little he had thought of Henry, his best friend and the man who legally possessed the woman of his musings.

James continued to battle with his emotions for several hours while watching Margaret dance with various notable guests. He then summoned Leonard and Margaret for the drive home. Quite a few guests were still enjoying the revelry, but James knew they could slip out a side door. Margaret chatted on the ride home, while James remained quiet and pensive. Upon arriving at the estate, James commanded Margaret to join him in the solarium for a drink.

Margaret was tired and had already consumed a few glasses of wine that evening, but she knew she could not refuse the invitation by his tone of voice.

"You've been quiet this evening," she commented.

"I'm sorry. I didn't mean to be so distant. I've had a lot to think about."

"Business?" Margaret asked.

"No, pleasure."

"Oh," she responded, wondering, as her emotions began to flutter, what his next words would be.

"Margaret," he began, "we've been behaving like husband and wife over the past week. I must admit it has been wonderful. I find myself thinking about you constantly."

Margaret was surprised to hear his revealing words and how they mirrored her own feelings. She said, "I've felt the same way. You've made me feel like a woman again, and it's been so long since I've enjoyed those feelings."

"Margaret, I may be confined to a wheelchair, but I'm still a man." Margaret looked directly at James and listened as he went on. "What I mean is that polio claimed my legs and only my legs. I can make love to a woman. The disease didn't rob me of that pleasure. Still, I've never found a woman that I truly loved, that I couldn't live without, or that I thought didn't have some hidden motive for her attentions. At least, not until now …" His voice broke on his last words, and a tear gleamed in his eye.

Margaret sat down on the couch next to James and reached over to put her hand to his cheek. He covered her small hand with his own and then placed a lingering kiss into her palm. He reached out and folded her into his powerful embrace. She trembled with anticipation, lost in the moment as she looked into his beckoning blue gaze. His lips touched hers in a passionate, exploring kiss. She could feel white-hot desire pulsing through her being. James was astounded at her heated responsiveness. His lips trailed over her cheek to plant kisses in a burning line down the gentle curve of her neck.

Her breathing was rapid, and James opened his hooded eyes,

dark with passion, to watch her breasts moving up and down with her quick, shallow respirations. He wanted to see more of her in the dim light of the fire. While leaving a longer trail of soft kisses upon her bare shoulders, he reached behind her to pull down the zipper on the back of her dress. The dress fell down to her waist to reveal her soft breasts. Margaret reached over to quickly unbutton James's tuxedo shirt, wanting to feel the warmth and sinewy strength of him against her skin. She was lightheaded from the wine, and it caused her to be uninhibited.

They engaged in a deep kiss that released a flood of desire. James cupped her breast in his hand and bent his head to taste her delicious skin. Margaret groaned with desire and felt a warm moistness between her legs. She looked down to witness a rising mound under James's tuxedo pants. He continued to touch, taste, lick, and suck at her delicate, enchanting breasts now full with excitement. His broad, muscled shoulders moved as he raked his hands over the one woman he wanted, the one woman he loved. As words of love were about to fall from his lips, Margaret snapped out of the erotic moment to reach out and touch his chest with her outstretched palm. She pulled up her dress to cover her breasts and choked out the words, "No, James, we can't. I just can't do this to Henry."

She arose from the couch and ran from the solarium, up the stairs, and into her room. She closed the door behind her and stood gasping with her back pressed against the door. In a few moments, she heard the whirring sound of the elevator reaching the second floor as James retired for the evening. Margaret half expected him to knock on her door, such was the intensity of their desire. No knock came. Margaret then fell, sobbing, onto the bed.

Her thoughts raced, and she felt so confused by her emotions. She knew she loved Henry. She thought she loved Henry. But how could she feel so passionate and filled with desire for another man? The bitter bile of her betrayal arose in her throat as guilt invaded her. Margaret's only wish was to leave this fairy-tale castle.

She looked at the clock to see that it was three in the morning. Margaret knew that sleep would elude her for the rest of this now short night. She dried the tears from her eyes and arose to begin packing all of her things. When she had finished, she walked down the hall in silence to the nursery and packed Matthew's and Aaron's belongings in the dim glow of the night-light.

Margaret forced herself to stay in her bedroom until nine o'clock, hoping to avoid seeing James at the breakfast table. She took the time to write him a thank-you note that she left on the dresser in her room. After a light breakfast, Leonard told her that James had gone into the office very early that morning. Margaret informed the staff that she and the babies needed to leave at once. A look of surprise came over Leonard's face, but he followed her wishes and arranged for the airplane to fly her back home that morning.

It was not until later when the plane was winging its way back to Georgia that Margaret breathed a ragged sigh and resolved never to let down her guard in such a manner again.

Chapter 7

Jakarta, Indonesia
May, 1945

The ache in Ma Le's back never seemed to go away. She reached down and around to massage the small of her back but was unable to do so because of the heavy, sleeping bundle she had strapped to her shoulders. The day was warm, forcing her to mop the beads of sweat from her brow with one of Henry's handkerchiefs. She looked down at the embroidered initials, H.M., on the now dingy handkerchief. The beautiful evening attire she was so accustomed to wearing when employed by Ben Tre at the White Dragon was now replaced with homemade work clothes roughly sewn by Madam Ky. The easy life she had created in Jakarta, via her old Vietnamese benefactor, was gone.

Ma Le looked over at her mother working alongside her in the rice patty. The lines in the older woman's face were deep, much deeper than one would expect, giving testimony to the difficult challenges she had stoically faced throughout her life. But Ma Le did not look at the woman with pity on this day. The loss of her former life had begun to wear on her. Worrying about when and if Henry could deliver them from the impoverished, war-torn region had caused Ma Le to often speak harsh words to her mother. The hardworking Madam Ky had taken her daughter's hurtful words in silence, understanding the source of her troubles. Over the past few

The Locket

months, Madam Ky's quiet, reserved, and subservient nature had allowed Ma Le to regard her as an intentional victim. What little respect she had held for her mother in the past was dwindling.

Henry had worked on a convoluted plan to send all three females to the States. He had made promises to always care for Ma Le and Susan, but Madam Ky's fate was still undecided. Fighting on the outskirts of Jakarta had escalated. In recent evenings, Ma Le and Madam Ky could hear artillery fire that seemed to get closer and closer. The hut would not be safe much longer.

Again, Me Le looked through her dark lashes at the older woman who incited her fury each day. She surmised that Madam Ky was the reason Henry's plan was not complete. Henry had not said this, but the corporal he had bribed to process the necessary paperwork for their departure was now stalling. He wanted more money, much more money than Henry had anticipated. Ma Le knew the extra money was because two adults would be leaving the country, not just one with a baby.

At that moment, Ma Le's thoughts were disturbed by the crying of her eight-month-old daughter, Susan. She released a heavy sigh, knowing the hour had grown late and that Susan's shrill cries stemmed from her hunger. Ma Le untied the makeshift papoose she had strapped to her back to carry the baby on her right hip. She spoke in a short stream of Vietnamese to inform the older woman of her intentions to return to the hut for the necessary feeding. She welcomed the rest from the hard work she was forced to complete day after day just to survive. Ma Le hated her existence. It made her remember the painful childhood she had endured in the impoverished fields of Vietnam.

"Come, little one," she said to Susan. "Mother will make everything right."

Speaking English aloud felt wonderful on her lips. Everything she said to Susan was in English, a preparation for the new life they would have in that faraway land she had seen only in her dreams or in *Life* magazine. Ma Le despised speaking Vietnamese but was forced to communicate in this manner with Madam Ky, as the wizened old woman had never learned a word of the language her daughter held in such high regard. Therefore, their conversations were minimal, which appeared to suit them both.

When they reached the hut, Ma Le rummaged through several burlap bags to produce a few small morsels of food for little Susan. She knew it would not be enough. As Susan sat on the floor eating bits of food, Ma Le walked to the crude door to look again for Henry. The sun was beginning to set, and he had promised to come by with more supplies. Yet the air was warm and still, and she could not hear the familiar whirring of his jeep engine. Another cry came from Susan. Ma Le clenched her jaw, as she knew that very little, if any, food remained in the hut. With a weary look, she walked over to her baby, unbuttoned her rough homemade blouse, and brought the baby to her breast.

Susan sucked hard, and Ma Le leaned back against the side of the hut, hoping Henry would come soon with more supplies. The little food that was left would not last through the next day. The waiting and the uncertainty continued to gnaw and eat at Ma Le, and her desperation was rising every day, every hour, every minute. Henry had read the signs. The war was coming to a close, and he would soon be transferred back to the States. Ma Le was determined not to be left behind. Again, she looked down into the dark eyes of her Asian American child, realizing Susan's importance to her deliverance from this wretched place.

Just then, as the shadows had grown longer in the hut, Ma Le looked up to see the silhouette of Madam Ky in the open door of the small dwelling. A bitter taste of hatred began to rise in the younger woman's throat. It startled her. Never before had she felt such intense hatred for another individual. But for the moment, she kept silent, thinking, always thinking, her mind racing in desperation for a way out.

Ma Le placed Susan back down on the hut floor and again walked to the door to look out in useless anticipation for Henry, her savior. It was now dark, and the promised visit had not occurred. The worry, the uncertainty, made Ma Le feel like an animal in a cage. Madam Ky lit the last candle left in the hut and offered her daughter a few morsels of food. Ma Le refused the food, saying she would eat later. She paced back and forth in the small, square space and continued to return to the door every few moments.

Madam Ky broke the silence with her Vietnamese words: "Stop looking for the soldier. He won't be coming tonight. He has never come this late." Then, with an evil glint in her eye, she added, "Perhaps they have already sent him back to America."

Ma Le snatched her head around to glare at the old woman who voiced the young woman's fears. Their long, stony silence was broken on this evening. In retaliation for Madam Ky's hurtful words, Ma Le blurted out in the Vietnamese tongue, "You are the reason we are still here! The corporal wants more money to complete paperwork for two adults to leave Jakarta. As it is, his friend James has sent him all the money that he will give. You must stay here. You've lived your life. I can take you to Jakarta. Ben Tre will give you a job cleaning. He may even let you sleep in the kitchen pantry."

At Ma Le's last statement, Madam Ky wrinkled up her nose and spat on the floor to indicate her disdain for the selfish plan. "You will not leave me behind. I may be old, but I can journey into Jakarta on foot. I have done it several times already. The authorities will be told of your planned passage. I will do that. Then perhaps you will never go to America. You will live and die in this squalor, just like your mother."

The old woman's acid tongue turned Ma Le's stomach and caused her to whirl around and walk quickly into the cooler night air. She breathed in deeply, wanting to calm her rising desperation, all the while knowing that the feelings would not leave her until their departure. Something had to be done. Her pulse raced, her breathing was rapid, and an uncomfortable tightness in her chest made her feel as if she were choking. At that moment, a small seed of a plan was planted in her mind, her only way out. A slow and wicked smile crossed her face as she began to feel some relief from the physical symptoms her desperation had caused. She noticed that Madam Ky had extinguished the thin flame of the candle, which announced her entrance into slumber.

Ma Le walked back into the hut and stretched out upon her sleeping mat to wait. She covered Susan's small form with a light, roughhewn blanket. She heard the loud snores of the old woman, snores that had robbed her of needed sleep. The woman would rob her of nothing else. Ma Le waited for at least two hours before she heard the elderly woman stir. Madam Ky then arose to relieve her full bladder, a ritual that Ma Le had witnessed several times each night. It would take five to ten minutes because the old woman always walked hundreds of feet away from the hut over the uneven ground to complete the necessary function.

Ma Le arose following her mother's departure and walked over to the left side of the hut. She untied one of the burlap sacks and reached in to pull out a large, sharp knife. She held up the knife and saw the full moon glisten on its sharp edge as the light poured in through the open hut door. It was a clear, bright night, which might help or foil Ma Le's plan.

She walked out of the hut to sneak around its side to be certain of her mother's location. The old woman was walking back to the hut, so Ma Le began walking toward her, keeping the knife hidden by her side, hoping her mother would not see the moon glinting on the steel edge of the weapon. Madam Ky showed no fear, assuming her daughter was leaving the hut to relieve herself as well.

As Ma Le and Madam Ky were about to pass each other on the rocky ground behind the hut, Ma Le quickly turned, raised the knife that the old woman never saw, and plunged it deep into the belly of her mother. An audible groan was wrenched from Madam Ky's throat, and Ma Le witnessed the wideness of the woman's disbelieving eyes from the light of the moon. The warm wetness of profuse blood loss was felt on Ma Le's right hand and arm as she turned the knife to the right and then to the left, ripping the flesh and internal tissue. Madam Ky fell to the ground, and Ma Le grabbed the knife from its initial point of destruction. As the old mother appeared to still be moving, her only daughter raised the knife once more to plunge it deeply into the soft flesh of her vulnerable neck. Ma Le felt the spray and wetness of the fresh blood on her arms and face. A silence then ensued; not even the rustle of wind was heard. Ma Le removed the knife from her mother's neck and walked back to the hut with an unusual calmness.

Once inside the hut, Ma Le packed a burlap sack with a few provisions for the anticipated journey on foot. Then a thought came to her that someone might come upon Madam Ky's body within a few days if it were left out in the open. She walked out of the hut back to the bloodstained area of ground where her mother lay, now dead. Ma Le grabbed the heels of her mother's body and dragged the lifeless form several feet into the woods. She then covered the evidence of her murder with large branches and pieces of underbrush. The area was remote, and it would be many days before any human traversed this land. If the British and Japanese soldiers reached this area, they would assume a stray sniper had killed the unfortunate woman who had led a solitary existence in the now abandoned hut.

Ma Le looked down at her bloodstained hands. It was difficult to see in the darkness, but the clear night illuminated the dark wetness of the bloodstains. The amount of blood on her clothes appeared excessive, if her fabricated story was to be believed. Therefore, she removed her blouse and washed her upper body with some water that was left in the hut. She took the soiled blouse and rubbed some of its blood onto the shirt she planned to wear for the anticipated journey by foot. Ma Le then lit the half-burned candle to survey her handiwork.

Just enough blood to believe that I held my dying mother in my arms during those last few moments, she thought to herself.

Ma Le then collected the bloodstained blouse and walked behind the hut. There she piled together some brush and laid the offensive blouse upon the top of the small pile. The brush pile lay over the bloodstained earth that witnessed the gruesome murder. Ma Le lit several matches and threw them onto the pile of debris. She watched the cleansing fire for long moments, not knowing that she would never feel clean again. When the flames began to recede and Ma Le was satisfied that evidence of her crime was sufficiently covered, she extinguished the fire with more water retrieved from the hut. She then walked back to the hovel she had shared with the old woman and gathered together various items to place them in the burlap sack that she strapped around her waist with a small coil of rope. She heard Susan stirring on the other side of the hut and knew she would not have time to stay there and bring the little one to her breast. So she unbuttoned her blouse and fashioned the papoose toward the front of her torso to enable Susan to suckle while Ma Le began the long journey into Jakarta by foot.

As they left the hut, small fingers of light were beginning to appear on the horizon. The distance to Jakarta was approximately ten miles. Ma Le knew the journey would take her at least six hours, with a few rest breaks, as the baby's presence would slow her down. Within the first thirty minutes of the trek, Ma Le was able to transfer Susan's cumbersome bundle to her back, which was more comfortable and allowed the pace of her stride to increase.

As the day wore on, the heat began to rise but did not become unbearable. Ma Le was now satisfied that the hard work she had endured over the past several months had prepared her body for this physical insult. During the first two hours, she refused to stop for rest in spite of Susan's indignant cries. When her back felt that it might break, Ma Le stopped to remove the papoose and allow Susan to sit on the ground. She removed a mango from her burlap bag, drank every drop of its juice, and devoured the fruit that would give her the physical strength to push forward.

Again, she gathered Susan onto her back and continued on, stopping every hour or so to drink a few small swallows from a canteen that was near empty. Ma Le began to lose all perception of time but knew that it must be deep into the afternoon. Blisters began to form on her sandal-shod feet, blisters that broke open to weep with water and then blood. Every step she took caused shooting pains through her feet and legs. At times, she became dizzy, which threatened to topple her and the baby to the ground.

Ma Le's strong will and determination, coupled with the darkness

The Locket

of her nature, kept her upright, pressing on, oblivious to the intensity of her pain.

At the moment she knew she could go no farther, she heard someone approaching from behind. It was a farmer traversing the path to Jakarta in a small horse-drawn wagon. The bed of the vehicle was filled with seasonal vegetables that he planned to sell in the city. The farmer stopped and offered the young woman a ride, and she accepted with a grateful and weary smile. Ma Le seated herself beside the man and placed Susan in her lap to rest the tired muscles of her back. The farmer looked at the baby, noting her American features, then observing the dingy but elegant, embroidered handkerchief Ma Le used to dab at her bleeding feet, all the while reading more about this mysterious young woman than she would have liked.

By the time Ma Le and the farmer reached Jakarta, the afternoon was growing old. Ma Le asked the farmer to leave her four blocks from Henry's hotel, anticipating that the walk could give her time to restore the disheveled look that would tell the story of the obstacles she had faced on that fateful day. It would also provide additional moments for her to fabricate a believable look of intense emotional upset at the death of Madam Ky. Her lies were already woven into a well-planned tapestry of deceit she would deliver to Henry as soon as she devised a way to lure him outside of the hotel without the knowledge of his friends and colleagues.

With every step bringing her closer to Henry's hotel, Ma Le conjured up disturbing personal images in her mind—selfish images of the wretchedness that would be her destiny without Henry's deliverance. These vivid images proved to create the appropriate look of distress she planned to expose to her lover, designed to elicit a speedy response.

Ma Le reached the hotel with tears streaming down her face, now smeared with dust and dirt from the road. The trails of wet tears left small, clean pathways descending down her smooth cheeks. She walked behind the hotel to the back door that would lead to the kitchen. She stood and waited beside a large uncovered garbage can, knowing a hotel employee would soon exit the door to empty kitchen scraps. Even though the stench was almost unbearable, Ma Le's stomach growled from her intense hunger. Atop the pile of offensive refuse in the large garbage can, Ma Le spied a half-eaten piece of fish that looked somewhat uncontaminated. Her hungry eyes darted back and forth. Desperation made her reach for the discarded seafood. She shoved the morsels of food into her mouth and swallowed without tasting.

Just as she was about to place the last few bites of food in her mouth, she heard a rustling behind the garbage can. Ma Le then looked over to witness a large black rat running out from the refuse heap. She gagged as waves of nausea arose in her throat. She fought it, vowing to keep the needed nourishment in her stomach.

At that moment, the back door of the hotel flew open, and a young boy walked out carrying a smaller garbage can ready to be emptied. He spied Ma Le and gave her a questioning look. She walked over to the boy with a beseeching expression and spoke quickly in his native tongue. She asked for his help in locating Colonel Henry Montgomery within the hotel. She stressed the importance of relating her presence to the army officer during a private exchange, so as not to alert others. Ma Le promised the young boy a monetary reward from Henry upon completion of the desired task. He turned around to follow her instructions.

Ma Le then slumped down to sit and rest on a small brick wall built to hide the piles of refuse she had just dined from. She held Susan close, hoping the young boy could locate Henry without too much delay. Susan slept in her mother's arms. Me Le looked down at her, a child born to release her mother from the squalor of her present existence. A smile stretched over her dirty, wicked face, and she released an audible, resounding laugh. The laugh was then followed by deep sobs that wracked her entire body. Large, salty teardrops fell onto Susan's sleeping face. The baby awoke to witness her mother's distress and also began to wail. Rapid footsteps were heard. Ma Le jerked her distraught face upward to encounter Henry's handsome, well-dressed maleness.

A look of concern covered Henry's face, and he rushed up to

The Locket

embrace his illegitimate family. "Ma Le," he began, "what has happened?"

"Henry," she choked out between sobs. "Mamasan is dead! She was killed by gunfire from a sniper who made his way to our hut. Susan and I were in the fields when it happened, but I heard the gunfire, and I saw the man. He went through our hut. He found nothing since our supplies were so low. Then he left." Ma Le continued her fake sobbing between each line of her fabricated story. Henry listened as she pressed on. "I held my Mamasan and she died in my arms. So much has been taken from me!" She then looked at her lover with wildness in her eyes. "Don't let them take Susan from me!"

Ma Le buried her head on Henry's chest. He comforted the woman who had afforded him so many nights of unbridled passion. After a few moments, he raised her head from his chest to say, "I'm so sorry about your mother. Casualties of that sort are the saddest part of war." They both stared at each other in silence, one believing the lie, one knowing the truth. Henry then went on to say, "I may be able to put you both on a military plane out of here at daybreak. I'll take you to the White Dragon now. If I pay Ben Tre enough, he'll let you stay in his apartment above the establishment for the night. I'll be there early tomorrow morning to take you both to the airfield. We must act quickly. I need to alert the corporal to go ahead and process the paperwork tonight, and I need to send a telegram to James. He'll take care of everything once you reach the States."

Ma Le allowed a bit of hope to enter her gaze, and that seemed to please Henry. The army officer then took his family over to the side of the hotel and into his awaiting jeep. He drove straight to the White Dragon and parked behind the bar that stood in readiness for its evening guests. Ma Le and Susan waited in the jeep while Henry entered the White Dragon to complete the necessary transaction. Within fifteen minutes, he reappeared and informed Ma Le that everything was settled. The young Vietnamese woman marveled at how easily each step of their plan was unfolding.

Ma Le and Henry then walked up the tall flight of stairs behind the White Dragon to the apartment occupied by her former boss. Ben Tre had never allowed her to view his private living quarters. Even though the apartment was small, only four rooms, it was well furnished. It resembled rooms she had seen in finer hotels within Jakarta. Henry appeared to be pleased that Ma Le and Susan would be safe for the night.

Henry broke the silence by saying, "Ben Tre said for you to use his facilities to wash up. He also told me that a few of your old garments would be hanging in his closet. He has plenty of food, so eat what you want." At his last remark, Susan let out a wail to announce her hunger. Henry then looked with tenderness at the pair. He touched Ma Le's face and kissed her full lips.

Henry turned and walked out of the apartment to complete last-minute details for his family's departure. Soon, he thought, the ordeal would be over, leaving him with a clearer head to contemplate his life with Margaret and his legitimate family following the war.

Ma Le immediately located some food for her daughter to silence the grating cries. She placed Susan on the floor of the bathroom to play while she undressed and washed her entire body. Following her cleansing, she thrust the offensive, bloodstained garments into a wastebasket. She then covered herself in a beige skirt and simple white blouse that she had retrieved from Ben Tre's closet. Ma Le surveyed her appearance in a mirror. Another deep laugh arose in her throat to see the irony of her masquerade in white, a pure color she hid behind so as not to reveal the evil strain in her soul that had committed murder under the cloak of darkness just hours before.

The evening wore on, and Susan was soon asleep following her bath. Ma Le's weary shoulders began to sag, so she stretched out her small frame on the couch. Her burlap bag lay nearby on the floor. Ma Le's dreams were fitful and filled with bloody images. She continued to feel the spray of warm, wet blood on her body. Just as she again witnessed the wideness of Madam Ky's disbelieving stare within her nightmare, Ma Le felt something heavy descend on her small form. Her eyes flew open to see Ben Tre leaning down to unbutton her pure white blouse. Ma Le smelled the strong stench of liquor on his breath.

Her right hand reached down to the burlap sack on the floor. Within seconds, she raised the long, sharp knife she had previously plunged into Madam Ky's flesh. She turned the knife sideways and placed the sharp edge under Ben Tre's nose as if she would surely cut the bulbous appendage away.

"Get away from me," she hissed. "Don't lose your life trying to get me to spread my legs."

Cold fear gripped Ben Tre, and he shuddered at her words. He retreated in silence to his room and slammed the door. Ma Le never saw Ben Tre again.

Just before daybreak, Ma Le heard the sound of Henry's jeep, and she gathered her burlap sack, placed some flat black shoes on her sore feet, and walked out the door with Susan filling her arms. Henry and Ma Le did not talk during the drive to the airfield, choosing to listen to the whirring of the jeep engine and the familiar sounds of early morning. Upon arrival at the airfield, Ma Le watched numerous soldiers boarding an American military airplane. Henry walked to the plane and spoke with another officer for a moment while Ma Le gathered her small parcel of belongings from the vehicle. Henry strode back to his lover and folded her close into a tight, intimate embrace. He kissed her full lips and looked down into the beautiful face that masked her ugly nature.

"Remember," he professed, "that I will always love you and Susan. I will take care of you forever." He was astonished at the intensity of his emotions and at the certainty of his commitment to this woman, a commitment that now felt much deeper than the one he had made at home. Henry went on. "My friend James Walsh is sending someone to meet you when you land in the States. He will take care of everything. You'll see me again after my assignment here ends and I reach the States. I'll think of you every day."

Ma Le remained silent, as was her custom. She kissed Henry and then turned to board the plane. She sat in a seat by the window to watch Henry's form become smaller and smaller as the airplane winged its way to her new life in the United States. Ma Le released a long, slow sigh, realizing that she would never again walk upon the Asian soil.

Chapter 8

Barnesville, Georgia
August, 1945

    The sun was bright and hot as Margaret and Granny Harrison rocked in unison in the old cane rockers within the gazebo located in the backyard of the Harris family home. Margaret looked over at Granny and saw her constantly dabbing at the streams of blue-tinged sweat that continued to pour from her sweet silver-rinsed hair. Margaret had long ago abandoned any further attempts to persuade Granny to stop using the offensive blue-tinted rinse. She had to turn her head away to hide the grin and giggle that accompanied her musings. The two women, one aged and one young, were enjoying their view of the twins toddling throughout the expansive backyard in their matching blue sun suits. Hawk and Pierce were forced to redirect the small boys as they ventured into the garden while practicing their new walking skills.
    Margaret surveyed her twins with scrutiny. Matthew had continued to thrive and dominated Aaron in the physical sense. His weight gain had been steady, to the point that he now had reached twenty-six pounds just prior to his first birthday. Aaron's weight gain had been much slower over the past six months. His small frame had barely reached the seventeen-pound mark at his pediatric checkup last week. Margaret's brow furrowed as she recalled how

Dr. Whitlock had dismissed her fears at Aaron's failure to thrive and match his brother's impressive weight gain.

"He's just active," were Dr. Whitlock's words. "He's probably burning off all of those calories with his new walking skills. Don't you fret now, honey. Aaron will catch up to his brother over the next year or two. You've got to remember, he started out a little on the puny side, my dear."

Margaret attempted to console herself with her memory of the physician's words and his flippant air utilized to erase all traces of worry. However, something nagged at her heart, and disturbing thoughts continued to surface each time she witnessed the two toddlers playing together.

"Granny," she began, "do you think there could be something wrong with Aaron? Something that might be keeping him from gaining weight?"

"What did Doc Whitlock tell you at their last checkup?"

"He assured me everything was fine. He just attributes his small frame to the fact that he came into the world a little on the puny side." In her mind, Margaret again reviewed the conversation with Dr. Whitlock to search for anything she might have missed, anything to calm her worries.

Granny's voice interrupted Margaret's thoughts. "Believe the doctor, sweetie, and just enjoy your little ones. We have seen nothing to lead us to believe that Aaron is ill in any way. Don't waste your days with worry. In an instant, those two will be grown men. But if you really pay attention, even to the little things, you will have glorious memories to keep you company when you're old like me." Granny smiled and patted Margaret's youthful, unlined hand with her gnarled arthritic one to soothe the anxious tone in her granddaughter's voice.

"I know, Granny," Margaret responded. "I'll try to stop my worrying. It is counterproductive. I'm going inside to get some lemonade. Would you like some?"

"That would be so nice, dear. Just what we need on this scorcher of a day." Granny then pulled out a new clean handkerchief to continue dabbing at the streams of blue perspiration pouring from her hairdo.

The Locket

Margaret smiled as she turned away from the gazebo to walk into the house. Mattie was busy in the kitchen, snapping pole beans for dinner that evening. Mattie swayed and snapped each bean while she listened to some upbeat, big band music on the radio. The beat was infectious, and both women began tapping their feet and swaying to the music as they completed their tasks. Margaret poured the extra-sweet lemonade into two tall glasses. She picked up the glasses and turned to back out of the screened kitchen door when a news bulletin interrupted the rhythmic beat of the song.

Margaret paused with her backside against the door and her hands full of freshly poured lemonade to hear, "Japs surrender, World War II is over." Both glasses of lemonade fell from her fingers to come crashing to the floor. Margaret ran, ignoring the splintered shards of glass that now covered the kitchen floor, into the backyard where Hawk and Pierce were still minding the twins and Miss Winnie had joined Granny in the gazebo.

Just before Margaret reached the gazebo, she yelled, "The war is over! The war is over! The Japanese have surrendered! That means Henry is coming home soon!" Margaret grabbed Miss Winnie and gave her a tight hug. Granny Harris received the second hug. Margaret then ran toward the garden and scooped up each twin, in turn, winging each boy high in the air and announcing the homecoming that would soon occur. She then shouted the news to Hawk and Pierce.

Hawk responded, "It sho' will be a happy day when Mr. Henry done walk trew dat fron' do'. Praise da good Lawd, he made it trew safe."

Margaret then remembered the lemonade mess she had left in the kitchen. She placed Aaron back on the ground and raced to the kitchen to clean up. When she reached the kitchen door with her eyes alight, she breathlessly noted that Mattie had already dealt with the sticky mess.

"Oh, Mattie!" Margaret exclaimed as she fell into the rotund embrace of the nanny she had known all of her life. "The war is over, and Henry will be home soon. I haven't felt this happy in a long time. Before long, I'll have the family life I've dreamed about." Tears gleamed in the young woman's eyes. The same joy was reflected in Mattie's gaze while she held the woman who felt like her own daughter. "I'm sorry about the mess. You should have left it for me to clean up."

"Don't ya fret, chile," Mattie responded. "I poured mo' lemonade fo' ever'body outside. Go ahead an' take it out on dat tray. Enjoy it now." Mattie watched Margaret back out of the door with the heavily laden drink tray. She continued to watch the beautiful young woman, consumed with joy, from the kitchen window. It always felt so sweet to enjoy a rare expression of true love from one of the Harris family daughters. They were daughters she loved as if they were her own. It was a pure, natural love that knew no racial rules.

The rest of the afternoon and evening was a whirlwind. Friends and neighbors dropped by to share the joy. Charles broke out several bottles of champagne from the cellar to celebrate the glorious news. The excitement welling up inside Margaret was more than exhilarating, a feeling she had forgotten. It was a feeling that bombarded her in waves and would take her through the next coming days or weeks until Henry's safe return. A tiny glimmer of disappointment did slip into her thoughts as she realized that Henry would probably miss the first birthday celebration for the twins, which would occur in less than a week. That was just another thing the war had taken from her. She dismissed the small discouraged feeling with the knowledge that the man she adored would soon be with his family for good.

An image of James entered her thoughts at that moment. It had taken many months to erase his burning presence from her mind since her Christmas holiday in Connecticut. With much determination, she thrust her preoccupation with the enigmatic man aside to contemplate the certain brightness of her near future.

Chapter 9

It was an early September afternoon that found Henry Montgomery alighting from a cab on Seventeenth Street in Atlanta. He took a deeper breath and felt a chill in the air. Henry paid the cab driver his fare and then turned to survey his surroundings. The street was short, just a block long. It was lined with large oak trees that stood tall against the blue sky. On the left side of the street, there were several large frame homes. On the right side stood two small brick apartment buildings, each housing four single-family dwellings. The buildings had been built in the early 1920s and had been designed to exude an air of southern elegance that belied the fact that they were broken into apartments. Most of the apartment buildings of the current day were much more institutional looking. Henry was pleased to discover that Ma Le and Susan were enjoying surroundings that were reminiscent of Old World southern traditions akin to what he had experienced as a boy.

He walked up the concrete steps of the small, two-story apartment building and opened the glass-paned front door. Large gold-lettered words on the glass pane read "The Maryland." Henry walked into the white-tiled foyer and noticed mailboxes located to the left. Ma Le's name was visible on the mailbox for apartment D. He also spied a door that must have led to the property manager's office. Henry made a mental note to pay the manager a visit prior to his departure later that afternoon.

Henry knocked on the front door of apartment D. Within

moments, the door swung open to reveal Ma Le's beautiful face and form. Her eyes grew wide, and her mouth flew open to reveal the glorious surprise his unexpected visit had created. She threw herself into his arms, almost knocking the gift he held onto the floor. The couple engaged in a deep kiss for long moments, drowning in the taste, touch, and scent of their forbidden actions.

Henry released his tight embrace, and Ma Le spoke first. "I did not know you would be here today. This is so wonderful. It makes me happy that Susan will see her papa on this special day. Come in. Share some cake with us."

Henry walked into the apartment. James had informed him that a furnished apartment had been secured for Ma Le, but Henry knew his friend must know the owner of the building to have obtained a dwelling of this caliber. The floors were hardwood and gleamed from a fresh coat of wax meticulously applied by Ma Le just the day before. Large area rugs were scattered throughout the living room. The furniture was comfortable and exuded a homey atmosphere that belied the true circumstances surrounding their relationship. Susan was seated in a high chair near the dining table. A birthday cake sat in front of her. The solitary candle atop the cake had just been lit by Ma Le.

"Come over here, Henry," Ma Le beckoned. "Let us sing the traditional American 'Happy Birthday' song to our daughter."

Henry smiled as he recognized Ma Le's diligence in adopting traditional American customs and values. He had noted her transformation since Susan's birth and was pleased by her tireless efforts to carve out a new life.

Ma Le paused before the ritual and said, "Let me go wash my hands first." She then walked into the kitchen and performed the necessary cleaning. She returned, and they broke into the song, a new tradition for the two females, an old, comfortable custom to the tall, good-looking man standing before them. When the song concluded and the candle had been blown out, Ma Le said, "Now we can all have some delicious cake." Ma Le articulated the English words with pride. Henry was amazed at her excellent command of a language foreign to her ancestry. She had become quite fluent in English over the past year. At times, it was difficult to believe that she was not a native of the United States. "But first," Ma Le went on, "let me go scrub my hands."

A frown crossed Henry's face as he wondered why Ma Le felt the need to cleanse her hands once again, when the ritual had been completed just minutes before. But he said nothing while father and daughter awaited her return. Ma Le then returned to cut and serve the cake. She passed out the pieces of cake and disappeared into the kitchen again for a few minutes. Upon her return, they all enjoyed the sweetness of the cake. Susan squealed with glee while she smeared the birthday confection all over her face and dark hair. Henry chuckled to witness the sight as Ma Le attempted to wipe the sticky mess from the toddler's hair and face. When Ma Le was satisfied with her cleanup job, she took Susan from the high chair to place her on the floor. The little girl toddled off into the living room while Ma Le disappeared into the kitchen once more.

Henry crouched down near Susan on the floor and placed the gift in front of his only daughter. She giggled, and they both tore into the paper together. Ma Le returned to the living room as Henry opened the top to a rectangular box. Inside the box, a beautiful doll with curly blond ringlets was nestled within a mound of tissue paper. Susan squealed again with joy and snatched the doll to hold it tightly in her arms. She touched the doll's face with wonder. Henry demonstrated how the doll's eyes closed when she reclined to allow her to sleep. Susan was captivated.

"I know this has been an exciting day," Ma Le said to Susan. "But it is time for a nap. You can take your pretty new friend to bed with you." Ma Le picked up Susan with the doll, and Henry followed them into the bedroom. Ma Le placed Susan into her crib. Her eyelids drooped. She fell asleep just as her body stretched out onto the small bed. Henry watched her innocent face sleeping in peace with the doll clutched in her arms. Ma Le kissed the child's forehead.

Susan's eyes opened for a moment, and she murmured, "Mama," a word filled with sweetness.

"Here is Daddy to tell you to sleep with peace," Ma Le whispered.

Henry reached down and placed a similar kiss on the soft skin of Susan's forehead. Ma Le pointed to the decorated army officer and said, "This is your daddy. Daddy," she repeated with an upward inflection, asking for imitation.

Susan murmured, "Daddy." She then closed her eyes to sleep. The two adults looked at each other and exchanged a knowing smile.

The couple turned and walked arm in arm into the living room. They sat down on the couch. Henry spoke first.

"Is everything all right? Are you and Susan fine in every way? Tell me. I've been thinking about you both every day."

"We are fine. Your friend James brought us here. It was all very simple, nothing like life in Jakarta. That all seems like bad dreams now."

"James is wealthy," Henry replied. "And wealth means power. He has friends all over America. I'm certain one of his friends extended a favor to him to lease this apartment at a reasonable rate."

"You are probably correct," Ma Le responded. "He told me the first six months' rent had been paid. James also found me a job."

Henry was surprised and pleased at her last comment. "What kind of job?" he asked.

"I complete alterations and mending on clothes from a large store here in Atlanta. The store is called Rich's." Henry nodded, as he was familiar with the department store. "Rich's lets me bring the clothes here for me to complete the work. Susan and I ride the street car to the store on Monday and Friday to take the clothes back and get more items to alter. I make a little money. It is enough to pay our living expenses." She looked nervous. "But there is not enough to pay the landlord each month."

"I know. I plan to pay your rent in six-month installments. I don't want you to ever worry again. You've suffered far too long, all your life. But I'm glad you're working. It will help because I can't pay for everything." They looked at each other in silence, both remembering Henry's heavy obligations to his legitimate family, living just a few counties away.

The Locket

But Henry did not want to think of Margaret and the twins at that moment. He had become quite adept at pushing those thoughts aside. Liquor helped. It helped numb the rising guilt that always threatened to engulf him. He asked his mistress for some whiskey. He gulped down the fiery liquid that gave him a radiating warmth. Thoughts of Margaret began to recede. Ma Le's presence beside him became intoxicating. All cares and inhibitions were thrust away to allow him to fold the small temptress into his passionate embrace. Henry lowered his head to rake over Ma Le's lips with a burning kiss. When the kiss ended, they both recognized their dark, smoldering desire and were unable stop.

Henry picked up Ma Le's small frame and walked across the hardwood floor to the master bedroom. He placed her on the bed, loosened his tie, and walked over to close the door, to shut out the cares and obligations of the outside world, even if only for a few hours. Their lovemaking then ignited but not with the intensity of eroticism they had so enjoyed in Jakarta. Henry blamed this decreased depth of feeling on his obvious fatigue from days of brutal traveling. Ma Le surmised that motherhood, with its constant demands, had diminished her ability to fully enjoy such moments.

When their lovemaking had ended, Ma Le immediately stood up from the bed. "Where are you going?" Henry asked.

"Oh, I just need to wash my hands. They don't feel clean." Ma Le held up her rough red hands that had become dry and cracked from excessive cleansing. "I'll be back in a moment."

She then donned a robe and turned away to once again wash her hands. Ma Le passed by the bathroom that was across from the master bedroom, choosing to wash her hands in the kitchen sink, as usual. She meticulously scrubbed each surface of her hand, each finger, each fingernail, and extended her symbolic purification up to the elbow of each arm. After ten minutes, the ritual was complete. She then walked back down the hallway past the bathroom, ignoring her full bladder. *I can hold it a bit longer*, she thought. Ma Le's existence had been governed by these unusual rituals since her arrival in America. Constant handwashing never produced a clean feeling. The warm spray of fresh blood was always felt on her skin. The simple act of relieving her bladder evoked bloody mental pictures of the ghastly murder her mother had endured when returning to their hut from completing that bodily function.

When Ma Le returned to the bedroom, her lover was dressed. "Do you have to leave so soon?" she asked with a disappointed tone in her voice.

"I'm afraid so. I need to catch the Nancy Hanks at four o'clock to get down to Barnesville. Don't look so worried. Remember, I never want you to worry again. You've spent enough time suffering in your short life." His words struck a hollow chord in Ma Le. Yes, her suffering was over, but at what price? The horrendous secret she kept locked away in the deepest recesses of her heart was proving to wear down her psyche. She would continue to devise elaborate rituals in an attempt to stifle her disturbing, obsessive thoughts.

Henry followed Ma Le from the master bedroom to Susan's room for one last glimpse of his beautiful, innocent daughter prior to his departure. Henry could now see more small flashes of resemblance to him. The couple stood over the little girl in silence, both creating a mental picture to hold onto. A slow smile crossed Ma Le's face with the realization that she was stealing another treasured moment from Henry's faceless wife and family. The couple walked arm in arm to the door. Henry bent down and folded

Ma Le into his strong embrace. He touched his lips to hers in another deep, passionate kiss that left Ma Le breathless. Following his intimate touch, Henry said, "I'm going to stop by and see your property manager downstairs and make the necessary arrangements to pay the rent in six-month installments." Ma Le nodded. He placed another small kiss on her forehead. "I probably won't be able to come and visit for several months. Nothing can ever look too suspicious. Margaret might find out. If you ever need to send me a message, call James Walsh, and he will know how to contact me."

Henry placed his large hand against Ma Le's smooth, small cheek in a loving caress. He then turned from the door to walk down the stairs. Ma Le put her hand to her lips to hold the feel of Henry's exploring kiss for a bit longer. She closed her door when her lover's image had disappeared into the property manager's office.

Henry stood just inside the office and tapped on a bell to alert the superintendent of his arrival. An older woman walked out from the back office. Her makeup and jewelry were heavy, a look created in vain to hide the lines that had appeared in the usual places for a woman her age. Her name tag read, "Rita Nelson." Rita's hair was bleached to create the effect of a platinum blond, and a cigarette dangled from her fire-engine-red lips as she said, "Oh, sorry. I didn't hear you come in. Just takin' a smoke break, you know. What can I do for you, soldier?" Rita gave a wide smile to the tall, good-looking officer with the piercing green eyes.

"I'm here to make arrangements to pay the rent for apartment D."

"Well," Rita began her well-rehearsed line, "it's due by the fifth of each month. And we charge a five-dollar late fee if it's received after that."

"I understand totally. I wonder if you would allow me to pay the rent every six months?"

"Oh sure, sweetie." Rita smiled up at Henry. "Let me just check the books." She pulled out a large ledger and then said, "Looks like the apartment is paid up through November. Would you like me to bill you? That would be no problem. If you'd just give me your address."

"No!" Henry barked back in response. "I'm sorry. I mean to say that you won't need to do that. I'll keep up with it all. If there are ever any problems, contact this gentleman in Connecticut." Henry gave her a slip of paper containing James's name, address, and telephone number.

"Whatever you say."

"Thank you for your time." With that, Henry walked out of the office to catch a street car that would take him to the train station.

Rita watched the handsome man's purposeful stride up to Peachtree Street from her window. "So that's the little gook's boyfriend," she said aloud. "Wonder what the missus at home would have to say about that half-breed kid upstairs." Rita shook her head and walked away from the window to crush her cigarette in the large, butt-filled ashtray she kept on the counter.

Chapter 10

It was dark by the time the Nancy Hanks rolled into the Barnesville train station. Henry stepped off the train to leave the sounds of its whirring, hissing steam engine behind and locate a telephone. The ticket taker directed Henry to the nearest telephone, where he placed a call to Tim Spencer, a close friend of the Harris family. Henry asked Tim for a ride to the Harris family home so as to surprise Margaret and the two toddlers he had only met in photographs mailed to him overseas. Tim agreed to be of service, so Henry sat down on a bench outside the train station to wait. He took deep breaths of the cool autumn air to calm the nervous, jumpy feeling that had invaded his gut. How would he react to Margaret? What were the boys like? How would he go about starting a new life with this ready-made family? So many other questions bounced around his head. Henry had allowed Ma Le and Susan to become a part of him, and their arrangement had become a comfortable one. Thoughts of Margaret, the beautiful young woman to whom he had professed his love and whom he had betrayed, brought the bitter bile of guilt to his throat.

I'll just have to put on an act so no one will ever suspect the nature of my actions in Jakarta, he thought. *I put on the act for my army buddies overseas. I'll just continue it here, and no one will ever know. Before long, the act will become real, and there won't be any more worries.* Henry was satisfied with his thoughts, certain that this act would never be perceived as insincere and would cleanse him of any further guilt.

His relationship with Ma Le and the fruit of that coupling, Susan, could easily be hidden forever. As Susan got older, Ma Le would find better employment, and his financial assistance would decrease over the years. He would begin to nudge his Asian mistress down that planned pathway over time.

At that moment, Tim arrived in an older Ford automobile Mr. Harris had sold him before the war. Henry placed his suitcases in the trunk and then sat down in the passenger side of the front seat. Tim and Henry chatted in a jovial manner that served to somewhat ease Henry's normally unruffled countenance. Before long, the car turned the corner onto Stafford Avenue. Henry asked Tim to leave him two doors down from the Harris home so as not to spoil the surprise of his arrival.

He walked the short distance to the house and then placed his bags down on the front walkway. He stepped up the four front steps that led to the porch. Henry peered unnoticed into the picture window to witness the comfortable, extended family scene. He saw Mattie in the dining room clearing away the dinner dishes at the far end of his limited view and realized that she must be working late that night. Closer to the picture window, he saw Charles smoking his pipe and reading the newspaper, while the largest twin boy started to toddle toward his grandfather. Joan sat at her rolltop desk, writing a letter. Granny Harris was beginning to nod off in her favorite overstuffed easy chair. Margaret sat on the floor, dressed in beige jodhpurs and a casual white blouse, playing pat-a-cake with the smallest twin boy. Her eyebrows winged provocatively over her shining, dark brown eyes. Margaret's dark hair curled to frame her face and served to make her seem too young to be the mother of twins. Even from his distant view, Henry could see that a change had begun to occur in the beautiful woman he called his wife. At that moment, Margaret sensed someone watching her, and it caused her head to turn toward the picture window. In an instant, she recognized the tall stance and silhouette of the man she had fallen in love with years before.

Margaret let out an audible gasp and then immediately bolted from the room to the front door, causing Aaron to whimper and poke

The Locket

out his trembling bottom lip. She flung open the door and raced out onto the front porch into Henry's awaiting embrace. Tears streamed down Margaret's fine, porcelain-like face. They kissed for a long moment, as Margaret wanted to erase the long months of forced separation that had befallen their fledgling union. She molded her body to his, feeling the crispness of his uniform and the metallic hardness of the medals that decorated his coat.

The attire caused a flash of anger to enter her countenance. The trappings of war enraged her. They were symbols of a government that had robbed her of so much. The feel of Henry was no different from before. His voice as he murmured, "I love you," sounded the same. He looked fit and healthy. The taste of his lips on hers was deeply familiar. The scent of his aftershave had been forever branded in her mind. But as Margaret stood back to survey her husband, she realized there was a new strangeness about him. There was a difference that could not yet be defined. This difference set off alarms in her heart, but her head ruled victorious to allow her to dismiss the disturbing perceptions.

The entire Harris family household stood with their noses almost pressed against the pane of the living room window. When Henry released Margaret, they both looked through the window with a laugh at the ogling faces. The couple walked inside for Henry to receive his formal homecoming. There was rejoicing. Margaret introduced Henry to his twin sons. She placed Aaron in his arms. The toddler looked uncertain at first, but his mother's enthusiastic, accepting glances gave him the nonverbal cues to smile broadly at his father. Margaret then said, "This is your daddy." She said, "Daddy," again, asking for imitation. Aaron repeated the sweet word Margaret had spent long months wanting to hear. Henry hugged the little one and kissed him on the cheek.

"Where is your brother?" Henry asked the smallest toddler.

Joan brought over Matthew, who wore a very frightened look. As Henry reached for his other son, Matthew let out a wail and clutched his grandmother's neck.

"All of this excitement has made him upset," Joan explained.

"Both of them are so tired, Henry. Margaret, if you want me to, I'll have Mattie put them both to bed."

"No, Mama," Margaret replied. "I know Mattie's ready to go home. Henry and I will put them to bed in a minute."

Henry shook hands with Charles, and they began to talk. Margaret took Aaron into her arms and then walked over to Mattie, who stood on the edge of the family reunion. Mattie wore a somewhat stern expression on her face that surprised Margaret. "If'n Mr. Charles want me to," she began, "I can go git some o' dat fancy champagne he keep down in da cellar."

"Don't worry about that, Mattie," Margaret replied while searching the old woman's face for the source of her stern look. "I know you're tired. I can have Daddy drive you home right now."

"No thank ya, ma'am. I think I be walkin' tonight. It be so clear an' bright. Go on now. Enjoy yasef." Mattie then took off her apron and disappeared into the kitchen to leave out the back door, as was her custom. Margaret thought of how her family would never have stood for her to walk home unaccompanied in the dark. The same type of consideration was never extended to a woman of color.

Margaret was a bit surprised at Mattie's speedy departure. Normally, she joined the Harris family celebrations with gusto. Margaret dismissed Mattie's unusual behavior and attributed her actions to the fact that it was late on a Friday evening. *Mattie must be tired.* Margaret stood in the kitchen thinking about Mattie and the terrible lot in life she and others of her kind had inherited based only upon the color of their skin. It made her shudder to think of what the Negroes endured each day. Her thoughts moved to the disturbing conversation she had embarked upon with James regarding the plight of the southern Negroes. She was beginning to see the wisdom of his words.

James had invaded her thoughts almost every day since last Christmas. Margaret had attempted to fight the constant emergence of his image, but her efforts had failed. She had begun to regard his ever-present spirit as a friend to consult and give advice. At times,

The Locket

she had mock conversations with James in her mind. *If anyone knew that*, she thought, *they would think I'm crazy.*

When Margaret returned to the dining room, Charles had champagne glasses lined up on the mahogany table. He poured everyone a glass of the sparkling golden liquid that always teased Margaret's nose. She walked over to her husband, feeling like a shy, uncertain bride again. Henry smiled down into her face and placed his arm around her to draw his wife and young sons into the warmth of his regard. Again, Margaret sensed a stiffness, something elusive she had never felt before. Charles distracted her from the mental searching to begin his toast.

"May our family now remain complete and forever be blessed with long, healthy lives and continued happiness." Everyone murmured their agreement to his confident words, assured in their belief that complete and total happiness was now just a moment away for the fledgling Montgomery family that had been separated by war.

Then the entire Harris and Montgomery family sat down to enjoy one another's company. Margaret did not want to miss a moment or to let Henry out of her sight just yet. So she allowed the boys to fall asleep on the couch, knowing she and Henry would put them to bed when they were ready to retire themselves. Tears glistened in her eyes when she thought about how Henry had never had the opportunity to enjoy that particular nightly ritual that she cherished so much. A flash of excitement entered her countenance as she thought of the night ahead, anticipating a joyous release of pent-up passions she had suppressed for so long.

Charles and Henry spoke at length about some of his war experiences, while the women continued to sip champagne and listen to the conversation about a faraway continent they had never seen. It was hard for Margaret to tear her gaze away from her husband's handsome form. She longed to feel his skin against hers. The yearning in her eyes was impossible to mask. Before long, Joan recognized the look in her daughter's eyes, and this was the older woman's cue to give the young couple some privacy.

"Charles," she began. "It's late now. They want to turn in. Anyway, you've got work tomorrow."

"All right, woman," he replied. "I get the hint. We'll get out of your way so y'all can start about the business of being a real family now. Good night, all." He again shook Henry's hand and gave Margaret a quick good night kiss on her smooth forehead. Charles then looked around the room and said, "I guess Granny just slipped off to bed without saying good night. That champagne must have put her in a good sleeping mood." Joan then pushed her chatty husband out of the room.

When Joan and Charles had left the room to head upstairs, Margaret and Henry looked at each other in silence for a bit, both feeling somewhat alone even though they were now together. Margaret spoke first. "I can't even describe how much I've missed you, Henry." Henry nodded his mutual understanding. "It was so hard, especially with the boys and all." Tears welled up in her eyes. "I was always so worried about you, thinking you might not make it back." A small tear moved down the curve of her cheek. "Please promise me that the government won't ever take you from us again. Please." She looked up at the man she loved.

Henry reached over to touch the stray tear on her cheek. He noted the haunted look that had entered her dark brown gaze. "We will be together for always. I love you so much. There will be no more separations. Don't fret now. Our bond will never be broken." Henry held his wife in a deep embrace. He was amazed at how easily the words had tumbled from his mouth. The act was working. He watched the lines of worry leave Margaret's young face. Henry marveled at how mere words could serve to erase his wife's anxious thoughts—words so similar to the ones he had spoken just hours before to his mistress. *If I can just keep the act going*, he thought, *then I'll start believing it myself. There won't be any more guilt. My betrayal can be hidden forever.* Henry felt certain he could hold steadfast in his resolve to purge the guilt from his soul as he looked down into the loving face of the woman he had chosen for his bride.

"Come," he beckoned. "Let's tuck these two in and go to bed

ourselves." The two angelic faces were still enjoying peaceful sleep when Margaret scooped up Aaron's thin, slumbering form. "You'll have to carry Matthew. He has gotten way too big for me to carry him upstairs."

"I hope he won't wake up and start screaming like he did before."

"Don't feel bad about that," Margaret said in a reassuring tone. "Matthew is always frightened of new people. He'll warm up to you soon enough. He just has to get to know you. Now Aaron, on the other hand, never meets a stranger."

Margaret led the way up the stairs as they carted the two sleeping boys. They entered the nursery that was lit by a dim night-light. Margaret placed Aaron in his crib, and Henry deposited Matthew in the other crib. Mother and father then stood arm in arm, gazing at their sons together for the first time. Margaret took a deep breath, knowing there would be many more treasured firsts to enjoy over the coming years.

"Aaron is so much smaller than Matthew," Henry observed.

"I know," Margaret whispered, so as not to disturb the sleeping toddlers. "Dr. Whitlock has assured me that he's fine. He was just so small at birth. It will take him several years to catch up, I suppose."

The couple then stood for long moments in silence, just looking at their sons. Margaret knew she could engage in this blatant admiration of their children for hours and never grow tired. But tonight, she wanted to lose herself in loving Henry. She took his hand and led him from the nursery to the bedroom she had occupied throughout her childhood. It was a room that had many times been a safe haven from those turbulent outside forces that often serve to disrupt a young girl's emotions. Somehow, she felt like that young girl again tonight. Margaret and Henry had spent many nights making love in that very room since their marriage. So this night should be no different. But it was. A tinge of embarrassment entered Margaret's cheeks when she looked up into Henry's dark, brooding eyes.

"Let me get changed, and we can turn in," Margaret said. She walked over to the chest of drawers to retrieve the lovely white peignoir set she had worn on their wedding night five years before.

Margaret then walked down the hall to the bathroom. She took great care to look her best for Henry. This was a night she had dreamed about for so many months. Margaret was surprised that some outside force had led her to dress in the bathroom like a wide-eyed, trembling virgin. Indeed, her hands shook as she fastened the small pearl buttons of her gown. She then looked into the face staring back at her from the mirror. Feelings of change were churning inside of her these days. At times, it was bewildering. Her values, beliefs, and emotions were in constant conflict as never before in her life.

The light from the vanity mirror glinted on the locket James had given her last Christmas. Her trembling hand touched the locket, and fiery, passionate images of James leapt into her mind. Margaret's head told her that searing thoughts of James and their night of passion were wrong. She fought to push the thoughts away to the deepest recesses of her mind, but she knew she could never make them disappear. James's memory haunted her each day.

Margaret walked slowly from the bathroom, hoping that Henry could erase her constant musings about a man who had been a dear friend to both of them. When she entered the bedroom, Henry was already undressed and reading the newspaper as he lay between the sheets. The sight of Margaret's undeniable beauty swathed in the filmy white fabric made Henry admire the wife he had chosen, but it was not arousing to him. The bitter bile of guilt arose again in his throat, keeping images of Ma Le and Susan branded in his mind. He resolved to push those thoughts aside. But this night, his efforts would be futile, in spite of the amount of champagne he had consumed.

Margaret turned on the closet light and cracked its door. She turned off the bedside lamp, as had always been their custom before lovemaking. She allowed the outer robe of her peignoir set to drop provocatively from her shoulders to the floor. Margaret slipped between the sheets to feel the warmth of Henry's masculine form beside her. She molded her body into his embrace. Henry lowered his head to kiss her, exploring her sweet mouth with his lips and tongue. Her hands ran over his shoulders and chest as they were

The Locket

illuminated in the dim light. The sight of Henry's strong, sculpted body had always incited deep erotic thoughts within Margaret. But this night was different. The images of James continued to bombard her mind. She found herself comparing the two men. The feel of the locket James had given her was a constant reminder of his presence in her life. Something always kept her from removing the necklace.

Henry's hands did not explore her body in erotic waves as in the past. Margaret reached down over his muscular, flat stomach to touch his manhood, which, to her surprise, was not aroused. Her hand recoiled, and Henry sensed her rightful dismay by the quick movements of her body. His guilt had consumed him and would not allow him to enjoy the pleasures of his wife on this night.

"I'm sorry, Margaret," he stated simply. "I don't know what's wrong. I guess I'm just exhausted from all of the traveling. Maybe we should just rest. I'll be fine in a day or two. You know how much I love you."

Margaret's voice quivered as she said, "I understand." In a way, she was relieved that Henry found it impossible to perform sexually that evening. They both turned away from each other to fall asleep. A fitful, dream-filled sleep came to Henry. The peaceful slumber Margaret desired eluded her that night while she listened to Henry twitch and turn like a caged animal. When small fingers of light peeked over the horizon, Margaret arose from the tortuous bed and silently dressed in a rust-colored sweater and skirt set. She walked downstairs to the kitchen.

When Mattie arrived for work, Margaret was sitting in the kitchen, stirring her cup of coffee. Mattie gave Margaret a knowing look and said, "Well, chile, ya done got up early dis mawnin'."

"It was hard to sleep after all of the excitement last night." Margaret never looked up from her stirring, not wanting to meet Mattie's piercing gaze.

At that moment, they both heard the cries from the toddlers upstairs. Both women responded to enter the nursery within seconds. Matthew was standing in his crib, reaching out to be readied for the day. Aaron was lying on his side, whimpering and crying, which was not at all like his usual happy countenance. Margaret picked him up to soothe the mournful cries that were reminiscent of his first few weeks at home. She smelled the odor of a terribly soiled diaper.

"You need to be changed, little buddy." Margaret wrinkled her nose. She placed Aaron on the changing table and removed his clothes to change the offensive diaper. What she then saw caused her to gasp and to call for Mattie's attention. The old nanny responded to the tone in Margaret's voice. When she reached the changing table, Mattie viewed bright red bloodstains on the diaper and feces filled with pus, producing an unusual stench. Margaret then looked into Mattie's eyes as they each shared a desperate, frightened gaze.

Chapter 11

Margaret and Joan sat in the car outside Dr. Whitlock's office, awaiting the elderly physician's arrival. Margaret allowed Aaron to play and climb around the spacious back seat while her eyes kept darting back to the street Dr. Whitlock would be driving down. She had immediately called the doctor she had known all her life following the disturbing discovery in Aaron's diaper. Dr. Whitlock had seemed a bit inconvenienced by the early-morning telephone call since his chronic rheumatism made getting up and out in a speedy fashion quite difficult and somewhat painful. The sound of panic in Margaret's young voice made him realize there would be no delaying this Saturday-morning office visit.

"I'm getting way too old for this," the doctor muttered while walking to his automobile. A roll of thunder broke loose above the old man's head. "I knew that was coming," he said. "I always feel it in my bones." He then chuckled and said, "Guess I'll just start predicting the weather for everybody in these parts as soon as I retire next year."

Dr. Whitlock's black Ford sedan turned the corner to the clinic he had occupied for years. It was an old white frame farmhouse he had renovated into a medical office when he was a much younger man. It now needed a new coat of paint in addition to internal remodeling he had chosen to forego since retirement was so near. Margaret spied the familiar automobile and alerted Joan. They got out of the car to wait for the doctor on the porch of his clinic office.

When Dr. Whitlock had climbed the four steps leading to the

porch, he encountered two women with matching frightened gazes and a happy, smiling toddler nestled in his mother's arms. He tickled the toddler under the chin to produce a giggle and said, "Well, he looks fit as a fiddle, Margaret. Don't tell me you've been letting Mattie put crazy ideas in your head. I'm sure he's fine, but come on in and let's take a look-see."

As he unlocked the door, Margaret rushed into her explanation of the problem. "I know he looks fine now, but the diaper was horrible. It was filled with blood and pus. I've never seen anything like it. Please check him out thoroughly. You know how worried I've been about his weight gain and all."

"Don't forget to tell the doctor how he was acting," Joan prompted her youngest daughter with growing concern in her eyes.

"Oh, yes," Margaret responded. "He was whimpering and crying like he was in pain when he awoke this morning. Then I opened the diaper and found the blood." Margaret's dark eyes were wide with worry, and her brow remained furrowed.

Dr. Whitlock pulled out a thermometer and instructed Margaret to hold it under Aaron's arm for several minutes. He then left the room to locate the toddler's medical chart. When he returned, he asked several questions regarding family history. Margaret could easily deny any similar problems in her family but was uncertain regarding health problems experienced by Henry's family, as his parents had been deceased for more than ten years. The situation made her yearn for Henry's love and support. Henry had been sleeping so soundly, Margaret had chosen not to disturb him that morning. Looking across at Joan now, she felt quite childish for having asked her mother to accompany her to the doctor's office.

The physician checked the thermometer and announced that Aaron had a normal temperature. He then asked Margaret to undress her son to begin the entire physical examination. Margaret watched Dr. Whitlock closely, feeling helpless and wondering why Aaron now displayed no obvious signs of distress. The doctor poked around on Aaron's abdomen, listened to his heart and bowel sounds, and then said, "I don't see a thing wrong with him, Margaret. All I can say is that he was probably constipated, and his straining caused the bright red bleeding." He then moved over to scribble something on a prescription pad. "Here, take this over to the apothecary. It's a stool softener. He's just fine. You go home and tell Mattie to quit scaring the living daylights out of you and me. Why, Mattie and Joan were over here every other day when you and your sister were little."

"You don't think we need to do any additional testing?" Margaret asked.

"No, dear, I don't," the doctor responded.

Joan then said, "If I remember correctly, I think Anne had this problem as an infant. I had to give her mineral oil. Then I started giving her prune juice every day, and there weren't any more problems."

Margaret could tell she was outnumbered. Her intuition must have been incorrect on this particular day. She looked down and started dressing Aaron so as to hide the warm, rosy hue that had entered her cheeks, an outward sign of her embarrassment. It also made her a bit angry to be patronized by the old physician. But Margaret went ahead and made her apologies to Dr. Whitlock for having disturbed him so early on a Saturday morning for an ailment that had proven to be nothing serious.

Joan and Margaret then paid Dr. Whitlock, gathered up the little one, and climbed into the car for the drive home. A light rain covered the windshield. Margaret was quiet and reflective, choosing to be isolated with her thoughts. It seemed strange to her that she was unable to shake the feeling of worry and concern over her son's condition. Dr. Whitlock's words should have provided reassurance. Looking over at Joan, Margaret realized the physician had erased any traces of apprehension that her mother might have had regarding Aaron's health. Margaret chose not to speak her remaining fears.

Joan broke the silence. "Your father and I were talking last night. You know, Tim Spencer has been telling us we could use his mountain cabin whenever we want. It's up in Elijay on Walnut Mountain. I'm sure he wouldn't mind if you and Henry went up there for a few days. It would be sort of like a second honeymoon. We'll take care of the boys." Joan could see another flash of concern in her daughter's eyes. "Now, Margaret. Dr. Whitlock said Aaron is fine, and I've never known him to make a mistake. Believe him. Go on up to the mountains. Y'all can leave right after lunch. You can come back in the middle of the week."

Margaret sighed and said, "All right, Mama. If Henry wants to, we'll go." A small spark of excitement began to rise in the young woman at the anticipation of a few romantic days alone with her husband.

"I'll call Tim when we get home," Joan replied with finality in her tone.

The car turned into the driveway of the Harris home. Mattie and Granny Harris rushed out onto the front porch with matching looks of worry etched into their faces. Joan stepped up onto the porch and announced, "Aaron is perfectly fine. Just a little constipation, exactly like Anne had when she was little." The look of worry melted from Granny's face, reflecting her trust in the doctor she had known for forty years. Mattie's expression never changed. She held out her arms, and Aaron accepted his nanny's embrace.

"Come to Mattie, chile," she murmured to the sweet boy who felt like her own grandson. Margaret and Mattie again exchanged worried glances. The younger woman looked away to help dispel the distressing concerns.

Margaret entered the house to find Henry sitting in the living room, drinking black coffee and reading the newspaper. Upon her entrance, he put away his paper to ask, "Is everything fine with Aaron?" Margaret was pleased to see his obvious interest in the well-being of his son.

"I suppose so," she replied. "I guess Daddy told you what I found in his diaper." Henry nodded. "The doctor said it was a simple case of constipation and too much straining." Henry then looked relieved. "By the way, Mama said we could leave this afternoon to spend a few days at Tim Spencer's cabin up in Elijay if we want to. Everybody here can take care of the boys. It might be good for us to have a few days by ourselves. What do you think?"

The Locket

Henry's piercing gaze looked down at his wife. "I think that would be nice."

"It will be about a three-hour drive," Margaret announced. "Are you rested enough for more traveling?"

"Sure. If I get tired, I'll just let you drive for a while."

"I guess I should go on and start packing." Margaret then turned to walk upstairs and begin the chore of packing the necessary suitcases. Within an hour, she was satisfied that each required item had been stowed away for the trip. Margaret walked downstairs just as Charles had returned from the Spencer house with the key to the mountain cabin. He gave the key to Henry.

Margaret then walked into the kitchen and found Joan, Granny, and the boys eating their lunch. "We're all packed and ready to leave," she announced. "It's such a long drive, and we would like to get on the road. Do you think we could take a packed lunch?"

"It be ready right here, Miss Margaret," Mattie replied.

Margaret looked over toward Mattie's voice to spy a basket. She walked to the kitchen counter and opened up the basket to reveal chicken fried to perfection with pimento cheese sandwiches and syrupy sweet iced tea packed in mason jars. Margaret looked up at her dear nanny's face and said, "No one can pack a lunch like you, Mattie. My mouth is watering just looking at this feast." With tears sparkling in her eyes, she hugged the now old woman. Margaret looked deeply into the wise face before her.

"Ya gonna be awright, Miss Margaret?" Mattie asked with lines of worry visible in her expression.

"Yes, Mattie," she responded. Then she said in a whisper, "The war may have changed him, but it's over now, and we can start afresh. So much is ahead of us." Mattie was satisfied that her substitute daughter was managing the return of her soldier husband. She turned back to the chores before her.

"Well, I guess we'll be leaving as soon as Henry puts the bags in the car," Margaret stated. "Let me tell the boys goodbye." She walked over to the two toddlers ensconced in their high chairs, busy smearing food all over their faces and hair. She bent down to plant lingering kisses on the velvety soft skin of each small forehead. After kissing Aaron, a look of worry entered her face, causing her to pause and wonder if the short trip was a wise idea.

Joan noticed the look and responded, "Don't worry about a thing. We know how to reach you if there are any problems. Mattie raised three daughters, and she and I did a fine job raising you and Anne. I think you know we have an awful lot of good sense and judgment. When you get up to Walnut Mountain, check in with the caretaker, Mr. Moses. He has a telephone. There won't be a telephone in Tim's cabin. But if we needed you, we would call Mr. Moses. He'll come and fetch you if anything goes wrong."

Margaret nodded. Every detail had been taken care of. There was no need to worry. It just felt strange to be leaving the babies behind. Never a night had been spent without them since their birth. Would they cry all evening? Could Aaron fall asleep without the rocking he always needed? Should the trip be postponed until they were a little older? The questions that bounced around in her brain were interrupted by Henry.

"Everything is loaded in the car," he stated. "Are you ready to leave?" Margaret nodded. She grabbed the basket, while Henry scratched Matthew's scruffy head and tickled Aaron under the chin. She followed Henry from the room, avoiding direct glances at those gathered in the kitchen. Margaret felt a need to conceal the strange apprehension she was unable to shake.

After telling everyone farewell, the young couple sat in silence for the first few minutes of the journey. The silence was deafening, making Margaret feel nervous. A need to converse engulfed her, so she began with, "I've really missed the long conversations we used to share. Your letters were wonderful, but they don't take the place of a real conversation, do they?"

"No. You're right. I've missed that too," Henry added truthfully remembering Ma Le's initial struggle with English and the reserved nature of her culture. Henry had always been a somewhat quiet man. However, Margaret's frank, straightforward manner coupled with her conversational finesse had been a quality he considered attractive.

It would also be an asset in her future as a colonel's wife, a position that would carry heavy social obligations.

"Henry," she began. "I love you so much. I want us to make a happy life together. We hardly know what it's like to truly live as husband and wife. And now you come home with a ready-made family. I just worry that the war has robbed us of too much."

"It hasn't," he replied in a reassuring tone. "Think of this as just a new beginning. I know I've missed a lot with the twins, but they're so young. They will never remember that I was away at war during the first year of their lives. Now, it's time to start afresh."

Margaret admired the determination she heard in his voice. His words brought reassurance, but there were still so many unknown things ahead of her, allowing her to feel trepidation. This prompted her to ask, "Where do we go from here?"

The frankness of her question caught Henry a bit off guard. "To be honest with you, I'm not really certain yet." Margaret frowned at his answer. "I should be receiving a letter any day now delineating my new assignment. Before leaving Indonesia, I received several letters from General Wheeler discussing various positions. All of them were acceptable, but remember, I'm a career army man. I've always been honest about that. I'm sure you understand that means moving a great deal. Think of it as an adventure. You haven't spent much time out of the South. It will be good for you. I don't want to tell you the different positions and locations yet, because I have no control over the final decision. I don't want you to get your heart set on a particular place and then get disappointed. We'll both find out soon enough. Let's just enjoy this trip and the month of leave the army has granted me."

Margaret was a bit irritated that her husband had chosen to withhold information from her. She had always envisioned long discussions regarding family decisions. But she consoled herself with the fact that they had no real control over Henry's new assignment. They just had to wait for the orders from General Wheeler.

Henry noticed Margaret's irritated look and said, "Enough of the worrying. I'm sure the letter will probably be waiting for me at your parents' house when we return." His words caused a flash of excitement. The uncertainty was titillating when she took Henry's advice and viewed the situation as a new adventure.

Margaret looked out the window as the car was now going through the city of Atlanta. The presence and majesty of its tall buildings always made Margaret catch her breath. Being a small-town girl, she had often wondered what it would feel like to live in the city. She again looked over at Henry, realizing that his new army orders might require moving to some large, urban area.

"Before we get out of the city," Henry began, "I need to stop and get some bottles of whiskey since all of the counties around Atlanta are dry." Margaret looked surprised. She had never known Henry to be much of a drinker, but she kept her silence. Henry turned down Peachtree Street, and Margaret watched signs for Fifteenth, Sixteenth, and Seventeenth Streets pass by before the car slowed to a stop in front of a small liquor store. Margaret remained in the car while Henry entered the establishment. A few moments later, he walked out of the store carrying a box in his hands. With bottles clinking, he stored the box in the floorboard of the back seat for safekeeping. Margaret looked back to note that the box contained eight large bottles of the strong spirits.

Soon they were back on the road. They sat in silence for a while. As the tall buildings of Atlanta were left behind, Henry broke the silence. "Have you spoken to James recently?"

Margaret almost jumped from her seat at the mention of the powerful man's name. She had worked so hard to erase the scorching memories of his touch. Margaret broke the long pause with, "No, I haven't talked to him since Christmas." "Oh yes," Henry replied. "You and the boys spent last Christmas up there. Did you have a good time?"

"Yes." Margaret's hand reached up to touch the gold locket that served as a reminder of James's warmth and the deep passions he had ignited. Just taking off the necklace would have helped her forget James. But taking it off, Margaret thought, might make her longing for his embrace even more difficult to manage.

The Locket

"It would be nice to pay James a visit," Henry stated. "I haven't seen him in several years."

"Let's just worry about where we'll be going next. I want to get our family settled before we plan another vacation." Margaret hoped her words would kill any further talk of a visit to Connecticut. Her emotions were still too fragile. She needed more time to cool the fire that burned beneath her skin at the mere mention of James Walsh's name.

Margaret glanced down at her watch and realized that the trip would last another hour and a half. Her stomach was empty, and that reminded her of the packed lunch sitting in the back seat. She reached back to retrieve the picnic basket. She opened one side of the basket, and the aroma of Mattie's prize-winning chicken filled the car. They both munched on chicken and pimento cheese sandwiches and quenched their thirsts with the sweet, dark tea Mattie had poured into mason jars.

With a satisfied stomach, Margaret's eyelids became heavy. She moved closer to Henry to rest her head on his strong, muscled shoulder. Her warmth beside him made a slow smile cross his face. He looked down into the sweet, angelic face of his sleeping wife. Regrets for his actions with Ma Le and the fruit of their union arose in him. He then tried to release those feelings of regret and betrayal, feelings his wife knew nothing about. Embarrassment at having to call on James for help to conceal the evidence of his betrayal also surfaced. He needed to talk to James soon. He had to make certain the secret they were keeping would remain just that, a secret.

Before long, they had reached Gilmer County and the small mountain community of Elijay. Margaret awoke when the car came to a halt at the foot of Walnut Mountain, just in front of a small log cabin belonging to the caretaker, Mr. Moses. She watched as Henry walked from the vehicle to meet the old man who emerged from the dwelling smoking a corncob pipe. The contrast of the tall, handsome army officer and the mountain hermit made Margaret wish she had a camera to photograph the unlikely pair. A bit of worry furrowed

Margaret's brow as she prayed that Mr. Moses kept his telephone in working order in case of any family emergency.

Henry sat back down in the Ford and maneuvered the automobile onto the winding mountain road of dirt. Halfway up the mountain, just after a sharp bend in the narrow road, stood the solitary Spencer family cabin. Henry parked, and they both emerged to smell the fragrant, North Georgia air.

Henry unlocked the door to the weekend home, and Margaret walked inside the rustic dwelling. "Tim said things might be a little musty since no one has been up here in several months," Henry remarked.

Most of the furniture was covered with white sheets. However, Margaret could already envision the home's charm seeping through the dust and almost forgotten memories. The empty fireplace begged for a light. An old sled on the hearth could tell stories of daring snowball fights held between Christmas and New Year's in the past.

"Well," Margaret stated, "let's get going and spruce things up a bit so it will seem more inviting." She then looked down at her sweater and skirt set together with the high-heeled pumps she had donned that morning. "I think I'll change first into something a little more suitable for cleaning up."

Margaret walked across the hardwood floor into the bedroom where Henry had already placed their suitcases. Henry began pulling the sheets off of various pieces of furniture in the large family room. Margaret could see him through the open bedroom door. In a purposeful manner, she unbuttoned her sweater, unzipped her skirt, and allowed the garments to fall to the floor. She then removed her slip and stockings to stand in her lacy bra and panties. Henry looked up from his work to gaze at her for an instant. Margaret yearned for his gaze to linger, but his eyes moved back to his chore, seemingly unaffected by her feminine form. A look of disappointment entered Margaret's face as she remembered earlier days from their marriage when Henry would have instantly raked his hands and lips over her body with much less of an invitation than the one he had just been given.

The Locket

She then sighed and reached over to her open suitcase to retrieve a pair of beige jodhpurs and a burgundy blouse. The rich color of the blouse brought out the creaminess of her skin. Margaret surveyed her appearance in the dresser mirror. Again she noticed the locket hanging from the graceful lines of her slim neck, another visual reminder of the enigmatic man who entered her thoughts each day. In a flash of anger at her thoughts, she unhooked the chain that seemed to scorch her neck and let it fall onto an ornamental doily covering the dresser before her.

Margaret joined Henry to complete all of the necessary chores for them to settle in comfortably for the night. Henry brought in the last few remaining items left in the car. Margaret looked up as he peered into a paper sack.

"Look, Margaret," he commented. "It seems that Mattie did sneak in a few groceries. She knew we wouldn't be near a store. I tell you, I don't know what y'all would have done without her over all these years."

Margaret smiled at the mention of Mattie's name. "I know," she replied. "We all take her for granted at times. But I can tell you I'll miss her just as much as my own mother when we move away from Barnesville. It makes me teary-eyed knowing that Mattie won't get to see the boys grow up the way she did with Anne and me." She paused a moment and then added, "Now give me that sack, and I'll see what I can do about dinner. You know I'm not a great cook, but I try."

Margaret rummaged through the sack to discover two large mason jars of Mattie's homemade vegetable soup, a box of crackers, a jar of peach preserves, a loaf of bread, half of a cream cheese pound cake, and some coffee. She reminded herself to retrieve the remaining fried chicken from the picnic basket, to be eaten with the vegetable soup, for supper. Margaret continued to get familiar with the kitchen while Henry poured his first glass of whiskey for the evening and sat down to read the latest issue of *Life* magazine.

By the time the smell of simmering vegetable soup wafted throughout the cabin, Henry was pouring his second glass of whiskey. Margaret looked up to see her tall, heavily muscled husband pick up his drink and walk out onto the front porch to breathe in deeply and savor the cleansing mountain air. She imagined that the quiet, still atmosphere must be a welcome change from the war-torn region of the world he had just left behind. Margaret followed him out onto the porch. She reached around his waist from behind in a loving caress. Henry lowered his head to place a light kiss upon the soft bloom of her parted lips.

When the short kiss ended, Margaret murmured, "I've got supper ready on the table." They walked together from the half darkness of early evening into the cabin.

They sat down to enjoy the meal, and when the main course was completed, Margaret cut two slices of pound cake to bring a sweet end to the meal. Henry then poured his third glass of whiskey, which was surprising to Margaret, but she kept quiet. She poured herself a steaming cup of black coffee, and they both sat down upon a large, overstuffed couch.

They talked in an easy manner about unimportant things, just catching up on events Henry had missed since his last leave. Margaret's thoughts then flew to the long, moving conversations she had shared with James in Connecticut last Christmas. She wondered why those exchanges had seemed so much more satisfying than her recent talks with the man she had been married to for several years. She thought about the content of her discussions with James to realize that no subject had ever been forbidden. Her frankness had been appreciated in James's eyes. James had treated her with great respect, as an equal, someone whose opinion was important and valuable. Margaret now realized for the first time that, although Henry appeared to enjoy her talkative nature, he often treated her as if her knowledge was limited to the point that she could not form an educated opinion on matters of importance. Margaret was a woman. Henry treated her as such.

Margaret was lost in her thoughts when Henry interrupted them with, "Guess we better turn in. It's getting late." Margaret dismissed her musings to follow her husband into the bedroom.

The bed loomed large and served to rattle Margaret's nerves

The Locket

as she remembered the rejection she had confronted the previous evening. Henry undressed and slipped between the sheets. He watched Margaret remove her clothing while admiring the luminous curves of her sensuous, strong body. Suddenly, Henry's gaze aroused a hint of embarrassment in his young wife, prompting her to reach over and extinguish the bedside lamp. Unbeknown to each other, they both felt relief to realize the cloak of darkness would hide the apprehensiveness they shared for separate reasons.

Margaret slipped naked beneath the sheet and blanket. She felt the warmth of her husband's taut, muscular form lying beside her. He reached over to pull her into his embrace. Henry trailed kisses down the slim column of her fragrant neck. His hands touched her full breasts, and he lowered his head to kiss and suck those creamy orbs. Margaret's mind raced to the last man who had touched her in such a manner … James. A comparison of the two men sprang to her mind as she struggled to thrust away the forbidden thoughts.

Margaret felt the hardness of Henry's manhood against her thigh. He raised his body and entered her. His entrance was difficult, feeling foreign and dull. It was as if she were making love to a stranger, which ignited a feeling of violation. Margaret closed her eyes, wishing the ordeal was over, but their coupling took quite a long time before Henry's climax was reached. Margaret enjoyed very little, if any, arousal and certainly nothing close to erotic fulfillment. Henry rolled his powerful form away from Margaret's sensuous flesh to turn with his back to her and fall into a deep, alcohol-induced slumber.

Sleep would not come quickly to Margaret that night. Their union on this evening could not be called lovemaking. Where had the depth of emotion gone? Margaret searched her memories. The tenderness, the love had been there before, hadn't it? How had her memories of Henry's passion cooled when the fire of James's erotic touch could be felt as if he were still beside her? Again, Margaret reached up to touch the locket that seemed to have become a part of her. When her hand touched nothing but her throat, she remembered removing the locket to place it atop the dresser.

Margaret arose naked from the bed to walk over to the dresser.

In the darkness, her hands found the delicate chain and locket. She then walked into the bathroom and turned on the light. Margaret read over the inscription again, wondering just what James had meant by the words "Eyes Opened by Truth. Pain Healed by Love." With trembling fingers and longing in her heart, she hooked the gold chain around her neck, vowing never to remove it again.

Chapter 12

"I think this is what we've been waiting for," Margaret said to Henry as she held an official-looking letter in her hand. They had arrived back in Barnesville that Tuesday afternoon, a bit earlier than anyone had expected. Margaret and Henry had just walked in the front door to find no one home but Mattie puttering about in the kitchen, preparing the evening meal. Mattie had informed the couple that Joan and Granny Harris had taken the twins over to Sadie Samuels's home for a visit. They were expected back any moment.

Upon discovering that the twins were fine but not at home, Margaret scrutinized the unopened letter. She was eager to read the contents of the correspondence that would dispel any further uncertainty regarding the location of Henry's next assignment.

Margaret handed her husband the letter with trembling hands. He opened it, and Margaret watched his eyes dart back and forth as he read the letter.

"So," she said with impatience. "What does it say?"

Henry let out a whistle and replied, "Well, I never imagined I would get this swank assignment. You had better start practicing putting on airs, Mrs. Montgomery, because your husband has just been assigned to a position at the Pentagon." Margaret's eyes grew wide with anticipation regarding the prestigious appointment.

"What exactly will you be doing there?"

"The letter says I'll be heading a division of the Army Corps of Engineers devoted to planning future military bases throughout Europe." Henry's voice resounded with excitement.

"So we'll be living in Washington," Margaret stated.

"Not necessarily," Henry answered. "We could settle down in the suburbs. There are quite a few nice bedroom communities in that area. General Wheeler has mentioned some of them in his letter. He recommends Alexandria, Virginia, and has given me the name of a real estate agent there. I guess we will need to go on up there next week to search for a house."

Margaret was grateful she had something to look forward to following the feeling of strangeness the pair had developed over their short vacation, one that should have been a romantic interlude. Plans for the upcoming move would distract her from distressing thoughts about Henry and the sense of longing she often felt for James.

Henry broke through her thoughts to say, "I think I'll run over to Tim's house now to drop off the key to the cabin. I'll be back in a little while." Margaret nodded her agreement, thankful for a few minutes of solitude to think about the changes that would soon occur in her life.

Margaret stood in the living room before the picture window and watched Henry drive away toward Tim Spencer's house. She then sank down in a chair, not really knowing what to do next. Her thoughts whirled around as she attempted to create a mental picture of her life to be. It was difficult, and the mental exercise left her feeling frustrated. She felt the need to tell someone about their future plans. Her first thought was to have a long chat with Mattie. Her comfortable old nanny had a quirky way of viewing life and its many changes. Long chats with Mattie in the kitchen always eased Margaret's concerns about life's transitions.

It was then that the young woman was struck with the silence that permeated throughout the house. Margaret had heard the screen door from the back porch slam a few minutes earlier. She looked at her watch to see that it was four fifteen, too early for Mattie to have gone home for the evening. Hawk and Pierce never worked on Tuesdays, so their familiar sounds were also absent.

The Locket

Margaret walked out of the living room, through the dining room, and into the kitchen. Mattie was nowhere. An eerie feeling of dread overcame Margaret, making her heart beat faster. She had the feeling of strange, flickering, cold fingers running up her back while she stood in the suffocating silence. Her next thought was to search outside for the old woman. Margaret noticed the kitchen garbage can was missing, which allowed her to realize that Mattie must have gone into the backyard to empty it into the large trash can out back.

But something made her press on in search of Mattie. She walked through the kitchen door and out onto the screened back porch. It was then that her eyes fell upon Mattie lying facedown in the middle of the backyard, half way between the house and the large garbage cans. The full kitchen trash can had fallen from her grasp, and garbage was strewn about on the ground by her crumpled form. Margaret ran from the porch screaming Mattie's name, hoping she would hear a response from her still body lying on the ground.

Margaret yelled for help at the limits of her voice, knowing that someone on Stafford Avenue would hear her cries. When she reached Mattie, Margaret pulled the woman's body onto her back to cradle her dark head and to look for any response. Mattie's face was distorted, her mouth drawn down on the left side with a steady stream of saliva falling from her lips. It was as if one side of the old woman's face had fallen an inch or more. Mattie's eyelids fluttered, and her eyes moved about uncontrollably.

"Mattie!" Margaret screamed into the elderly woman's face. "Can you speak? Talk to me, Mattie! It's me, Margaret! You're going to be all right. I'll get help. We'll get you to the doctor." Frantic words tumbled from Margaret's mouth as she held Mattie in desperation.

Mattie appeared to understand who was holding her and the words Margaret had just spoken. Her eyes focused upon Margaret's face while she spoke in slurred tones. "Miss Margaret," she choked out. "Tell my girls I loves 'em. Look after Maggie. She need help. Remember, I loves you, chile, jus' like my own. Jus' like my own …" Her voice trailed off, she made a choking sound, and her eyelids fluttered while her eyes rolled over to one side.

Tears streamed down Margaret's cheeks as she continued to frantically reassure the now lifeless form she held in her arms. "You're going to be fine, Mattie. Mattie! Keep talking to me, Mattie!" Margaret realized that the small spark of life she had just witnessed in Mattie was now forever extinguished. Her heart told her that this was so, but she allowed her mind to take over the horrendous situation and allow her to cope with the sudden tragedy through denial.

Margaret's arms remained frozen around Mattie's shoulders and head as she clutched the woman who had meant so much to her throughout her entire life. A steady stream of tears continued to trail from Margaret's wild-eyed gaze onto Mattie's soft, dark skin. A familiar lullaby Mattie had sung to the Harris girls and to the Montgomery twins came to her mind. Margaret began to rock Mattie's lifeless body while singing the sweet lullaby in a trembling voice. She knew that if she kept the lullaby going, Mattie would surely open up her eyes and join her in the childish tune.

Margaret's voice became hoarse, but the tune went on without interruption. Thirty minutes later Joan, Granny, and the boys arrived home. Upon finding the house deserted and a burned roast in the oven, a sense of dread overcame Joan.

"Granny," Joan commanded, "keep the boys in the house. Something is wrong. Let me see if I can find Mattie." Joan turned off the oven. She walked out onto the back porch. Her gaze immediately flew to the disturbing scene between Mattie and Margaret in the backyard. Joan turned quickly to Granny, who stood in the kitchen. "It's Mattie. She's collapsed in the yard. Call Doc Whitlock right now."

Joan slammed the door to the kitchen to keep the toddlers away from the morbid situation. She then walked slowly toward the pair, hearing Margaret's raspy singing of the old familiar lullaby. When Joan reached them, it was clear that Mattie was no longer alive.

"Margaret," Joan said in a soft voice and touched her daughter's shoulder. "We need to let Mattie rest now. I think it will be best if you come on inside. We've called Dr. Whitlock. He'll be here soon."

The Locket

The singing stopped. "No, Mama. I can't do that. Mattie can't rest without her lullaby. You go on back to the house. I'll be in as soon as she wakes up." Margaret's eyes were wild and unseeing. The hoarse voice that threatened to leave her began singing the lullaby once more.

Joan felt nausea rising in her belly as her entire body trembled, not knowing what she should do next. She reached down to take Margaret's arm in an attempt to force her away from the corpse lying on the ground. Margaret quickly snatched her arm away from her mother's grasp.

"No!" she barked out. "Leave me alone!" Joan stepped back with tears brimming in her eyes. She looked up to see Charles striding across the backyard. Joan walked up to her husband to whisper a quick explanation of the situation. There were sounds of cars screeching to a halt before the Harris home.

A chilly breeze blew leaves across the backyard as Dr. Whitlock walked toward Margaret and the nanny she clutched in a tender embrace. Upon viewing the physician's presence, Margaret displayed a look of relief. "She's asleep now, Doc. I know you can wake her up. She doesn't want me to let go of her." The doctor reached down to Mattie's neck to feel for the pulse he knew was gone.

"I know you're tired, Margaret," the doctor simply stated. "I can take care of Mattie here. Let me give you something that will help you rest. Then your father can take you on into the house."

The doctor reached down into his black bag to hold up a long syringe. He plunged the syringe into Margaret's arm. Her strength was such that the prick of the needle was unnoticed. Relieved that the physician was now present, Margaret allowed her father to lead her away from Mattie's body. She walked an unsteady gait with Charles's arms tightly around her for support. Within a few moments, the sedating drug engulfed her, causing her knees to buckle and the world to go to black.

Chapter 13

"I just don't think this is a good idea," Joan commented to Charles. They were both in the process of dressing to attend Mattie's funeral, which would begin in less than an hour. "It's been so hard for Margaret. I always knew she loved Mattie, but I never imagined she would become so upset over losing her. It's like she just snapped. Charles, I'm afraid she'll make a spectacle of herself today."

"Leave her alone, Joan," Charles responded. "I think anyone who witnessed the death of their own nanny would behave a little strangely. Now, she has been fine over the past few days. I know she's been a little down, but she's collected herself. Margaret wants to pay her respects, just like the rest of us. It might even help her get over the loss a bit quicker."

"Just visiting the funeral home would have been enough. Mattie was a dear old soul to us all, but I just don't know about attending a colored funeral. I've heard they sometimes dance in the aisles of the church. It just doesn't feel right." The worried look never left Joan's face as she clipped a simple strand of pearls around her neck. "I know we'll be the only white folks there."

"I'm sure you're right about that," Charles replied. "It won't hurt any of us to learn a bit more about the colored folks' culture."

Joan knew there would be no keeping Margaret away from the funeral. At times, Charles and Margaret became staunchly united regarding certain issues. Joan had witnessed this over the years, and she knew better than to fight a battle she would surely lose.

The Locket

Downstairs, Margaret sat looking somber, gazing out the living room picture window. She had already taken the boys next door so Miss Winnie and Robert could babysit during the funeral service. Margaret remembered Henry's attempts to avoid attending Mattie's memorial. A hot flash of anger had welled up inside Margaret at his obvious disregard of the love and respect she held deep in her heart for the old colored woman. While Henry appeared to appreciate Mattie's hard work for the Harris family, the color of her skin made a public show of respect unnecessary in his eyes. A few well-delivered comments from Margaret's newly acid-filled tongue had persuaded the tall army officer that his presence was required.

Within moments, they were all ready to leave. The five adults climbed into Charles's dark blue Ford for the short drive to the colored Baptist church. They were planning to meet Anne outside the church just prior to the service. Charles turned the Ford down the old Mt. Zion Road. Margaret's tired eyes, framed with dark circles, looked out the window of the automobile to witness the flying dirt and leaves. Margaret knew that driving down this dirt road would forever remind her of the loss of Mattie. Doc Whitlock had said it was a stroke. There was nothing anyone could have done to save her.

Charles turned the car around a bend in the road. Before them stood an old wooden-framed country church standing among a grove of trees. The Rose of Sharon Baptist Church had originally been painted white, but peeling paint and weather wear had turned the structure to more of a gray color rather than its original pristine state.

Anne got out of her vehicle to join her family when their car pulled up to the church. A few of the Negro church members were still standing outside talking. They all walked together silently up the steps and into the dimly lit sanctuary. Most of the seats were taken, as the service was to begin in a few minutes. Therefore, the small group of white faces were forced to file into the last pew at the back of the church. All of the colored people present that day were resplendent in their Sunday-best finery. Margaret had always heard that colored funerals were different, as they felt cheated if a very public display of grief was not realized. Nothing could be more foreign to the white community, which chose a reserved type of grief designed to hide true depths of emotion.

Reverend Paul Johnson then walked to the podium to say, "We come here today, my brothers and sisters, to grieve mightily over the loss of our beautiful sister in Christ, Miz Mattie Lewis." His booming voice resounded through the congregation, filling the small structure to its rafters. "We will begin today by singing 'What a Friend We Have in Jesus.'" Everyone then stood to sing the old spiritual hymn. Joan and Anne looked down in search of hymnals, but the poor Negro church had none. The entire colored congregation broke into song, and the familiar melody shook the church. Margaret easily joined in, knowing the words by heart from her church choir days. Joan and Anne had never enjoyed music and singing as Margaret had throughout her life. Margaret looked over to see the two women struggling to remember the words. Granny Harris and Margaret stood proud and strong, singing each word fully with perfect pitch. The white men remained silent, as was their custom.

Margaret gazed around the small country church. Mattie's casket was simple, made of oak, and covered with a blanket of pink carnations. Pink had always been her favorite color. There were several other large sprays of flowers in stands and pots surrounding the open casket that nestled Mattie's body, now in eternal repose. Margaret watched the congregation sway back and forth to feel the music through their entire bodies. Some of the colored women began to yell out phrases such as "Amen, brother" and "Praise the Lord Jesus." Margaret's body began to sway as she stood at the end of their pew just next to the center aisle. Henry's eyes grew wide to note that Margaret was unconsciously joining their unusual swaying and gyrating, which would have been highly unacceptable in her own church. He reached around to grasp her arm firmly and staunch the rhythmic movements he hoped no one else had witnessed. Margaret felt embarrassed and childish following the simple action and the disapproving look he wore.

Following the familiar hymn, Reverend Johnson walked down among the flowers and announced which families had purchased a

The Locket

floral gift. The reverend then indicated that there would be several solos to come. A tall Negro man then stood to sing "Leaning on the Everlasting Arms" in a rich baritone voice. An upbeat version of "Shall We Gather at the River" was presented by a young colored woman blessed with a full alto voice.

After the solos were complete, Reverend Johnson began to deliver Mattie's eulogy in the melodious tones of a southern preacher. Mattie's husband had passed away when Margaret was a teenager. However, she left behind two adult daughters, Alice and Virginia, in addition to her youngest daughter, born late in life to Mattie, and who had just reached the age of eighteen. The youngest, and possibly the dearest, as some folks had always surmised, was named Margaret after Joan's youngest child. Everyone called her Maggie, and it seemed to suit her. The three women sat in the first pew listening to the reverend's words and looking visibly shaken regarding Mattie's tragic death. Margaret yearned to be sitting near the women, especially Maggie.

The eulogy was moving, and it served to bring a tear to most every eye in the small country church. A steady stream of tears flowed from Margaret's haunted eyes. Henry glared at his wife from time to time, hoping to stop the very public display of emotion. Colored women wept openly and stood to hold their hands upward toward the heavens or to shout out more "Amens" or "Yes, Jesus." It all seemed so natural and fitting to Margaret. It all seemed quite strange and foreign to the rest of her white family.

Following the emotional eulogy, the entire group again stood to sing a rolling rendition of "When The Roll Is Called up Yonder." During this musical interlude, every Negro form wildly swayed and clapped to the catchy beat of that colored version of the familiar Southern Baptist hymn. Some people did dance in the aisles of the church. Joan's eyes were wide with amazement at the spectacle before her.

The congregation continued to sing the hymn several times to give the entire group time to file out of each pew and walk by Mattie's casket to say their goodbyes. Even the white members were expected to follow suit. And so they did. Margaret watched friends and loved ones cry bitterly over Mattie's body, kiss her, and caress her face, not wanting to let go just yet. The tears that would not seem to stop almost choked Margaret when she reached the open casket to see Mattie. The old Negro woman had never looked more beautiful. She was dressed in a pink suit that would certainly have been her choice. Instead of the everyday cotton handkerchief she normally tied around her head, Mattie's hair had been well greased and formed into a very becoming style. Her work worn hands were demurely covered in white gloves. Margaret bit back an urge to scream.

After everyone had viewed the body, the reverend stood again to speak. "I will now call up Mattie's lovely daughters to bid their mother a last farewell. Her dear child Maggie will sing before we dismiss to lay our sister's body to rest and her soul to Jesus."

All three women stood before the mourning crowd. Alice and Virginia gathered close by the casket to weep and touch their mother for the last time. Maggie's sweet, pure voice arose to heaven singing the beloved hymn "It Is Well with My Soul." Margaret sat in her place on the back pew, feeling miserable and left out of her dear nanny's beloved circle. Acting on impulse, Margaret was compelled to rise from her seat. She did so and walked purposefully toward the group of colored women. Alice and Virginia held out their arms to welcome an additional daughter.

Margaret and Mattie's daughters stood arm in arm, black and white, in a semicircle around the head of the casket. Margaret bent down to caress Mattie's cheek and to place a lingering kiss on her brow. She continued to stand with the women, arms interlocked, until Maggie completed the beautiful melody. Margaret could feel the shocked gazes of her family upon her, but she chose to ignore them. Henry and Joan squirmed in their seats, knowing this spectacle would be retold over and over all about Barnesville in the coming weeks. Henry could hear the men at the barbershop calling his wife horrible things. He was happy they would be moving from this small town soon.

When the last notes of the song ended, Margaret hugged Maggie and murmured heartfelt condolences. The congregation mingled about the sanctuary and then began moving, with the casket, toward the burial plot in the cemetery behind the church. Margaret walked back to her family feeling renewed, with a load of grief now lifted from her.

Henry took her arm sharply and said, "I've had about enough of this. We're not staying for the graveside service." Margaret surveyed her family. Only Joan shared Henry's disapproving look. They all bid Anne farewell and then filed out to their automobile. The family rode in silence back to the house. Margaret walked straight over to Miss Winnie's to gather up the boys, who were probably getting hungry for their supper. When she entered the house, Miss Winnie was holding Aaron in her arms. He was whimpering and fussing.

"What's wrong?" Margaret asked with a concerned look on her face.

"I don't know," Winifred replied. "He just hasn't been himself today. I even wonder if he has a fever. A little while ago, I heard his stomach rumble something awful. But he won't eat anything. Maybe it's a stomach virus. I think I smell a messy diaper."

Chapter 14

Margaret sat impatiently in the waiting room of the Egleston Clinic in Atlanta. The nurses had forced her to leave the examining room during the last few tests. They explained that the procedure might be upsetting to the young mother. Margaret then inquired if Aaron would experience a great deal of pain. She was assured that he would be given a mild sedative and would never remember the required medical tests. The nurses had been correct. No cries from Aaron's small frame were heard in the adjoining waiting area. The silence disturbed Margaret even more.

The wait had been a long one. Mother and son had spent most of the day at the clinic. Margaret sat thinking of the argument she and Joan had engaged in regarding the trip to Atlanta. Joan had been appalled that Margaret would even consider taking Aaron to the medical clinic unaccompanied. As the weeks had been going by, Henry was forced to leave for Alexandria, Virginia, in search of their home prior to the start date of his new assignment at the Pentagon. Margaret and the boys would be joining him as soon as there was some resolution to Aaron's illness.

Margaret threw down the magazine she had been thumbing through. She walked over to a window to stare at cars passing by just outside the clinic. Disturbing thoughts of Aaron and the very real possibility that he might have a serious medical condition bounced around in her brain. It was all she could think about.

Margaret's head jerked around when she heard the door leading

The Locket

to the inner offices swing open. A short, stout nurse beckoned for her to enter the physician's area. Margaret did so and was ushered back into an office that loomed large and unfeeling; an austere, uncomfortable atmosphere permeated the walls. She gazed up at the various medical degrees and certifications held by Dr. Jackson, all seeming to be impressive but meaning very little to the young mother who sat there with fright in her dark brown eyes. She wondered why they had not brought Aaron back to her, but she remained silent until the physician arrived.

The middle-aged doctor, who wore thick, dark-rimmed glasses, entered the room followed by a young intern. Margaret pounced on the pair to ask, "Where is my son?"

"He's resting in the examining room with one of my nurses," Dr. Jackson replied. "It will take several hours for the sedative to wear off completely. I'm certain he'll sleep for your entire drive home this afternoon. Let me introduce you to a colleague of mine. This is Dr. Wilding. He has just completed an internship at the Mayo Clinic and is now beginning the first portion of his residency here at Egleston. I hope you don't mind if he observes our discussion today. He was a big help with little Aaron in the examining room."

"That will be fine," Margaret responded as she gazed over at the friendly, fresh face of the young man who obviously loved his work. "Now tell me what's wrong with my son."

"Well, Mrs. Montgomery," he began. "We completed a battery of tests today. I even asked the lab to do a rush job on some of the blood tests since you live so far away from here. From the testing completed, I see no disease process in this little boy. I believe he has simply had some recurrent bouts of constipation, which would account for the bright red bleeding."

Margaret wore a look of surprise on her face. "Are you certain there is nothing wrong at all?"

"Right now, I can find nothing amiss in his bowel function. We'll just have to wait and see if the symptoms you've described persist or if any additional problems arise. Then we'll take it from there. Here is an instruction sheet in how to deal with recurrent constipation. My office telephone number is at the top of the sheet. Contact us if there are any further problems."

The doctor rose to shake Margaret's hand. The hand she offered him was cold and clammy, reflecting her nervous mood. It was unreal to her that she appeared to know there was something very wrong with her child, but no one else seemed to recognize that. She looked into the blue eyes of the young intern. He wore a look of concern but averted his gaze from hers, hoping his mentor had not noticed the nonverbal sign of disagreement with the senior physician's resolution to the problem at hand. Margaret thought she saw that flash of concern but felt further questioning of the somewhat united pair would prove to be fruitless. It was clear that the young doctor would have to follow the lead of the senior physician or his residency there would be short-lived.

Margaret murmured her thank you to both doctors and turned to follow the nurse back to the examining room where Aaron was resting on the table. "You'll have to carry him out to your automobile. Do you need me to help you?" the nurse asked.

"No. I'll be able to manage it." Margaret picked up the sleeping boy and was then led down the hall and out of the suite of offices by the nurse. Margaret thanked her and said goodbye.

The load she carried consisting of Aaron's sleeping form, a baby bag, and her purse was awkward and unevenly distributed. She stopped in the hallway to place her purse and bag on a chair and adjust Aaron's slumbering weight. Just as she did so, Margaret looked up to see the young resident walking quickly toward her. Margaret's heart began to beat faster as she witnessed the urgency in his gait.

"Mrs. Montgomery," he called. "Could I speak with you for just a moment?"

"Of course."

"If you don't mind, let's step in here to talk." He took her arm and led her around the corner, then into the small clinic chapel. He closed the door, and they sat in the last pew.

"I had to come and talk to you before you left," he began. "I disagree with Dr. Jackson's assessment of Aaron." Margaret's eyes

The Locket

grew wide. "I've done quite a few pediatric gastroenterology rotations at the Mayo Clinic. I truly believe there is something seriously wrong with your little boy's colon. You know I'm still in my residency, but I've observed the masters in Rochester, Minnesota. Dr. Jackson did not complete all of the necessary battery of tests on Aaron today. That's because we're not equipped here for this type of problem. If my diagnostic skills are walking down the right path, then you need to take Aaron to the Mayo Clinic. It's the only place where he will get the proper diagnosis and appropriate treatment."

Margaret looked gratefully into the kind blue eyes before her. "I can't thank you enough for being so honest with me."

The young physician, whose blond good looks reminded her of James, then squeezed her arm and said, "I've got to get back. I don't want Dr. Jackson to realize what I've told you. I could lose my residency over this." A tear sprang to Margaret's eyes as she realized the risk this man had taken. She watched him walk away from the chapel.

Margaret gazed up at the illuminated cross before her. A tear escaped her dark brown eyes to roll down the soft skin of her cheek. She closed her eyes as she held her sleeping son and said a fervent prayer for the child. She hated the helpless feeling that permeated the very core of her being.

~ ~ ~ ~ ~ ~

It was three in the morning when Margaret awoke to a piercing scream coming from the nursery. She flew from her bed and rushed down the hall to find Aaron lying on his right side, crying in pain. Margaret then heard the strange rumbling coming from his stomach just as Miss Winnie had described. She picked up the toddler to realize that he felt feverish. At the same time, she smelled another offensive diaper. Joan entered the room to witness Margaret cleaning up the boy from yet another diaper containing signs of a serious illness.

They exchanged worried glances. "I've got to get him to the

Mayo Clinic, Mama. It's the only way to get to the bottom of all this. We still don't even know what's wrong with him. I'm going to fix him some of that syrup water and then take him to bed with me."

Margaret carried Aaron downstairs to the kitchen. She sat him on the counter to watch her mix water and Karo syrup together in a bottle, just as Mattie had done many times before. He didn't take a bottle very often any longer, but it seemed appropriate on this night. She carried him upstairs into her bedroom. Margaret propped up pillows and leaned back in the bed to give the little one his sweet water. Aaron sucked on the bottle and consumed six ounces, which pleased Margaret. His head felt cooler. Then they both nodded off into restless slumber.

Margaret awoke at six. Aaron was still asleep. She quietly rose from the bed to don her robe and slippers. She padded down the stairs in the house that no longer enjoyed Mattie's morning sounds to the telephone at the foot of the staircase. She raised the receiver to place a call. Within moments, the rich, deep tones of James Walsh's voice came over the telephone line. "James," Margaret began. The man immediately recognized the voice of the woman who captivated his thoughts on most days. "I need your help."

Chapter 15

Margaret stepped from the sleek black automobile onto the Connecticut soil of James's estate, now covered in a blaze of autumn colors. She held Aaron, who was bundled up against the crisp, piercing wind. She walked up the steps to greet Leonard, now awaiting their arrival at the door. Attempting to forget her worries over Aaron for a moment, she planted a warm smile on her face to greet the old friend.

"Margaret," Leonard started. "Aaron has grown so much. I think he is beginning to look like you. He's always had your personality."

"Now, Leonard." Margaret smiled. "I don't think you were able to tell if he had my personality when we were here last Christmas. He was only a few months old. I must admit, though, now that he's fourteen months old, I do see a little of myself in him from time to time."

"Let me take your coats. James is waiting for you in the solarium." Margaret stood Aaron on the marble floor. She removed her camel-colored cashmere coat and then took off Aaron's dark blue coat and hat. Margaret had chosen to wear a navy wool dress that day, which seemed a bit severe when she surveyed her appearance in the mirror that morning. But the severity of the dress suited her mood. The constant worries over Aaron's health, together with Mattie's recent death and the rift that had grown between her and Henry were beginning to wear upon the young woman. Margaret had dropped quite a few pounds. The circles under her eyes were becoming more difficult to disguise each morning when she applied her makeup.

Aaron ran ahead into the solarium before his mother reached the cheerful room. His small form came bounding around a couch. When he unexpectedly ran into James's wheelchair, he raised his hand and said, "Hi." James smiled at the exuberant toddler. Aaron spied several toys Mrs. Oliver had brought down from the nursery. He sat on the floor and began playing with them.

Margaret walked into the room. Although her loveliness could not be denied, the thin lines of her body and the strain around her eyes looked very out of place in a woman of her age. James chose not to comment on her obvious physical changes.

"Hello, James. It's good to see you." She looked around the room, feeling as if she had just returned from a long journey. "I know it's been less than a year since I was here last, but it seems like ten years. So much has happened."

"I know," James agreed. "I spoke with Henry on the telephone today. He told me about Mattie. I was sorry to hear about her death. Her place in your heart can never be filled." Margaret nodded as a lump rose in her throat. She reached up to touch the locket that always adorned her neck, only to remember that she had placed the locket under the collar of her dress. It was a childish gesture designed to hide the fact that she did, indeed, wear the locket every day. It would have been easier to just remove the piece of jewelry, but something always kept her from doing that.

James looked at the woman who entered his dreams each night. It was clear that major changes were occurring in her personality. He remembered the stiff, hurried telephone conversation he had exchanged with Henry earlier that day. Henry had made it obvious that Margaret harbored not even a hint of suspicion regarding Ma Le and Susan's existence. Upon sensing disapproval in James's voice, Henry began to verbally rationalize his actions and to even make believe that the affair was really over. Henry, in his own words, was simply meeting his obligations to the child by providing for this outside family. Henry was attempting to regain some measure of favor in James's eyes. There would be none. James could never

The Locket

condone his old friend's actions. He would remain silent, but there would be no approval or even a measure of masculine understanding.

Again, James surveyed the woman before him, the woman who was being so deceived. This served to place a hardness in his jaw. Margaret did not deserve treatment of this sort. At times, he wanted to shout the hideous information at her, as he realized it could become a means to win her heart. But winning her heart in that particular manner would be unthinkable for a man who had never achieved any goal with an unfair advantage.

Margaret broke the silence with a question. "What have you been able to arrange at the Mayo Clinic?"

"Through several different friends, I was able to get Aaron an appointment to see Dr. Hugh Sterling. He is purported to be the leading pediatric gastroenterologist at Mayo and quite possibly throughout the world. You're in good hands. The appointment is for one o'clock the day after tomorrow." Margaret sighed as she sat down on the couch, knowing James was a solid rock to lean upon. It was a feeling that felt very good and one that she had not experienced in a long time.

James continued, "I took the liberty of booking us both rooms at a nearby hotel. If something serious is wrong with Aaron, you may have to stay several days or more. I hope you don't mind if I accompany you. You may need someone to be with you since Henry couldn't get away from his obligations at the Pentagon."

"I think it's all so wonderful and generous of you, James." Tears began to sparkle in her eyes as she gazed down in an attempt to hide her emotional upheaval. James wheeled his chair over to her. His strong hand encircled her thin, delicate one. Margaret gazed into his hypnotic blue eyes. She brought his hand to her cheek in a loving caress and then placed a light kiss into his palm. Their attraction was electric. They both had to fight a strong urge to fall into a deep, exhilarating embrace that would lead to more, much more. Margaret murmured the words, "Thank you, James. Thank you for everything."

The interlude was broken by Mrs. Oliver's entrance. Margaret gave her a warm greeting and was comforted by her familiar, caring manner. They chatted for a while to finalize plans for the flight to Minnesota in James's new private plane, complete with modifications to accommodate his handicap. Mrs. Oliver would be accompanying them to help care for Aaron. For the first time in weeks, Margaret felt a measure of security and some peace.

"James," Margaret said, "I want to get Aaron settled in the nursery and talk to Mrs. Oliver about his symptoms. They show up every day now. We probably need to go on upstairs."

"Go right ahead," James asserted. "Rest for a while in your room. We won't be having dinner until eight tonight. I'll see you then."

Margaret spent the next hour with Mrs. Oliver and Aaron in the nursery. The older woman appeared to have a wonderful way with an ailing child. She was able to soothe Aaron's fussy cries with ease. Another offensive diaper had to be changed. Margaret saw fear in the nanny's eyes when she witnessed evidence of the boy's illness. Aaron had lost several pounds, and his clothes were becoming loose. Margaret explained her usage of the syrupy water concoction when the child refused all food.

Margaret kissed her young son so she could retire to her bedroom for a little while before dinner. As she walked from the nursery, she heard Aaron say, "Bye, bye, Mama." The words were like a sweet melody to Margaret. Aaron's verbal skills had been increasing so fast in the past few months. He was beginning to string two words together, which was amazing to his mother.

Margaret walked down the hall to the familiar yellow-and-white bedroom she had occupied on her last visit. She closed the door while recalling the heated passion James had ignited within her on that winter evening almost a year ago.

Not really feeling the need to rest, Margaret opened a nearby armoire to discover her toiletry case. She opened up the case to retrieve a hardbound book. In a drawer of the bedside table, she found a black fountain pen. The book she held in her grasp was not a new novel that captivated her attention. It was a journal she had started writing in since Henry's arrival back home. Shattered images

The Locket

regarding the family life she had always expected had been hard to accept. Margaret needed a friend. But she had lost touch with most of her high school girl friends. Motherhood complete with a set of twins had taken away most of the free time she could have devoted to a meaningful friendship. So, the journal had become her friend, her therapy, her release.

She picked up the pen and began to write feverishly, putting all thoughts and feelings down upon the unadulterated paper. Margaret could feel the tension seeping from her body. The curve of her script, the movement of the pen, and the quick stroke of punctuation felt enormously satisfying to her hand. She wrote until her fingers were frozen and her shoulders ached from the awkward position she held upon the bed. A soft knock allowed her thoughts to run free. It was Leonard reminding her of the time and informing her of James's request to meet her in the solarium at seven thirty.

Margaret knew she would not have time to soak in a hot bath. So she removed her clothes to freshen up in the adjoining bathroom. After reapplying makeup in an attempt to hide the haunted look in her eyes, Margaret slipped into a form-fitting, black, wool crepe dress that skimmed over her curves. The neckline rose high, but the back of the dress dipped seductively into a V, revealing a heady expanse of creamy skin. She slipped simple pearl earrings onto her earlobes and left the room to check on Aaron in the nursery with Mrs. Oliver.

Upon her entrance to the nursery, Margaret found Aaron sleeping in the capable nanny's embrace. "Has he been fine?" Margaret asked the older woman.

"Oh, yes," she answered. "He ate most of his supper. I had the cook prepare him some items that would be easy on his stomach. He seemed to enjoy it. I think he doesn't have much energy these days."

"I know," Margaret said with sadness. She had witnessed the slow deterioration of Aaron's health over the past few weeks. "Come and get me from the dinner table if there are any problems. If need be, I'll sleep here in the nursery tonight."

"Go ahead and enjoy your dinner. I can handle things here."

Margaret obeyed the command. She walked down the curved

staircase to meet James. She reached up to touch the locket and make certain that it was well hidden beneath her higher than usual neckline. When she reached the solarium, James was not there. A bottle of her favorite wine stood chilled in an ice bucket with two glasses sitting on the table nearby, waiting to be filled. Margaret went ahead and poured a glass for herself. She then picked up the long-stemmed glass to walk over and stand before the roaring fireplace. The flames were hypnotic.

She stood there alone for quite a few minutes, lost in her thoughts as she looked at the flames reflected in the golden hue of her drink. James wheeled into the room to gaze at the beautiful lines of Margaret's figure. The creamy skin of her back peeking out from her dress sent erotic warmth throughout his body. The movement of her shoulders when she shifted her weight made him catch his breath. It was difficult, but he knew he needed to control the urges within himself.

James reached over to pour himself a glass of wine. The clink of the glass made his lovely companion turn around.

"Is Aaron settled in nicely?" he asked.

"Yes. I feel so secure with Mrs. Oliver here. Again, James, I just don't know how to thank you for all of this."

James looked at the beautiful woman before him. "Aaron is my godchild. I take my role has his godfather very seriously. He's ill, and he needs specialized medical care. I just hope the physicians at Mayo will be able to come up with a definitive diagnosis and appropriate treatment quickly. It's clear that his condition is deteriorating."

"I know," Margaret responded with a frown. "It's all I can think about."

"Let's go ahead and have dinner," James commanded. "Give me a chance to distract you from those worries for a little while."

They entered the dining room and sat down at one end of the long, elegant table. A salad was served, and the couple began to weave yet another long, satisfying discussion. They discussed Henry along with his return to the States. Margaret shared her hopes and plans for the future of her family. James recognized a hint of despair in the elegant woman who sat before him. It wasn't difficult for him to see the disillusionment that had entered Margaret's thoughts regarding Henry. James wished that he could have avoided any involvement in hiding Henry's affair. But the debt he owed Henry, for years of physical assistance while they attended Georgia Tech, was one he could not forget. There was also a child to be considered. Though he had never met Henry's young daughter, James could not have allowed the innocent child to suffer in the squalor of Jakarta.

Margaret interrupted James's thoughts with a question. "Are you a religious man, James?"

"What do you mean by religious?" he queried.

"I mean, do you believe in God? Do you read the Bible? Are you a member of a church?"

"If you equate attending church regularly with being religious, then I guess my answer is no. But I don't think that's what you're really asking." Margaret shook her head. "My mother was very spiritual. She fostered belief in a higher power. So, yes, I do believe in God. Mother also opened up the mysteries of the Bible to me. It is a powerful text."

He went on, "You and I have talked about wisdom." James gazed over at Margaret's slim neck and was disappointed to see no evidence of the locket that now was hidden beneath the collar of her dress. "True wisdom comes from knowledge of and belief in the life lessons contained in that ageless volume. But simply reading it won't make an individual wise. It's necessary to really live the teachings. Also, wisdom comes through suffering. The obstacles you must overcome in life will make you strong and courageous, causing you to realize that a moral, deeply spiritual existence is a desirable one. It is at that point when an individual develops wisdom."

"So you're saying it's a learned process. No one is born wise." Margaret's interest in the conversation had caused that familiar spark to return to her gaze.

"If you follow the life lessons that are contained in the Bible simply out of fear or retribution from an angry God, then you do not have true wisdom. The suffering you must endure in life allows you to truly know that the conscious choice to lead a moral existence of perpetual spiritual growth is the right one. When you realize that suffering has a positive purpose, you are taking the correct path. When the suffering you've experienced teaches you the manner in which you should live your life, and your beliefs and actions become one in the same, you have gained wisdom."

"It makes sense, James. But the suffering part is hard to take."

"I realize that. Remember, there are three types of suffering—deserved, testing, and redemptive. Deserved suffering is punishment for sin. But a loving God doesn't punish sin. Sin punishes sin. Testing is a type of suffering designed to define your faith and belief system. Redemptive suffering is God's way of turning you away from sin to realize how He would like you to live. Only the individual who experiences the suffering knows which type he is going through."

Their conversation continued for several more hours, covering political issues, social ills, and financial concerns. They began to wind down with a discussion of Margaret's personal aspirations. She confided in James that she had not taken to motherhood easily. Her previous work as a high school English teacher had been quite satisfying. Margaret admitted that she missed her work. James was not surprised.

Margaret glanced down at her watch to realize they had finished their meal long ago. Her watch read eleven o'clock. "The meal and the conversation were both satisfying. Thank you so much, James." She reached over to take his hand and press it against the softness of her cheek. A fire burned in James, so he looked away to hide the desire that might be visible in his piercing blue gaze. Margaret released his hand to say, "Now, I simply must get to bed. There is so much ahead of us in the next few days."

She excused herself to walk up the staircase and straight to the nursery to check on Aaron. He was sleeping peacefully, so she returned to her room to retire for the evening. Within a moment, she had covered her sensuous form in a cream-colored chiffon and lace negligee that hugged each curve of her body. She slipped between the sheets, feeling warm, secure, and protected. For the first night

The Locket

in weeks, her sleep was deep and satisfying until a shrill cry awoke her at two thirty.

She rose from the warm bed to run down the hall and into the nursery. Aaron was lying on his side in obvious pain. His shrill cries ceased at his mother's presence, but he continued to moan and whimper. Following a diaper change, Margaret placed the boy in her arms and began to rock him in the nursery rocker. She softly sang Mattie's signature lullaby.

Her singing caused her not to notice James wheel his chair into the room. Looking a bit disheveled with a golden lock of hair falling over his forehead and clad in a deep burgundy robe, he startled Margaret with his soft, masculine voice. "Is everything all right?"

Her singing abruptly stopped. "Oh, you frightened me." Her hand went instinctively to her throat, as she realized James would notice the locket hanging there. He did. He also noticed her scantily clad breasts just beneath the treasured gift. Margaret's cheeks burned with embarrassment at her careless behavior. She groped for something to say. "I really need to go down to the kitchen to fix some of that syrupy water."

"Go on ahead," he answered. "I'll hold Aaron for you." She stood in the dim light to bring the toddler to his godfather. The silhouette of her nakedness beneath the filmy nightgown beckoned James. It was difficult to keep himself from touching the curve of her voluptuous breast as she leaned down to put Aaron into his awaiting arms. Margaret walked out of the room.

James held the boy close to his powerful chest. He spoke to him in soft tones. At one point, James was able to tease a smile out of the little one. If only he could take the child's pain away. The trip to Rochester, Minnesota, would hopefully bring a resolution to Aaron's problems. The Mayo Clinic and its Graduate School of Medicine was internationally known and respected. Although the Mayo brothers, William and Charles, both died in 1939, within a few months of each other, their traditions of medical teamwork and specialization were still alive. James made the pilgrimage each year for a complete physical and comprehensive postpolio assessments.

The physicians he had come to know there were aware of his active role in the March of Dimes. The Mayo medical community was aware of James's powerful yet caring reputation.

Margaret returned to the nursery with the promised bottle. She was now covered in a modest robe. James relinquished Aaron to his mother's embrace. He then excused himself to return to his own bedroom, knowing it would be difficult to contain the pent-up passions he held deep in his heart for the young woman who had much more living and learning to complete.

~ ~ ~ ~ ~ ~

Several days and sleepless nights later, Margaret and James sat in Dr. Hugh Sterling's office located at the Mayo Clinic. The physician, who had given them little information thus far, was ready to talk. He began with an apology. "I am sorry that it took several days for me and my colleagues to reach a definitive diagnosis. But I needed to be certain about several different aspects of Aaron's condition. That is why he had to be hospitalized."

He went on to say, "Mrs. Montgomery, your son has ulcerative colitis. It is a serious condition in that the patient develops ulcerations and abscesses in the lining of the large intestine. We feel that the ulcerations in Aaron's colon are extensive. He has been experiencing rectal bleeding over the past few weeks. There is a very real danger that he could develop blood poisoning, which could be fatal." Margaret's face became pale. James reached over to clasp her cold hand.

The doctor continued. "His condition is treatable. We can perform surgery to remove the ulcerated portion of his intestine. If the operation is a complete success, then he should go on to lead a relatively normal life, free of the disease. He would probably have several bowel movements each day, which is a little abnormal, but other than that, I would expect him to enjoy a happy, healthy life." His last words provided a measure of comfort to Margaret, but the serious news continued to make her thoughts whirl around in an uncontrollable manner.

The Locket

Dr. Sterling's voice broke through into her thoughts. "Aaron needs the surgery soon. Within the next week would be best. We should not allow his condition to deteriorate further."

Margaret understood. She knew she needed to think with a clear mind. She felt so torn with Matthew down in Barnesville, Henry in Virginia, and she and Aaron in Minnesota. It was time to bring things together. "Would it be possible for the surgery to be performed at the Walter Reed Military Hospital in Washington close to our new home?" James was happy to witness Margaret's decisive attitude.

"Actually," Dr. Sterling responded, "I believe one of my former colleagues is practicing there now. I feel certain he could handle the surgery there at Walter Reed. Let me make a few telephone calls, and I should have an answer this afternoon." Margaret looked over at James to gain some strength, knowing she would need it for the challenges ahead.

Chapter 16

Alexandria, Virginia
July 3, 1948

"Maggie!" Margaret shouted as she walked down the staircase of her Alexandria, Virginia, home. She was dressed in a navy pantsuit paired with navy blue flat shoes in preparation for the busy day ahead. Margaret searched throughout the house for Maggie and the twins to announce her departure for Washington. As there was no sign of them, the lovely young mother headed for the backyard, where her young sons could be found on most every bright summer day.

Margaret opened the French doors that led to their patio and backyard swimming pool to witness her twin sons splashing about in the shallow end of the pool. Maggie sat at the edge of the pool, keeping the two boys out of trouble while dipping her feet into the cool water.

Now, almost four years old, the boys looked like little men. Each had developed distinct personalities that were quite different. They were a complement to each other.

"Watch me, Mama!" Matthew shouted. He climbed from the pool dripping wet to walk back approximately ten feet. He then proceeded to run and jump, bottom first, into the deep end of the cool blue water. From the water, he yelled back at his mother, "Did you see me, Mama? I'm getting really good!" He climbed from the

The Locket

pool again to stand before his mother, threatening to spray her smart navy pantsuit with his dripping arms.

Matthew's dancing, dark eyes fell in disappointment, as his planned trick had been thwarted. He turned to find his brother and say, "Come on, Aaron. Let's see who can make the biggest splash." Aaron joined in while Maggie stepped back from the pool in anticipation of the rolling waves of water.

Margaret walked over to Maggie and said, "I don't even know why any of us try to stay dry around here during the summer. The boys simply live in the water. Before long, I think they will be growing gills."

"You may be right about that, Margaret," Maggie responded. "I love being out here with them in the summer. It gets all the cobwebs out of my brain, so to speak." Margaret smiled at young Maggie while feeling so secure that her sons were being cared for properly. She was amazed by the obvious changes Maggie had consciously made in her speech pattern. Maggie's southern Negro dialect was all but gone since the move to Alexandria. Maggie had become a close and treasured friend to Margaret, an easy extension from her mother's previous role. Margaret insisted that all domestic employees call her by her first name in an effort to dispense with nonsensical formalities.

Margaret knew Leonard might have been the catalyst for the changes she had observed in the young woman of color standing before her. The two had developed a very deep friendship that just might, as Margaret surmised, turn into love. Leonard and Maggie were constantly writing letters. James always made it known that Leonard would be accompanying him whenever he visited the DC area. So Margaret made certain Maggie was always given some personal time during those visits to spend with Leonard.

"I'm about to leave for the fairgrounds," Margaret announced. "There are a thousand details I need to take care of. You know Leonard will be coming tomorrow with James. Why don't the two of you just plan to spend the entire day together? Between Henry,

James, and I, there are plenty of people to look after the boys. You haven't seen each other in quite a while."

"You're right," Maggie agreed. "I think I would really enjoy that. Thank you, Margaret. You've got to be the best boss anyone could have."

"Don't mention it. I spoke with James last night, so he and Leonard already know about these plans."

Both women then looked back again to watch the boys cavorting in the water. The Montgomery sons shared their parents' dark hair, which was forever cropped short in a traditional GI cut for the summer months. The two women laughed at the antics they witnessed. Maggie piped up with, "It's hard to imagine that Aaron was ever gravely ill to look at him now."

"I know," Margaret responded as the old, haunted look crossed her face. "It all seems like a bad dream now. Let me get a picture of them out here by the pool."

Margaret ducked inside the house to retrieve her camera. She returned to the pool, and Maggie had already summoned the boys from the water for the appropriate posing. The children were now just about the same size. It had taken Aaron many months to truly look healthy following his surgeries. Regaining his mobility had been eased by Matthew's help. Their separation, due to illness, had been difficult for Matthew. Upon Aaron's return home, Matthew had assumed somewhat of a fatherly role with his twin brother, which had healed the wounds of separation for both children.

As Margaret stood before them, ready to snap the photograph, she could see the edges of Aaron's large abdominal scars peeking up from the waistline of his swimming trunks. Maggie also noticed them. Without any verbal command, the nanny walked over to Aaron and raised the waistband of his trunks to hide the visual evidence of his infirmity. It was very important to Henry for all tangible signs of any abnormalities to be closely hidden from the view of others. Very few, if any, of their social circle of friends knew of Aaron's previous illness. Henry had great plans for this favorite son, and nothing would spoil them.

The Locket

Henry's feverish demands to hide unpleasant things always nagged at Margaret. She was an honest, open individual who would have liked to seek comfort from close friends and confidants. However, her husband forced her into certain secrecies that seemed unnecessary to the straightforward woman. Her heavy involvement with the March of Dimes was also a delicate subject to Henry. It seemed that he considered this type of work as a parade of unpleasantness. James's disability had never made Henry uncomfortable during their college years. But somehow everything about James seemed to grate hard on Henry. Margaret had continued a close involvement with the powerful man from Connecticut, an involvement she felt compelled to keep alive. Her marriage was beginning to make her feel dead inside. Even short moments with James were treasured ones that helped her make it through the drudgery of her chosen union with Henry, a man so changed by war in the eyes of his vibrant wife.

Margaret snapped the picture, kissed her boys goodbye, and headed out the front door for Washington. As she drove, her thoughts covered the satisfying aspects of her work with the March of Dimes. The organization had made great strides in their search for an effective vaccine to prevent polio, but much more work was ahead before a vaccine would be available and the disease could be conquered. Margaret had served as president for the DC chapter of the March of Dimes over the past year. This outlet helped her forget the troubling aspects of her marriage and allowed her to focus upon the needs of others. Following Aaron's recovery, Margaret had soon realized that her life needed more, much more than it contained as a wife and mother. Her work for the March of Dimes had been her savior, filling part of the emptiness in her life, an emptiness that should have been filled by Henry.

Margaret spent most of her day taking care of details for the elaborate Fourth of July fair that would begin tomorrow morning at ten. The DC chapter of the March of Dimes had elected a slate of accomplished officers. The fundraising fair was sure to be a success. James would be speaking in the afternoon, along with several other

Washington notables. Good food, fun rides, raucous activities, and excellent entertainment had all been well planned.

Late in the afternoon, a weary Margaret became satisfied that her work was complete. She walked from the fairgrounds to her vehicle. The exhaustion in her bones made the drive home seem longer than usual. When she turned the automobile into their driveway, she noticed Maggie and Matthew playing catch on the front lawn, but Aaron was not in sight.

Upon stepping from the vehicle, Margaret walked up to them and asked, "Where is Aaron?"

"Oh, he's gone to walk with T.C.," was Matthew's quick reply.

Margaret's brow furrowed. She looked over to Maggie. "Who is T.C.?"

"He's this sweet old man who's been coming by most afternoons over the past two weeks. He doesn't like to talk much. He just needs a partner to walk with, and Aaron seems to be his choice. T.C. and Aaron like the walks. I guess you've been gone so much over the past two weeks, you've never gotten to meet him. They should be back in a few minutes."

Margaret was surprised that Maggie had allowed her son to leave their home with a stranger. Maggie saw the concern in her eyes. "It's all right, Margaret. We all went on the first few walks. He's just a lonely old man who enjoys little Aaron's company."

"Well, I want to meet this man before he leaves this afternoon," Margaret said curtly, feeling like a mother lioness watching out for her cubs.

She walked into the house to find Henry. Margaret found him in the living room, reading the newspaper and indulging in his first cocktail before dinner. "Do you know anything about this old gentleman named T.C.?"

Henry looked up from his paper to say, "What are you talking about?"

"Maggie has been allowing Aaron to go for a walk with some old man named T.C. most every afternoon over the past couple of weeks.

The Locket

It just bothers me. We have no idea who this man is. She tells me they should be back in a few minutes."

"Well, let's go look," Henry responded.

They walked to the large living room window that looked out onto their manicured front lawn. Within a few seconds, Aaron bounded up the sidewalk, followed by a tall, thin man who looked to be in his mid-seventies. He was dressed in an expensive suit, but he had loosened his tie, rolled up his sleeves, and now carried his jacket over his right arm.

"Good Lord," Henry said under his breath and then headed immediately out the front door. At that moment, the telephone rang, distracting Margaret from the mystery. She ran to answer the shrill ring. The voice on the other end of the telephone belonged to one of her fellow officers within the March of Dimes. It took several minutes to take care of the pressing matter before her regarding tomorrow's event. Margaret could still see Henry speaking with the elderly man as if they had known each other for years. The mystery intrigued her.

By the time she hung up the telephone and walked onto the front lawn, the aged gentleman was slowly making his way back down the street. "Who was that?" Margaret asked Henry with interest. He gave a chuckle.

"I don't think you have anything to worry about," Henry responded. "That was Supreme Court Justice Tom Clark." Margaret's eyes widened. "We had a little chat. It appears that his wife died over the past few years, and he now has very little family left. He seems to be quite lonely. I think he spends all day at the court, and then his daily walk with Aaron is his only bit of recreation. Then he returns home each night to continue his never-ending study of the law." Henry reached down and patted the prickly, short haircut on Aaron's head. "I guess he really likes your company, little buddy."

"You think so, Daddy?" Aaron asked. "He sure is quiet. I ask him questions. Sometimes he answers, and sometimes he doesn't. But he's real nice. He always brings us chewing gum. T.C. tried to walk with both of us the first day, but Mathew was too wild for him." They all laughed at Aaron's descriptions.

The family began to return to the house. Margaret stood on the sidewalk, watching Justice Clark's rambling gait. She wondered if he did, indeed, possess true wisdom. He appeared to be paying attention to the little things in life, just like Granny Harris used to describe. Margaret released a long, slow sigh while missing the wise soul of her grandmother. Granny Harris had been ever present in Margaret's mind since her unexpected death a year earlier. At times, Granny even filled her dreams with what seemed to be nonsensical messages. Margaret looked back at the now small image of Justice Clark walking away and then up at the heavens, wondering if she would ever fully understand the intricacies of life.

~ ~ ~ ~ ~

The entire Montgomery family, including Maggie, filed out of their vehicle to stand in the freshly cut, fragrant green grass and witness the beginning of the March of Dimes Fourth of July fundraising fair. The heat was intense, so Margaret had chosen to wear a white eyelet sundress with a straw hat bearing a band of the same material. Maggie had also chosen a sundress in a floral pattern. Matthew and Aaron were hard to contain at the prospect of the day ahead.

Looking across the fairgrounds, Margaret spied the familiar wheelchair and then recognized Leonard's tall, dark form. She looked over to see the unleashed anticipation glowing in Maggie's eyes. "Why don't you go on ahead," she whispered to Maggie. "You haven't seen him in several months."

"You sure you don't need me to take care of the boys?"

"We made this deal ahead of time. Remember? Enjoy your day."

Maggie ran over to Leonard and surprised him from behind. A slow, bittersweet smile covered Margaret's face at the memories of her own youthful love. The two dark-skinned adults embraced in their

The Locket

nonverbal greeting. James turned his chair to spy Margaret, Henry, and the boys coming toward him.

"You shouldn't have given her the entire day off," Henry stated in a gruff tone. "We pay her well, and this is one day we'll need several pairs of eyes on these two." He looked down at Matthew, knowing how annoying his rambunctious side could become.

Henry's words were like acid, but Margaret was not going to allow him to spoil the cheerfulness of this day. "If you hate all of this so much, just go on back home, and you can pick us up later this afternoon. I'll take care of the boys today, and we'll still have time to get ready for the party tonight."

Henry could hear the disapproving tone in her voice. Hundreds of people were milling about on the fairgrounds. He recognized several high-ranking Pentagon employees who might be able to assist him in the quest for a promotion he had been working toward for the past few months. "Oh, I'll stay most of the day, but we're leaving in the middle of the afternoon." Henry grabbed Matthew's hand to walk toward the Pentagon official he had just noticed. "I'll take one, you take one," Henry said over his shoulder to announce the division of labor for the day. "Meet me at the car at two o'clock."

Margaret was embarrassed that Henry had not even acknowledged James's presence just a few hundred feet away. The strange private grudge Henry held against James had continued for several years now. Margaret had stopped apologizing for his rude behavior a long time ago. It was hard to understand. But then many things about Henry were now difficult to comprehend.

Margaret greeted James and Leonard with a warm smile. Aaron climbed up into James's lap and was rewarded with a bag of popcorn. Margaret laughed and said, "You know he'll stay in your lap all day if you keep him supplied with popcorn and Coca-Cola."

"Yes," James replied with a grin. "I remember the days when I could be bought off that easily."

They all laughed. Margaret looked over at Leonard and Maggie, who could not tear their gazes away from each other. James noticed the longing in their eyes and said, "Go ahead and have fun, you two. Remember, it's your day off." The well-matched couple smiled and then walked off, hand in hand, to enjoy the festivities. Maggie had blossomed so in the last few years and had now reached the age of twenty-one. Life in the Northeastern United States agreed with the youthful woman of African heritage. The more enlightened atmosphere of the North suited her. Margaret knew it would be difficult now for Maggie to return to the South with its strictly drawn racial rules.

"Let Aaron and I show you around the fairgrounds. Hopefully, all the hard work will turn into massive donations. Let's keep our fingers crossed. I know you'll be able to move everyone with your speech today, James." They made their way through the crowded fairgrounds. Aaron insisted on playing most of the games but became frustrated when an elusive prize was not awarded. When James noticed the red fire engine Aaron wanted to win, he joined in the toy marksmanship game, determined to win the prize for his godson. The fire engine gleamed red and silver in Aaron's pudgy fingers after only three well-placed shots from James's toy rifle.

At lunchtime, they munched on hotdogs loaded with ketchup, mustard, onions, relish, and sauerkraut. Aaron's small hands could hardly hold the mammoth hotdog that was put before him. Small, ice-cold, green tinted bottles of Coca-Cola complemented the summertime cuisine. Aaron turned his Coca-Cola bottle up and guzzled several large swallows. He then said in a strangled little voice, "It tickles my nose, Mama. The Co-Cola even burns my eyes. But it sure tastes good." They laughed.

"Coca-Cola tastes even better," James announced, "with a pack of very salty peanuts at a baseball game in Yankee stadium. I'll take you and your brother to one of those games when you're a little older." Margaret smiled at James's plans.

When lunch was over, Margaret looked at her watch. "James," she said, "it's almost one o'clock. We had better get you up to that podium. It's about time to deliver the speech." They maneuvered their way through the crowd. Margaret searched for Henry and Matthew, but they were not nearby. Once James was ensconced in his

The Locket

rightful position, Margaret took Aaron by the hand to, once again, enter the crowd, hoping to find the rest of her family. She searched the sea of faces over and over and then gave up for a while as James began to speak. Margaret and her young son moved to the back of the crowd near where they had parked their automobile.

"I can't see, Mama," Aaron announced. "Pick me up so I can see."

"Honey," Margaret responded, "you're too big for me to carry around. Let's go over to our car. I'll let you sit on the roof so you can see better. But you must promise me you will be still, and you cannot stand up. I don't want you to fall off." Aaron nodded his understanding of her specific instructions. She went on to say, "I wish we could find Matthew and Daddy. We haven't seen them since before lunch."

Margaret hoisted Aaron's solid frame onto the roof of the Ford. He clutched the fire engine in his lap, which did serve to distract him. Margaret listened to James's commanding words with respect and admiration. Each eye in the crowd was riveted to his enigmatic presence. She was certain that those individuals present on that day would see James as a leader, a powerful man who could effect changes of great magnitude, not a broken man to be pitied for his disability. James was a man who preferred to be defined by his integrity and beliefs, not by a physical difference that he knew could never change the aspects of his character.

The speech was coming to a close when a strange feeling came over Margaret. It was a feeling that moved up her back almost as if someone were watching her intently. The sensation made her head turn to the left. A cool, refreshing breeze blew across her face. She heard automobiles whizzing by on the road located about ten feet from her vehicle. Margaret looked over to see a red balloon peeking up between two cars parallel parked beside the road. The vehicles obscured her view somewhat, so she became compelled to investigate the source of the strange sensations that now roamed through her body in waves. She picked Aaron up off the car.

"Aaron," she said, "can you stand here quietly by the car for just a minute, so I can walk right over there?"

"Sure, Mama."

A heavyset woman whom Margaret recognized as a member of the DC chapter of the March of Dimes stood nearby. "I'll watch him for a minute," the woman offered.

"Thank you," Margaret murmured. She made her way around their vehicle to walk toward the red balloon. As she moved, the balloon inched through a small crevice between the two cars and out onto the road. Just as the young mother reached the edge of the road, she witnessed the crimson balloon escape from a small, chubby hand and float up into the air. The small hand belonged to Matthew, who now stood unattended in the middle of a busy street. At that very instant, a dark blue automobile appeared from nowhere, it seemed, to speed down the road, heading straight for Margaret's young son. With strength she didn't know she had and with no thought for her own safety, Margaret lunged forward to push her child from behind and out of the careening car's path. It was as if time stopped to allow the courageous mother to steal precious seconds and avoid a terrible tragedy.

The vehicle screeched to a halt a few feet away from the two individuals now lying on the side of the street. Matthew had experienced that windless feeling from a hard fall making him struggle to gain his breath. When it returned, a loud cry was wrenched from his throat. Margaret hugged her son tightly to reassure him of his safety. She looked over his small body to see only scratches from the pavement and no evidence of serious injury. Margaret could feel the sting of scraped skin high on her left cheekbone. More abrasions were evident on her left arm and elbow. A warm wetness felt on her left leg proved to be a deep gash, caused by forceful contact with a portion of the vehicle's fender.

"Miss! Miss! Are you all right?" The voice came from the distressed face of the driver, a man looking to be in his mid-thirties.

In a dazed manner, Margaret responded, "It looks like we are." Matthew continued to wail and clutch his mother. A crowd of people surrounded them. Again, the driver spoke up. "Someone get some

The Locket

help. She'll need some stitches in that leg." Margaret looked up to see Leonard's and Maggie's faces.

"I'll get James," Leonard announced. "We'll get you to the hospital." He turned to Maggie, gave her his handkerchief, and then turned on his heel. Maggie knelt beside her dear friend to press the handkerchief against the deep gash and attempt to staunch the blood flow. Margaret saw the heavyset woman who was now holding Aaron.

Within moments, Margaret heard the purr of an automobile engine approaching. Leonard jumped out of the sleek vehicle to scoop up Margaret's small form as if she were a rag doll. He placed her gently onto the back seat. Maggie, Leonard, and the boys all climbed in to join Margaret. James was already ensconced in the front seat with a brooding look planted on his handsome face. With the window rolled down, James shouted to command a parting of the crowd so their vehicle could move on through to the hospital.

Henry stood on the other side of the fairgrounds, far removed from the podium where his one-time friend had just concluded the moving speech. He chatted and laughed with some of his buddies from the Pentagon while he swallowed the last drops of cold, golden-hued beer from a mug held in his hand. A young man ran up and grabbed him by the arm before he ever realized Matthew was not nearby. "Your wife has been hurt," the man reported. "The man in the wheelchair and his driver took them to Walter Reed. It seems she jumped out in front of a car to save your son from being killed." It was not until that instant that Henry realized Matthew had wandered away.

Soon, Leonard pulled the long, dark automobile up to the emergency entrance of the hospital. Again, he picked up Margaret's small form to stride purposefully into the medical facility. A nurse greeted them and directed them to an awaiting examination room. The doctor arrived as James, Maggie, and the boys entered the room.

Upon seeing Margaret's injury, the doctor made a faint whistling sound. "Pretty nasty gash you've got here. How did it happen?"

"She jumped out in front of a speeding car to save her son," James said. His brow was furrowed with worry over the woman that filled his thoughts. James reached over to clasp the brave woman's small hand. "What needs to be done, Doctor?" James asked. "Keep her in the hospital overnight if you suspect any other possible injuries."

"Oh, I doubt that will be necessary," the doctor responded, understanding the man's concerns. "Actually, the wound probably looks worse than it really is. We'll give you a shot for the pain and have you stitched up in no time."

Margaret looked around at all of the concerned faces, feeling the attention was way too much. "Doctor," she said. "Could you also examine my little boy to make sure he's fine? I pushed him pretty hard. I know he has some cuts and bruises, and the wind was knocked out of him."

"Certainly," he answered. "But let's take care of you first. I'm afraid I'll have to ask your husband and everyone else to wait outside while I attend to this wound." Maggie and Leonard exchanged knowing glances to realize the doctor's incorrect assumption. No one present corrected the physician. The group filed outside of the examining room as the doctor requested. Heads turned as Henry burst through the hospital's door. He walked straight to Maggie. "Where's Margaret? Is she all right?"

"She's fine," Maggie answered. "She has a deep cut on her leg and a few other scrapes. The doctor is stitching her up now." He looked relieved. Maggie then added, "Matthew seems to be fine too. Just a few cuts and bruises, but the doctor wants to examine him thoroughly."

Henry walked over to Matthew with a furious expression on his face. "What did I tell you?" Matthew's face turned red as he looked down at his feet. "I told you to stay right beside me! Now, look what you've done! All you are is trouble! You and your mother could have been killed!" Matthew's lower lip trembled, and large, salty tears rolled down his cheeks. Maggie silently walked over to pick up and comfort the traumatized child.

James wheeled his chair directly in front of his old friend. His face was brooding and ominous. "I think you've said just about enough."

He looked over at Maggie and said, "You and Leonard take the boys outside for a minute." They obeyed the command. James looked at the army officer before him with unleashed fury burning in his eyes. He could smell the alcohol on Henry's breath. "What the hell do you think you were doing today? A young child has to be watched closely. But I guess you were off loving the booze more than your son!" James could see his words hit a nerve. "You're a good-for-nothing husband and a horrendous father. I just pray that someday Margaret will see you for what you really are before it's too late for her to enjoy some measure of happiness in her life. Go home. We don't need you here."

Fright and fury filled Henry. Fright over the possibility that James might inform Margaret of the affair with Ma Le and fury over what he considered meddlesome behavior. "I've had enough of this March of Dimes bullshit anyway. I tell you this. Stay away from my family. My boys don't need a substitute father. It would suit me just fine if we never see each other again."

James knew he would have to honor the request. But he would leave the foolish man with some things to remember. "You won't be seeing me again. I will, however, check up on Margaret and the boys through various sources. If there is ever a time that I feel they are not being cared for properly or are in danger because of your unfortunate choices, I will reveal your affair. Believe this threat, Henry. It will be carried out complete with tangible evidence of your betrayal."

"Just stay away from my family," Henry replied. "Our lives will be perfect without your interference." He then walked out of the hospital to his car. Henry knew he needed time to fabricate a believable story regarding the day's events. He walked past Maggie, Leonard, and the boys standing outside without saying anything.

Two hours later, James's vehicle pulled into the driveway of the Montgomery home. Margaret had walked out of the hospital. The shot she had been given had erased her pain. She was feeling much better and was still experiencing waves of relief following their near tragedy. Maggie and the boys walked ahead into the house. Margaret stood by the open window of James's automobile.

"James," she stated. "Once again, you've been here when I needed you. Thank you for everything you did today."

"Business is really hectic right now," James announced. "So I may not see you for a while. I've had to scale down some of my work for the March of Dimes. Call me if you need anything. I know how you've developed a fondness for writing in that journal of yours. Write me a letter from time to time. You and the boys are so important to me. Always remember that."

Margaret murmured her agreement. James touched her hand and brought it to his soft lips to place a lingering kiss there. The familiar fire began to burn inside her. Margaret felt her stomach turn somersaults. Her knees felt weak, but she attributed the woozy feeling to her pain medication. She waved goodbye and walked slowly into the house.

A concerned-looking Henry rushed to the door. "Darling," he said. "Come sit down. I came by the hospital, but everything was under control there. You know General Wheeler expects me to be there at his party tonight. So I needed to get home. General Wheeler told me one of his secretaries would look after Matthew today while he and I were discussing my new assignment. I didn't realize how irresponsible that twit of a secretary could be. Had I known that, I would never have trusted her to take care of Matthew. General Wheeler has assured me she's going to be fired."

"I would hate for that to happen," Margaret replied with alarm. "I know Matthew is hard to contain sometimes. We're all fine. I'm sure the secretary was well intentioned and she didn't mean for anything bad to happen. Talk to General Wheeler. Convince him not to fire the poor woman."

Henry had a reluctant look on his face. "Well, if you insist, then I will. I still think the woman should be dismissed from her position. But the decision is his. Oh, and I'm sure you'll want to stay here tonight, rather than attend the party."

"No, I'll go. I will just have to wear pants. But it is an informal party."

"All right. But let's make sure you don't mention anything to

General Wheeler about his secretary. I think she has missed a lot of work lately due to family obligations. So she has been a sore spot for him for a while. I'm sure after I talk him out of firing her, he'll have her transferred to another department. So, there's no need to discuss it any further."

Margaret nodded. This type of coaching occurred before any social engagement. It nagged at Margaret and made her feel childish. It was several years into their marriage before she could define the conversational topics that were unacceptable to Henry. Margaret would be making a social mistake by discussing anything pertaining to religion, politics, money, health, or her work at the March of Dimes.

Desegregation of the military had been debated all over Washington that year. Margaret held strong opinions regarding the policy and supported Truman's efforts to encourage harmony among the races. She felt the military was an excellent place to start. Margaret could envision herself being drawn into various conversations at the party that evening. An inability to keep a tight rein on her tongue might prove to be troublesome. In a decisive manner, Margaret walked upstairs knowing she didn't have the energy to leave herself behind and act like the proper military wife on that particular evening.

She entered the bedroom where Henry was dressing for the party. "I think you're right. It will be best if I stay at home and rest tonight." Henry gave her an understanding look.

Chapter 17

Father's Day, 1953

Henry's plane would not be leaving from Dobbins Air Force Base until tomorrow morning. It would be headed for the Panama Canal Zone, where he had been ordered to spend the next two weeks. His work over the past year teaching at the War College in Carlisle, Pennsylvania, had brought him to a point where this trip was necessary for him to complete an important research study. The timing of his journey was such that it allowed him to lie to his legitimate family in Pennsylvania, so he could leave a day early and spend a rare holiday with his daughter in Atlanta.

Henry looked down into the pretty Amer-Asian face before him. He was often shocked at the depth of love he felt for Susan. She was quiet and mature for a youngster of only eight years old. She appeared to love her father unconditionally. Henry knew Susan wished his visits were more frequent, but the scarcity of his presence was never a source of conflict. The young girl before him was able to find quiet contentment in her unusual situation.

"How is school?" Henry asked as they walked down Seventeenth Street outside Ma Le's apartment. Susan walked beside the new bicycle her father had just given her. It had been a nice surprise for the child to receive a gift on a day set aside to honor fathers. She had presented Henry with a handmade, painted clay bowl to hold his keys and pocket change.

The Locket

"It's really nice. I think school is probably the best thing in my life. You may think this is strange, but sometimes I wish school was open all year." Susan's words were truthful.

"What's your favorite subject?" Henry asked.

"English. I love reading. It's fun to pretend you're someone else and get lost in a book."

Henry was grateful for the chance to talk to Susan alone. He had noticed a myriad of disturbing changes in Ma Le since her arrival in the States years before. In fact, the two lovers appeared to have very little in common any longer. Henry was able to visit only once or twice a year, so their once fiery physical relationship was all but nonexistent. Ma Le had developed what Henry termed as quirky behaviors. He wanted to find out more about Ma Le's daily life. Her strangeness was unsettling. Henry had planned to reduce his financial support over the years as Ma Le became more self-sufficient. Events were not unfolding as planned. He decided to question Susan.

"Tell me about your mother. How does she spend her days?" A look of fear crossed the young girl's face. Henry noticed it and said, "It's all right. I won't tell her anything you say." Susan still looked uncertain. "I promise," Henry added.

"She doesn't leave the apartment much," Susan began. Her long, dark hair shone in the summer sun. Susan's tawny skin was flawless. Henry could tell his daughter was becoming a great beauty. "She has to stay at home most of the time because there is so much to be done."

"What do you mean so much to be done? There are only two of you."

"I know," Susan answered. "But Mama likes everything very clean. The floors have to be scrubbed every other day, and that is a lot of work. Mama never changes her schedule. The landlord got mad at her last year. She told me Mama was ruining the hardwood with all of the scrubbing. That's when they put down the tile throughout the apartment. Miss Nelson said all of that crazy scrubbing wouldn't hurt the tile."

"Your mother still works for Rich's, doesn't she?"

"Yes. But it's hard for her to keep up because of all the cleaning she has to do at home. Her boss at Rich's says her work is the best. He's right. Her stitches are always perfect."

"Don't you think your mother would like a better job, one that pays better?" Henry asked, hoping to understand the woman he felt he hardly knew any longer.

"No. She doesn't like for things to change. The week they put the tile down in our apartment last year was a really bad time. I thought I would have to call that phone number you gave us. But then she started getting better."

A flash of fright entered Henry at Susan's last words. His falling out with James had made him apprehensive about Susan ever contacting the powerful man. "Remember, Susan," he admonished, "only use that telephone number in a real emergency, like if someone is hurt badly."

"I understand, Daddy." A sadness Susan should have been too young to experience colored her dark brown gaze.

"I need to get going now," Henry informed his daughter. "Tell your mother goodbye for me."

"Don't you want to come up and say goodbye yourself?"

Susan's beseeching gaze was hard to resist, but Henry's desire to avoid conflict won the internal struggle. "No. I need to be going. I have an appointment I can't be late for. I'll be seeing you soon." He hugged and kissed his only daughter.

Susan watched her handsome father walk across the street to his automobile parked a few feet away. The young girl wondered if she would ever see him again. His monetary support to pay the rent each month was a constant. His physical presence, in the form of visits, was rare. She loved the man for delivering her and her mother from Jakarta. But there was never a day in which her thoughts did not move to her father's real family. A conventional, happy home life was an eternal wish for Susan. At a younger age, she playacted her traditional, family-filled dreams with paper dolls. Now, she filled

The Locket

the void with books that took her away from the constraints she was forced to live under inside her home.

A long, slow sigh escaped her lips. Susan knew it was time to go back up to the apartment that felt more like a prison. She wheeled her new bicycle up the front walk, up the concrete steps, and into the white tiled lobby. The bicycle would have to be stored on the screened porch of their apartment. Her mother would not be pleased. Susan struggled but was able to hoist the bicycle up the stairs to their second-floor apartment. She then unlocked the door with the key she had tied to a string around her neck.

Before stepping on the floor, she called for her mother. Ma Le walked from the kitchen where she had just washed her hands.

"Mama," Susan began. "This is a surprise Daddy had for me."

Ma Le turned up her nose. "Now what will we do with that? It will need to be put on the screened porch. Be careful though. Don't let it touch the floor, or I'll have to scrub it today instead of tomorrow."

Susan struggled with the cumbersome load once again after removing her shoes to walk on the spotless tile floor. It was difficult, but she made it to the back door without allowing any part of the bicycle to come into contact with the floor. She was breathless by the time she closed the door to the porch.

"Where is your father?" Ma Le asked.

"He said he had an appointment he couldn't be late for. So he left. He told me to tell you goodbye."

A sour look was plastered upon Ma Le's face, but she made no comment regarding Henry's actions. The past few years had been hard on her. Wrinkles that were too deep for a woman in her early thirties framed her dark eyes. A pinched look was forever worn around her mouth, causing additional crevices to form in that area. Her once shiny, dark hair was now dull. Heavy streaks of gray hair now ran through her ebony tresses, making her seem ten years older than her actual age.

"I want to show you something," Ma Le stated. "Come here." She walked down the hallway to the bathroom, with Susan following behind. "Now, what is wrong here?" The sour look upon Ma Le's face deepened with each word that tumbled from her mouth.

Susan looked at the towel rack to see one solitary towel. She knew what was wrong. The towel's mate sat crumpled on the side of the sink.

"I'm sorry, Mama. I guess Daddy did it when he used the bathroom."

"You know you have to help me around here," Ma Le said with anger flashing in her eyes. Susan immediately retrieved the crumpled-up matching towel, smoothed out its edges, folded it in a particular manner, and then returned it to its rightful place upon the towel rack. "Go to your room for the rest of the day. I don't want any more messes around here. Remember, if this happens again, there won't be any visits to the library for the next two weeks."

"Yes, Mother," Susan said in a meek manner. She had learned long ago that life could be endured if she always followed her mother's wishes. Ma Le had an obsession with twos. As much as possible, all objects within the apartment were arranged two by two. A set of twin towels was always on the rack. Cans in the cupboard were arranged in clusters of two. Ma Le forced Susan to tie red ribbons around the neck of hangers that held her clothes in the closet. Of course, the ribbons allowed two hangers to be strung together. The telephone would be answered on the second ring. The door would be answered after the second knock.

Susan walked into her bedroom as commanded. She took deep breaths of the cleansing air. She opened her closet and untied a few of the bows. She mixed up a few pairs of her organized shoes. There were other twin objects around the room, but she knew better than to disturb them. It made her feel less stifled if she could destroy a small portion of the idiotic organization. But it had to be small. Ma Le checked her room several times a day. Susan had to remember to restore the couples to their rightful locations within the next hour.

At times, just being around Ma Le made Susan feel as if she were going mad. The library and her reading were her only ways to escape for just a while. She knew she could do nothing to interfere

The Locket

with her afternoon library visits. Life would be unbearable if they were taken away.

~ ~ ~ ~ ~ ~

"I'll need a shovel to clean up this mess!" Margaret shouted to her young sons. "All right, you two, I need some help!" Matthew's bedroom was in a shambles.

"But, Mama," Matthew whined. "Billy wants us to play ball with him this afternoon. Please let me go!" Matthew fluttered his puppy dog, brown-eyed gaze up at his mother. His manipulative manner always served to melt Margaret's determination. She smiled down at her son's face.

"All right, go on," she relented. Matthew's face began to glow. He rushed over to the desk in his room, retrieved his baseball glove, and bounded out the door while calling for his brother.

Aaron walked up quietly and hugged his mother around the waist. He was thoughtful and affectionate, a son who admired his mother, displayed gratitude for her kind deeds, and attempted to make up for his father's inadequacies. Henry's inadequacies were becoming clearer each day.

"I'll clean up both of our rooms if you want me to, Mama."

"No, honey, that wouldn't be fair. Go play with your brother. Both of you can straighten up your rooms tonight before supper."

Aaron smiled at his mother's warm gaze. He, too, grabbed his baseball glove and bounded out the door to catch up with his mischievous brother.

Margaret looked back at the horrendous mess before her. She missed Maggie. The woman had been an excellent housekeeper, just like her mother. Margaret's current housekeeper worked only two days each week in a somewhat haphazard manner.

When their planned move to Pennsylvania had been announced several years ago, Leonard and Maggie had immediately announced their plans to marry. Margaret was ecstatic to hear the news of an imminent union between her good friends. Mattie would have been so happy. Margaret remembered the words Mattie had spoken as she lay dying. This precious daughter of hers would now be well cared for and would enjoy a life that could not have been duplicated in Barnesville. The couple married two days before Christmas in 1948. Maggie now lived with Leonard on James's Connecticut estate and was employed by the powerful man in a domestic capacity. Margaret received frequent letters from Maggie. The couple now had a daughter, Olivia, who had just celebrated her third birthday.

Thoughts of Maggie and Leonard soon led to musings about James. Just as he had promised, his presence had been scarce since their move from Alexandria, Virginia. Margaret reached up to touch the locket that was forever worn around the delicate lines of her neck. She missed James. She missed his depth of character. She missed his wisdom. She wanted to draw on his strength. She needed his courage.

As these thoughts ran through her mind, Margaret walked into the master bedroom and picked up Henry's suit coat to hang it in their closet. Margaret smelled the coat and recognized the faint hint of liquor that lingered on the jacket. It made her feel nauseous. She wished the coat belonged to James. In her mind, she imagined smelling the maleness of the man she knew she truly loved but could never have. If this were his coat, she might put it on and wear it around the house for hours. Instead, she threw the offensive garment in the dirty clothes hamper.

Chapter 18

Mother's Day, 1958

"No! These stitches aren't straight enough!" Anger flashed in Ma Le's eyes as she looked at some of Susan's handiwork. The obsessive cleaning she felt compelled to engage in every day had become so cumbersome that she had been forced to solicit Susan's help in completing the weekly alterations from Rich's. Ma Le looked at her daughter and said, "You'll have to rip these stitches out and start over." The familiar sadness entered Susan's face, but she knew better than to argue.

Susan had now reached the age of thirteen and had just finished her eighth year of public education in the Atlanta City School System. As always, her time in school was treasured. It took her away from the strict boundaries of her existence at home. Susan's grades were forever exceptional, but she received no praise from her mother regarding her academic achievements.

Susan looked down at the skirt she had hemmed halfway around. She sighed and began to rip away the offensive stitches that did not meet her mother's standards. Since money was scarce in their household, Susan had resorted to sewing a handmade blouse as a Mother's Day gift for Ma Le. The older woman had not been impressed. Susan was certain the garment had been created utilizing her best efforts. She never gave less than her best to any project. But nothing was ever right for Ma Le, a woman who wanted perfection and order in life.

Ma Le roamed about the apartment dusting pieces of furniture repeatedly and checking to see if all doors and windows were locked and secured. Susan attempted not to watch her mother's strange behaviors. When she saw that Ma Le had checked the lock on the door ten times in thirty minutes, she had to stifle a very strong urge to scream. It had become almost unbearable for Susan to spend time in the same room with her mother. Even though it was Mother's Day, tonight would be no different from any other. Susan's offer to cook a special dinner had been rejected by Ma Le. Hot meals were becoming rare, due to the mess they produced. Ma Le ate very little anyway and had grown quite thin. Susan relished the hot lunch she was given at school but had to eat numerous cold plates at home. At times, she was given food that was spoiled, so she became diligent about inspecting what food was in the house to make certain she was not eating something that would make her ill.

Susan began to gather together the few, small items she had utilized to hem the skirt. Ma Le hardly noticed Susan walk, with quiet feet, back to her bedroom to complete the necessary alteration. She knew she would be happier there. In that room, she could enjoy the freedom to dream while she exercised her fingers for the meticulous handiwork.

In spite of her situation, Susan had dreams of a better life. She had devised a plan, of sorts, designed to further reduce the time she spent at home. Susan did not enjoy the sewing and mending. However, Ma Le was in danger of losing her job at Rich's if she could not keep up with the pace they had set. So, the help she provided to her mother was essential at this point. But it had reduced the time she usually spent at the public library. The librarians missed seeing Susan since she now only visited that beloved building on Saturdays.

Yesterday, the head librarian had approached Susan regarding an after-school job shelving books. Just thinking about the job lifted her spirits. Susan had explained to the librarian that she would give her an answer in a week or less, after speaking to Ma Le. The subject had not been discussed. As Susan began stitching the hem of the skirt again, she was reminded of her intense dislike for sewing. She felt an urgency to speak to her mother regarding the librarian's proposal.

Susan dropped her sewing onto the bed and returned to the living room. Ma Le was dusting the molding above their front door.

"Mama," she called. Ma Le looked down from her stepladder. "Can I talk to you about something?" Ma Le nodded and then stepped down from the ladder to sit in a living room chair. "Mrs. Morris, the head librarian at the public library, came up to me yesterday while I was looking for some books. She asked me if I might be interested in working for her after school. Mrs. Morris wants me to shelve books for her. I could work for one or two hours after school each day and then on Saturdays too. I wouldn't make a lot of money, but it might help us out since Daddy only pays the rent. Would you let me do it, Mama?"

Ma Le thought for a moment but did recognize the wisdom in her daughter's plan. Additional income was becoming a necessity. Her daughter would be at home for smaller and smaller amounts of time. That would mean less and less of her untidy activities. The idea was a good one.

"That will be fine," Ma Le responded. "But you may still need to help me with the alterations from Rich's."

Susan was ecstatic. She had not felt such excitement for many long years. For the first time, Susan began to see that there would come a day when her sentence in this prison on Seventeenth Street would be over. In an uncharacteristic move, she quickly hugged and kissed her mother, who displayed a shocked look at her daughter's affectionate response.

~ ~ ~ ~ ~ ~

"What the hell were you thinking?" Henry stood before a seated Matthew with fury blazing in his eyes. Margaret and Aaron sat in silence on a nearby couch in their North Carolina home.

Henry's agitation stemmed from Matthew's irresponsible and

dangerous behavior. Margaret had received a telephone call several hours earlier from a nearby hospital emergency room. It seemed that Matthew and several other teenaged friends had been caught driving an old flatbed truck down a lonely country road. The flatbed truck was just that, a flat bed and an engine. There were no seats left in the dilapidated vehicle. The four adolescents had fired up the engine for a joyride down a bumpy, dusty road. They had located a straight chair, which was placed in what they considered a secure manner, to allow Matthew to drive. After about thirty minutes of reckless careening up and down the dirt road, Matthew stopped the jalopy in an abrupt manner, causing two of his young friends to topple off the back of the flatbed onto the hard dirt road. One boy suffered only a broken arm, and another sustained a wrist fracture.

This was a Mother's Day Margaret would not soon forget. It had begun rather quietly that morning as Margaret awoke to breakfast in bed prepared by her twin sons. The breakfast consisted of very stiff scrambled eyes, two pieces of burned toast, undercooked bacon, and a cup of tepid coffee. Both sons beamed up at their mother with the pride that comes from an unbelievable accomplishment. Neither boy could ever have said they even knew how to boil water before that day. Although the meal was lacking in the palatable department, it was brimming over with love. Margaret had tears in her eyes as she hugged each of her children, who were now just about the size of full-grown men.

There was no smile on Matthew's face as he now sat with his eyes cast downward, listening to his father's verbal assault. Henry had already consumed at least four glasses of whiskey when the telephone call was received. Margaret had been able to talk him out of driving, but she knew the liquor would make his vengeance all the more fierce when she arrived home with Matthew that evening. Aaron had not been involved in the late-afternoon mayhem but had chosen to play basketball with some school buddies who lived near their Fayetteville, North Carolina, home.

Much of Henry's fury stemmed from the fact that he had given Matthew permission to cavort with the farm boy friends earlier in

The Locket

the day. Margaret had protested, anticipating that there could be trouble. She possessed an extra sense that could sniff out even a hint of impending danger to her boys. Henry's parenting was haphazard at best. At times, Margaret felt Henry just wanted Matthew out of the house and out of his way. The army officer's anger at his own inadequacies was now about to explode.

Henry looked at his son to say, "Those two boys could have been killed! This is just another mess I'm having to bail you out of! Why did you do such a damn foolish thing?"

Matthew looked at his father with something close to hatred reflected in his eyes. "We were just playin' around. They weren't hurt bad. I guess things like this wouldn't be happening if there was more to do around this hick town."

"There's plenty to do in this town," Henry retorted. "Your brother never gets in trouble. He went to play basketball with some school friends today and was upstairs studying when we got the telephone call from the hospital. Why can't you act more like your brother? Then maybe we could all have some peace around here."

"I'm sick of this shit!" Matthew spat out the words. The boy then stood up to stride away from the room and leave his drunken father behind.

Henry grabbed his son by the shirt collar and said, "Oh no. I'm not finished with you yet." Henry's face was red from the liquor he had consumed.

Alarm prompted Margaret to stand and shout, "Henry! Don't hurt him!" She could see the unleashed fury blazing in her husband's eyes.

Henry placed his face close to Matthew's. The boy could smell the offensive stench of his father's boiling-hot breath. In a storm of anger, Henry raged. "You will live by my rules in this house. If that doesn't suit you, just leave. You'll end up in jail by the time you're out of your teens anyway. We would all be better off without you. Some days, I wish you'd never been born because all you've given us is grief. Go ahead, since you think you're so smart, and do whatever the hell you want. I'll gladly haul you down to juvenile hall and let you rot down there, you sorry son of a bitch."

"Stop it, Henry!" Margaret screamed.

A mean glint entered into Matthew's eyes while his father still clutched a fistful of the boy's shirt. "Maybe I wouldn't be such a sorry son of a bitch if my father wasn't a drunk."

The words struck a sensitive nerve in Henry. He exploded at the bite of Matthew's truthful words to shove his son against the hard plaster wall in the living room. Matthew's head flung against the glass of a framed picture hanging on the wall. The glass shattered, the picture fell, and Matthew let out an agonizing groan as he slid to the floor.

Margaret ran to her son to place her body between the angry man and the boy who continually incited his fury. She looked up at Henry to plead, "Stop all of this, please!" Henry's fists were clenched because, in his mind, the assault had not been concluded. "You could kill him! It's all over! Leave my son alone!" She looked down at Matthew to see the extent of his injuries. The mighty shove had caused a nasty gash in the back of his head.

"Keep him out of my way, Margaret. Or I swear to God, I'll kick the hateful brat out of the house." Henry strode from the room to enter his study and slam the door. Margaret knew he kept extra bottles of whiskey in that room, so she did not have to guess what he would be doing.

Margaret turned to Matthew and said, "Come on back to the bathroom, and I'll take care of that cut." Both boys followed their mother to the bathroom in the hall. Mathew pulled down the toilet seat cover and sat down to allow his mother to bandage the laceration. Aaron sat on the side of the tub, shaken by what he had just witnessed. The silence between the two brothers was painful to Margaret. She knew they all needed to talk.

As she washed the broken skin, she said, "I'm so sorry all of this happened tonight. You know your father didn't mean those horrible things he said. It was the liquor talking. When your father isn't drinking, he never acts mean. You both know that, right?"

"But, Mama," Aaron responded, "I don't remember a time when Daddy didn't drink." The words were truthful.

Tears sprang to Margaret's eyes at the realization that alcohol had become her husband's mistress. His affair with the alluring spirits must have started during his last few years away at war. The boys had never known him as a sober man. Margaret had chosen to tolerate Henry's daily indulgences, to pretend they were not taking place. Even his fellow officers at Fort Bragg had seen several displays of his raucous, drunken behavior. There had also been times when Margaret had been forced to cancel party invitations at the last minute because Henry was too inebriated to attend and behave in an appropriate manner. Margaret always drove to and from social functions because of fear that Henry would have an accident. It was ironic that Henry used to coach her on appropriate and inappropriate conversational topics prior to an outing with his colleagues. Now, she continually attempted to cover up the unpleasant reality of Henry's alcoholism. She knew the cover-up could not go on forever.

"Just remember, boys," Margaret began with a quiver in her voice, "your father was once a great man. He still can be a great man if he can leave the bottle behind. I'll talk to him. Maybe it will make a difference."

"Good luck with that," Matthew said. "He'll never change. I wish he wasn't my father."

"Don't say such things!" Margaret's hands shook as she secured the bandage to Matthew's head. "I love you both so much. The two of you have unique and lovable qualities. I will always be here for you. I am your mother. But I want you both to promise me you'll try to stay out of trouble so we won't ever make Daddy angry like this again." It made Margaret feel better to talk in the "we" sense, so Matthew would not feel quite so singled out for ridicule. It amazed Margaret that Matthew held no real resentment for his brother, who was Henry's obvious favorite. The army officer already had mapped out a military future for Aaron. It was a future, she was certain, that did not suit Aaron's gentle nature.

Both boys nodded their agreement to Margaret's plan for keeping peace within the family. She sent them on down to their rooms for the night.

Margaret walked down the hall to the study. She knocked softly on the door. Henry responded, "Who is it?"

"It's me."

"You can open the door."

Margaret opened the door as commanded. Henry was seated at his desk. In his right hand, he held yet another glass of strong spirits. He was looking at an old photo album. With a slur in his speech, he said, "What happened to the fun in life, Margaret?" She noticed the photographs were from his college days and the very early years of his military career.

"I really don't know, Henry. I guess the stress and pressures of everyday living sometimes break us down. Then it's hard to recognize the joy in our existence." Margaret was surprised at the philosophical nature of Henry's query. It was out of character.

"Henry," she began, "I want to talk to you about something that has become a very real problem."

"I know I was too rough with the boy tonight. It won't happen again."

"You were too rough, and your words were unforgiveable. But thank goodness Matthew has a thick skin. I want to talk about something more serious, your drinking."

Henry's head snapped up from the album. "What do you mean?" His eyes narrowed a bit. A pinched expression entered his face.

"I think you're drinking way too much. Every day, you come home from work to head straight for the liquor cabinet. It's gotten to where you sometimes drink four or five glasses of whiskey a night. You've probably lost count tonight. You're even slurring your words. You would never have said those dreadful things to Matthew tonight if you were sober. Please stop the drinking. Do it for your family. Don't let it destroy us." Tears sprang to Margaret's tired eyes. A bit of fear entered her countenance, as she hoped her husband's inebriation would not cause him to lash out in a violent manner once again.

"I don't have to listen to this. My drinking is not a problem.

The Locket

Believe me, if I had been stone-cold sober, I would have said those things to Matthew. We're going to have to watch him closely, Margaret. He's conniving. Why, he even—"

"Stop this, Henry," Margaret interrupted. "Don't try to throw things off on Matthew. I'm here to talk about your drinking." Margaret trembled inside and tried to find some courage. "I want it to stop. I'm asking you tonight to put the bottle away and stop drinking. I know it will be hard, but I'll help you. If you need to, you can take a couple of weeks off work and stay at home. We can do this together, for us, for our family. Will you please stop drinking?"

The question seemed to hang in the air for long moments. As in the past, Henry walked down the path of denial with a shortcut to avoidance. He said through clenched teeth, "I don't have a goddamn problem with drinking. So shut up about it. I'm going to bed. Make sure I never hear another word about this again." Henry strode past his wife out of the room and down to their bedroom.

Margaret knew Henry well. The finality of his tone was real. His military training had prepared him to make those take charge kind of decisions. The decision had been made. Henry's love affair with liquor would continue. Margaret collapsed into an easy chair. Sobs began to wrack her body. The sobs were deep and wrenching. The smell of liquor permeated the room. Margaret felt like grabbing the bottle of whiskey and hurling it across the room to shatter against the wall. But she knew it would make her feel no better.

She touched the ever-present locket hanging from her neck. Another deep sob welled up inside her and was released into the loathsome atmosphere of her home. How could she take this loveless marriage any longer when all she wanted to do was run to the arms of another man? The physical love in her marriage was gone. Henry had not touched her in a year. Could she dare leave him? Divorce was unthinkable in her family. As far as she knew, there had never been a divorce. How would she support herself if she left Henry? Margaret had not worked for a living in a very long time. The boys needed a man around during these difficult adolescent years. Her head throbbed. She ached inside for James's loving touch but knew she would have to get through this on her own.

Margaret realized she was clutching the locket so hard the chain was about to break. She released the treasured gift, dried her eyes, and stood to walk down the hall to the bedroom she shared with Henry. She opened the door quietly to see her husband's form sleeping in the bed. His snoring was loud, and the room reeked from the heavy scent of alcohol. It made her stomach turn while waves of nausea engulfed her. She knew she could not spend another night in that bedroom.

Margaret walked over to the other side of the room to switch on a soft light. She knew Henry was too drunk to wake up in spite of the illumination. Margaret opened her closet door and gathered up an armload of hanging garments. She walked the clothes straight down to the guest bedroom and deposited them in the spare closet. The actions began to give her a small measure of inner peace. If she had to be trapped in this dreadful marriage for a few more years, at least she didn't have to sleep beside the drunken fool each night. Henry never seemed to care whether or not she was lying beside him anyway.

As Margaret arranged the last few items in her new bedroom, she heard feet shuffling down the hall. Matthew walked into the spare bedroom rubbing his sleepy eyes. He saw the evidence of her symbolic departure. The guest bed had been made up with fresh sheets and turned down for its new, regular occupant.

"What are you doing, Mama?" he asked.

"I thought it would be better if I started sleeping in here from now on." Matthew heard the sadness in his mother's voice.

"He's not going to stop drinking, is he?"

"No."

Matthew walked over to his mother and hugged her fiercely. It took her breath away. "I love you so much, Mama."

"I know, honey. I love you so. Don't ever forget that." She watched the sleepy young man walk out of her new private place. Margaret knew the next few years ahead would not be easy.

Chapter 19

February 1962

    Susan stood at the circulation desk of the Atlanta Public Library with the telephone held to her ear. She listened to the tenth, eleventh, and then the twelfth ring into the apartment she shared with her mother, knowing something was very wrong. Ma Le never left the apartment unless forced to do so. Every telephone call was always answered after the second ring. Susan had placed the call to inform her mother that Mrs. Morris had asked her to work later than usual that evening. The young woman now knew she needed to get home quickly. Ma Le had lost her job at Rich's the day before due to her inability to complete the necessary alterations on schedule. As the pressure in her work increased, so had the momentum of her obsessive cleaning. Susan had not been surprised that the prestigious department store lost patience with her mother.

    What had surprised Susan was the stricken look on her mother's face following a telephone call from Henry. Her father was angry about this new situation. Henry had taken the unusual opportunity to inform Ma Le that he was withdrawing financial support now that Susan had reached the age of seventeen. Ma Le was visibly shaken regarding his decision. Susan did her best to comfort her mother. She reassured Ma Le that she would immediately obtain a full-time job at the library, following high school graduation, in order to pay their household bills. They knew Susan would be unable to support them both on her meager earnings at the library. The rent on their apartment was not cheap.

Susan walked over to Mrs. Morris. The head librarian was in her midforties and had been employed by the public library for the past fifteen years. Mrs. Morris and Susan had grown very close over the past few years. The relationship had filled a void for Susan. She looked forward to seeing the older woman each afternoon when she arrived for work. Mrs. Morris, now deeply into a childless marriage, had found a certain satisfaction and joy in her connection with the young woman.

"I'm going to have to go home early," Susan stated with worry etched into her expression.

"What's wrong?" she asked.

"I don't know, really. I called home, and Mama didn't answer. She rarely leaves home. Something isn't right." Tears sparkled in Susan's dark eyes.

"There's more to this, isn't there?" Mrs. Morris asked. She knew Susan well.

"Mama lost her job at Rich's yesterday. It upset her so much. I was afraid to leave her and go to school today. But I went ahead."

"You need someone to go home with you," Mrs. Morris responded. "Let me go tell Sylvia she will need to close the library tonight. I'll drive you home."

Susan waited with a feeling of dread in her gut. In a few moments, Mrs. Morris returned from behind the circulation desk with her coat and purse in hand. The two walked out the door to head straight for the librarian's vehicle. Inside the automobile, the two women were silent, both aware there was something to be faced ahead. Mrs. Morris looked over at Susan. She had watched her mature into an impressive young woman, a young woman who had the potential for greatness. Susan's intelligence, her maturity, and her poise were remarkable in someone who should be experiencing excruciating growing pains. She was also a great beauty. Mrs. Morris had seen the young men swoon over Susan's dark-haired good looks while they watched her movements from behind heavily laden shelves of books.

The Locket

Within minutes, Mrs. Morris parked her Ford by the curb in front of the Seventeenth Street apartment building. The women stepped from the car to walk up the concrete steps of the building. Susan led the way up the staircase to her second-floor apartment. Mrs. Morris had taken Susan home on many nights but never ventured this far into their domain. When they reached the front door, Susan quickly located her key and unlocked the barrier to their entrance.

The apartment was silent. Both women walked slowly onto the tiled floor.

"Mama," Susan called out. There was no response. Susan walked ahead. The click of her low heels reverberated throughout the apartment. She went from room to room but saw no sign of Ma Le. Mrs. Morris was stricken by the clinically clean atmosphere she now observed. After going through most of the rooms, Susan saw the closed bathroom door. She walked to the door and knocked softly.

"Mama, are you in there?" Again, there was silence.

Susan turned the doorknob to discover that it was unlocked. She slowly pushed open the door while Mrs. Morris stood waiting in the living room.

Ma Le was sitting, naked, in the dry bathtub. She was hugging her knees tightly to her chest as she rocked back and forth. She whispered a word repeatedly while her body continued the rhythmic movements. As Susan came closer to her mother, she could hear the whispered speech.

"Mamasan, Mamasan, Mamasan, Mamasan ..." Ma Le whispered in unison with her rocking motions.

"Mama," Susan called for her mother's attention. There was no sign that Ma Le had even noted her daughter's entrance into the small room. Ma Le's eyes stared forward, unseeing, at the bare white wall before her. Susan stood for a moment, not knowing what to do next. She walked closer to Ma Le to stand beside the tub.

"Mama, let's go into your bedroom. You don't need to be in here now. You'll be fine if you just put on your nightgown and get some sleep. I'll help you get to bed." Susan reached down and touched

Ma Le's arm in an attempt to urge the woman toward the desired location. Ma Le recoiled at the unexpected touch.

"Don't touch me!" she hissed. "I'm dirty! I'm dirty!" Ma Le began to move her hands up and down her forearms in symbolic washing motions. "Mamasan's blood is everywhere! It won't come off! It won't come off! Mamasan! Mamasan!" Ma Le closed her eyes tightly, and the rocking began again. Susan knew the situation had escalated to something beyond what she could manage. She turned to walk from the bathroom and discovered Mrs. Morris standing at the door. Susan knew she had witnessed the bizarre encounter.

"Susan," Mrs. Morris began, "your mother needs medical attention. We need to get her to a hospital as soon as possible. They will know how to take care of her."

Susan followed Mrs. Morris into the living room. The older woman picked up the telephone to speak to the operator. "I need you to call an ambulance for me." There was a pause. "It appears to be a psychiatric problem. She may be having a nervous breakdown." There was another short pause. "Send the ambulance to Seventeenth Street. The apartments should be on your right when you turn off of Peachtree Street. They are called the Maryland. We are in apartment D, which is located upstairs."

Mrs. Morris replaced the receiver of the telephone back on its cradle. She turned back to Susan to say, "We should go watch your mother until they get here. She might hurt herself."

The women stood in the strange atmosphere of the bathroom, watching Ma Le rock and whisper in the bathtub. It was as if the deranged woman did not know they were present. Susan looked down at the cold, white tiled floor, noticing the pristine cleanliness. Yet, in spite of all the rigorous scrubbing, Ma Le still felt dirty. What, thought Susan, had tainted her so? She had spoken of Mamasan's blood. Susan did not understand any of this. She felt a strong urge to run from the frightening situation. Susan began to shake inside while a tear streamed down her cheek. Their future was so uncertain, and she was more afraid to relate the entire situation to Mrs. Morris, who stood beside her.

The Locket

Mrs. Morris stepped closer to Susan and folded the young woman into a tight embrace. She stood for eternal moments, holding Susan's shaking form. A loud knock was heard at the door. Mrs. Morris released Susan to answer the urgent summons. She opened the door. Two men stood there dressed in matching white uniforms. They pushed a gurney into the living room. Mrs. Morris directed them toward the bathroom. She stopped them short of entering the small room to ask a question.

"What hospital will you be taking her to?"

The men pushed past Mrs. Morris to witness the sight of Ma Le's frantic rocking in the bathtub. The taller man then said, "She'll be going to Grady Hospital. They'll probably put her in the psychiatric ward."

Mrs. Morris nodded her agreement. Susan's dark eyes loomed large with fright at the man's words.

"You may have some difficulty getting her out of there," Mrs. Morris warned the men. She turned to Susan and said, "Come out here in the living room. I want you to come home with me tonight. The doctors probably won't let you see her for several days." The fright in Susan's gaze worried the older woman. She placed her arms around Susan's shoulders to walk her into the living room. "The doctors will know what to do for her. At the hospital, she will be safe."

With a quiver in her voice, Susan said, "But she doesn't handle change well. It's going to be very bad."

At that moment, a piercing scream was heard from the bathroom, which caused Susan to flinch. Many more gut-wrenching screams were heard before the men were able to cover Ma Le with a white sheet and strap her down. When the narrow bed was wheeled through the living room, Susan saw that Ma Le's hands and feet were tied to the metal bars that lined the sides of the gurney. Mrs. Morris opened the door to aid the men. Ma Le's screams continued to reach a feverish pitch as she struggled against the restraints. Susan saw her neighbors across the hall open their front door to peer out, looking for the source of the commotion. She knew every neighbor that evening would be doing the same. The landlord might use this as an excuse to rid herself of the problem upstairs.

When Ma Le and the men were gone and the ear-splitting screams were silenced, Mrs. Morris turned to Susan. "Let's go to my house now. Don't worry about packing anything. I've got something you can sleep in."

A sudden calmness entered Susan's countenance. "Please, wait just one minute. I need to make a telephone call." Susan reached over to her purse to retrieve a small slip of paper from her wallet. She lifted the receiver of the telephone and placed the necessary call. In a moment, a voiced answered on the other end of the line. "May I speak to James Walsh?" Susan said with a quivering tone. "Tell him it's Susan, Ma Le's daughter."

~ ~ ~ ~ ~ ~

Margaret maneuvered her late-model Ford into a parking space at the white, public high school located in Milner, Georgia, a sister community to her hometown of Barnesville. Now, at the age of forty-one, Margaret was not the same woman who moved away from Lamar County years before. She was as beautiful as ever. Only a few small lines were visible at the corner of each shining, dark brown eye. A few small changes that come with age were present but served to create an aura of confidence, wisdom, and strength of character that had not been present during her young womanhood spent in the small kingdom of Barnesville.

She contemplated the changes that had occurred in her life over the last few years as she walked the length of the parking lot to the school. Margaret now taught senior English classes there since the move back to Barnesville last summer. That summer had been a difficult time. Henry's drinking had escalated to the point that Margaret made a conscious choice to no longer hide the secret of his alcoholism. The army officer had lost all respect for himself, which in turn caused most of his colleagues to regard him as useless in his position at Fort Bragg. When Henry eventually reported for work

The Locket

one day quite intoxicated, it was clear to his commanding officer that Colonel Montgomery would need to be relieved of his post. Since drinking now consumed his life, Henry was of no use to the army in any capacity. He was unfit to continue commanding the Twentieth Engineer Brigade.

General Wheeler, who had been a friend of Henry's since early in his military career, volunteered to formally relieve Margaret's husband from his position at Fort Bragg. The general had forced Henry to leave by announcing his retirement. It was a logical way out for the once great man now so broken by the passionate allure of the bottle. To soften the harshness of the situation, General Wheeler had paved the way for Aaron to receive a congressional appointment and scholarship to West Point. The powerful general had made a few telephone calls to various military officials. The final result was eradication of all hospital records pertaining to Aaron's treatment for ulcerative colitis. Though Aaron was no longer debilitated by the disease, Henry knew that full disclosure of his medical history would keep him from entering the prestigious military institute.

Margaret entered her school room just as the bell rang to herald the start of morning classes. Some last-minute students filed into the classroom and then settled down to their respective desks. The teacher looked over her classroom while mentally identifying students who favored her teaching style. She then took note of those students who enjoyed informing their parents of any controversial tidbits of information that might tumble from Margaret's mouth. Margaret had carved out a certain reputation for herself at the Milner High School and within the Barnesville community. She had become quite outspoken regarding her approval of equal rights for black people within the South. The civil rights movement was gaining momentum. However, sleepy little southern communities were attempting to ignore the inevitable. Margaret had spoken her views in her Sunday school class several weeks ago. Since that time, prominent members of the Barnesville aristocracy had openly shunned her.

The cold faces of people Margaret once thought of as friends now haunted her. But she was compelled to continue with her crusade—even in spite of threatening letters and telephone calls she had received of late. The threats disturbed the boys, who worried about their mother's safety. Henry, however, appeared unaware of anything outside a liquor bottle. His health was suffering from the abuse inflicted upon his body over long years of drinking. Margaret pushed thoughts of Henry from her mind.

She had discussed racism and integration of public school systems in a few of her classes. She had also been reprimanded by the principal of her school for doing so. Margaret had been grateful to her principal, Mr. Howard, for giving her this badly needed job. But still, she could not fight the compulsion she possessed to enlighten the ignorant fools who sat before her regarding social consciousness and the specific concerns of the time. After taking a deep breath, Margaret decided to press on.

"Class," she began. "I want everyone to take out several sheets of paper and your pencils. We will be writing our usual Thursday-morning, five-paragraph composition today.

"Before I give you the topic, I want to discuss an important woman in history. Her name was Margaret Sanger. She was a nurse practicing around the turn of the century, a visionary of sorts. Margaret Sanger clearly recognized the oppression our society had placed upon women. She realized that women would never enjoy equal rights, as compared to men, in our social order until they could exercise control over their reproductive health. In other words, until women could practice birth control, their inequality would persist." Margaret heard a few of the immature seniors giggle in the back of the classroom.

"Now, I tell you this because there are parallels between the oppression of women and the oppression of blacks in the United States and, most of all, here in the South. Because of her activism regarding women's rights, Margaret Sanger recognized that the greatest challenge we could be forced to face in the twentieth century would be racism. Now, this is not a history class. I don't expect you to know the life history of Margaret Sanger, who was a white woman with a multicultural perspective. I brought her up to merely give you food for thought.

"I want everyone to write a composition today about the positive aspects of integrating our public school systems. I want you to imagine what it would be like if blacks and whites attended school together, not separate. Imagine that this classroom was comprised of twelve white students and twelve black students. But do remember that I asked you to discuss the positive aspects of integrating whites and blacks together in our educational system."

A freckle-faced boy sitting in the very back of the classroom raised his hand. "Yes, Billy," Margaret responded.

"But what if there ain't no positive aspects, Mrs. Montgomery?" He smiled as he asked the ignorant question. Margaret cringed at the horrendous grammar. A few other students giggled their agreement to the boy's query.

"Then I guess you would not be following my instructions," Margaret replied, "which would easily land you a failing grade. I don't think anyone here today would like to see what an F would do to their grade point average."

Margaret watched the students begin their assignment. A few of the students whispered back and forth but were silenced by a stern gaze from their teacher. Margaret gave her class the entire hour to complete the assigned composition. It was clear that many of the students were struggling for words after being forced to examine a different perspective regarding current educational traditions. Before long, the bell rang, and much of the class had not completed their composition.

As the students stood to leave, Margaret said, "You will be given time in class tomorrow to finish your compositions." The students did not looked thrilled at the stated plans.

Five more times that day, Margaret repeated the writing assignment to her English classes. Reactions were varied. Margaret had half expected some of the students from known racist families to refuse the assignment and walk out of the room. This did not occur, but she knew some parental outrage would take place.

At the end of the school day, a deep exhaustion had entered the teacher's body. She gathered the completed papers and again walked across the parking lot to the old Ford that would soon be a candidate for the junkyard. Margaret's family had always enjoyed frequent purchases of new cars, due to her father's ownership of the Ford motor car dealership in Barnesville. She missed her father. His sudden death from a heart attack two years before had been a stinging blow to Margaret and Anne. Joan never really was the same after her husband passed away. She was plagued by numerous health problems, and then her life ended following a bout of pneumonia in February of 1961.

When the Harris family home in Barnesville no longer enjoyed an occupant, Anne had suggested that Margaret and her family move into the house on Stafford Avenue. Henry's retirement was imminent, and the arrangement worked out well for all involved. Finances had been tight in the Montgomery household over the past few years. Henry had always taken care of their money, and he had made it clear that his pension alone would be difficult to live on. The opportunity to live rent-free in the Harris family home was ideal. Anne and Margaret had agreed not to sell the Barnesville home until the Montgomerys' financial situation had improved. Attendance at Gordon Military Academy, a private school, was tuition-free for white Barnesville residents, as a white high school was not located within the city limits. Their only expense for attendance at Gordon Military Academy was the cost of uniforms.

Margaret remembered the first time Aaron donned the crisp military-type attire. It looked quite strange. The trappings made him uncomfortable, and that was clear. At least it was clear to everyone but Henry. Matthew, on the other hand, had proudly strutted around the house in his new school uniform. Somehow, Margaret thought, seeing the garments on Matthew did please Henry and served to elevate this less than favorite son in his father's eyes.

Margaret pulled the Ford into the driveway on Stafford Avenue. She gathered her papers and her purse and walked to the mailbox before entering the house. There were some utility bills, a letter

The Locket

from Maggie, and an official envelope embossed with the name and business address of Senator Richard Russell. The official-looking letter filled Margaret with a sense of dread. She knew that it had to be the formal announcement of Aaron's congressional appointment to West Point. Henry would be thrilled. Aaron would not.

As Margaret turned the knob on the front door, she knew she had allowed the West Point plans to go way too far. She walked into the living room to find Henry reading the newspaper, while Aaron worked on a school project. Margaret dropped the senator's letter into Henry's lap. He looked at the envelope, and a broad smile became planted on his face. He ripped into what he knew would be the congressional appointment.

Margaret watched as Henry stood up with the letter and walked over to his son. "Well, son," he began as he waved the letter before Aaron's face, "this is what you've been waiting for." A nervous look crossed over Aaron's young, handsome face. It was a face that resembled his father's, but that was where the similarity ended. The personalities were quite different.

"Now," Henry announced. "This is just the beginning of an illustrious military career. There's no telling how far you'll go. Why, with my guidance, you could become a general on down the line." Henry's face beamed. Aaron's eyes were cast downward. A rosy hue entered the boy's cheeks, but he kept silent. Margaret knew she had to say something.

"Henry and Aaron," she began. "I want to discuss this congressional appointment. Henry, I know you want Aaron to do this. I realize you think it's best, that it's a wonderful opportunity. But I don't think you've ever really discussed it with Aaron. Perhaps Aaron's plans for his future are different from yours." She had opened a door for Aaron, but his silence persisted.

"The boy isn't stupid, Margaret," Henry replied. "He knows this is right for him. He'll go, and then before you know it, we'll have a West Point graduate. It will make a man out of him."

Aaron began to look antsy under his mother's close scrutiny and her blatant attempt to air his true feelings. She pressed on. "Aaron," she said, "is it your wish to attend West Point and then pursue a military career?"

Aaron looked very nervous when directly faced with the burning question. Margaret and Henry stood stone faced, waiting for an answer from their son. At that moment, their family discussion was interrupted by the shrill ring of the telephone. As a way to avoid confrontation, Aaron jumped up to answer the ring. He returned to announce that Henry had a telephone call. Henry left the room to answer the telephone that sat on a table near the foot of the staircase.

Margaret looked at Aaron. "I gave you a perfect opportunity to tell him how you feel," she whispered, so as not to alert Henry, who was just around the corner.

"I know," Aaron whispered back. "I'm just not ready yet. Let me think about it some more. I'll tell him in the next couple of weeks."

Margaret gave her son a look of warning. "Don't wait too long. He's already taken this way too far. I wish we had stopped this before it got to Senator Russell's office."

Margaret could hear just a few monosyllabic responses from Henry on the telephone. He then replaced the receiver back on its cradle and walked toward Granny Harris's old bedroom that was now his study. Margaret heard the door slam. She knew he kept his liquor in there. That suited Margaret. At least he wasn't constantly guzzling down the spirits in front of his boys any longer. But Henry's reaction had made her curious.

"Who was that on the telephone?" she asked Aaron.

"I'm not sure," he replied. "It was a man, and that's all I know. I'm going to finish this project up in my room."

Margaret walked into the kitchen and began preparing the evening meal. This kitchen that she remembered so fondly from her youth had always been Mattie's domain. Since the old kitchen had changed very little over the years, Margaret's memory of her substitute mother was still vivid in that location. At times, she felt as if she could still smell the spicy scent of the pomade Mattie had always used in her hair. The memories of Mattie made Margaret

The Locket

remember the letter from Connecticut. Margaret always enjoyed hearing from Maggie.

Margaret retrieved the letter from the living room. Her hungry eyes devoured Maggie's words as she walked back into the kitchen. There were a few lines about James, which caused tears to sting at Margaret's eyes, but she fought a possible flood of sorrow. Margaret's hand touched the locket she had worn now for more than fifteen years. Henry had never asked his wife where the locket had been purchased or anything about its significance. It was Margaret's secret to cherish, and she liked it that way.

Margaret's musings were interrupted by Matthew entering the back door. He and Aaron were now well over six feet tall.

"Hey, Mama," Mathew greeted his mother. He bent down to plant a kiss on her cheek. "I'm starved. Is supper ready?"

"No, not yet. I'm running a little behind. But I'll have it on the table in about forty-five minutes."

"Where's Aaron?"

"He's upstairs finishing that English project. Don't bother him."

"Don't worry. I won't. English isn't exactly my cup of tea, so to speak."

Margaret wrinkled her nose at the son who didn't share her love of reading and language. Matthew's grades were never exceptional, but he did enjoy life. He was quite popular at school, and his noteworthy good looks always kept him busy with a steady stream of Saturday-night dates. Aaron, the shy one of the two, sometimes doubled with Matthew on a date night but had never found a special girl. Matthew was quite content to date a different girl each week. Aaron had no appetite for his brother's fickle ways. But the boys remained close, nonetheless—a closeness that had grown, Margaret surmised, from a void created by their father, who loved liquor more than his family.

Margaret went about her work in the kitchen. As she had promised, the meal was hot on the table in forty-five minutes. She called up the stairs to tell the boys that dinner was ready. She walked to the study door and knocked softly.

"What is it?" Henry gruffly replied.

"I just wanted to let you know that supper is ready."

"I'm not hungry. Go on and eat without me."

Margaret knew it would be a difficult night. When Henry was disturbed about something, he would drink all evening without ever eating a bite of food. This made his intoxication much worse. Margaret sighed and walked away from the door. She was so weary of the entire situation. Her restlessness within the marriage had intensified since returning to Barnesville. She now felt very isolated in the small town that was comfortable to her as a child. There were many days when she regarded their choice to return to her childhood home as a mistake. There had been no alternative. Their financial situation dictated the move to the familiar Stafford Avenue home.

The three members of the Montgomery family present at the dinner table ate in silence. When they were finished, the boys helped their mother clear the table and wash the dishes. Matthew and Aaron then returned to their rooms to complete homework and begin to settle down for the night. Margaret sat down in the living room to read some of the completed compositions she had assigned that day. As expected, some students delineated only negative aspects of school integration, and the deep-seated hatred that dripped from those compositions shocked Margaret. The South had far to go. Margaret was no longer certain that she wanted to stick around and witness the South's unwilling transformation.

Margaret heard the door to the study open abruptly. She then heard Henry walk through the house and out the back door. She knew he would be quite drunk from the hours he had spent in the study alone with the liquor. Margaret feared he might be about to start the car, but that sound was not forthcoming. So, she returned her attention to her work for another fifteen minutes. When Henry had not returned to the house, Margaret decided to go and investigate.

She walked through the dining room, through the kitchen, and out onto the back porch. Margaret's eyes fell upon Henry, now in a crumpled heap in the middle of the backyard. She was certain it was another blackout. She wondered what he had been doing out there as she walked up to his inebriated form, partially illuminated by the porch light. Margaret reached down to turn Henry from his stomach to his side. He was still breathing, but the stench of liquor was overpowering. Margaret was reminded of the last time she found a different crumpled form in the backyard of this home. Henry's presence here somehow tainted Mattie's memory.

On the ground beside Henry was a flashlight and several sheets of paper, now damp from the chilly dew on the grass. Margaret looked up to see the storage shed door wide open. Henry had obviously entered the shed to retrieve the papers Margaret now held, before he passed out on his way back into the house.

Margaret went back into the house to call for the boys. This was nothing new to them. On many occasions, they needed to assist Margaret in getting their drunken father to bed. The boys, who were really now men, picked up Henry with little effort, while Margaret gathered the papers and the flashlight.

"He doesn't feel very heavy tonight," Aaron commented.

"I know," Margaret added. "He's eating less and less and drinking more and more."

Before long, Henry had been deposited onto his bed. Margaret took off his shoes and covered him with the sheet and blanket. The boys returned to their rooms. As she walked out of the bedroom, she heard a loud snore. Margaret always worried that Henry would die in his sleep from the amount of liquor he consumed. She knew she could not take much more of this.

Margaret walked back in the kitchen to retrieve the papers she had found beside Henry. She looked down at the yellowed sheets. The papers were a lease agreement for an apartment on Seventeenth Street in Atlanta. The last page of the agreement was signed by James Walsh and dated in May 1945. It was a mystery to Margaret. What did this mean? James had not been living in Atlanta in 1945. In May 1945, Henry had not yet returned from the war. A frown was etched into Margaret's brow. She wondered if Henry would even remember that he had located the papers. Margaret folded the lease agreement and placed it under the mattress in her bedroom.

In a few minutes, she climbed into her bed and turned out the light. Sleep would elude her that night.

~ ~ ~ ~ ~ ~

It was eight thirty on Friday morning. Margaret stared straight at her principal, Mr. Howard. She had been summoned from her classroom just after relating a continuation of yesterday's composition assignment. Margaret knew that assignment would be the topic of their conversation.

As Mr. Howard sat behind his desk, Margaret piped up. "I know you probably received some phone calls last night about the assignment I gave to my classes yesterday, but—"

"That's not what I want to discuss," Mr. Howard interrupted. "We need to talk about your chronic tardiness."

"My what?"

"Your chronic tardiness. I've documented it over the last month, Mrs. Montgomery. You've been at least ten minutes late on four separate occasions."

"Late? I don't remember being excessively late. I might have been a few minutes late because my car gave me trouble starting on cold mornings. But I was not aware that you perceived this as a problem. I'll be certain that it won't happen in the future."

"I can give you the specific dates if you like," Mr. Howard continued. "What I'm saying is that this can no longer be tolerated, Mrs. Montgomery. I'm afraid I'm going to have to let you go."

Margaret's mouth opened in astonishment. Still, Mr. Howard went on.

"You see, I need someone I can count on, always. I need all of my teachers to be in their classrooms a full thirty minutes before the first bell. I'm afraid you've let me down in that area, and that is why I am going to have to let you go." Mr. Howard would not look up from the papers he chose to rearrange on his desk.

Margaret stood and placed her hands flat upon the opposite side

The Locket

of the principal's desk. She leaned close to the small man before her. Mr. Howard was forced to look straight into the face of his employee.

"I see what's going on here," Margaret calmly stated. "You've received numerous telephone calls last night regarding my assignment dealing with the integration of the public schools. The parents asked for me to be removed from my position, didn't they? So, you made up this tardiness story, and I'm the only one to dispute your word. I lose. You and the racist parents win. It's a lovely world we live in down South. Mark my words, integration is coming, and you, along with all of these small-minded parents, won't be able to fight it much longer. It's all an issue of morals and professional ethics. You will regret the day you made the decision to relieve me of my position."

"I had hoped," Mr. Howard began, "that I would not have to mention the real reason I'm firing you." Margaret's face displayed a bit of curiosity regarding his last statement. "It seems that numerous faculty members and students have smelled alcohol on your breath here at school."

Margaret was more than livid when she said, "If you know what is wise for you, these false allegations will end with those last words out of your mouth. I'm leaving now. So you had better find a substitute teacher for my class. But remember this. Look ahead to your future. It will be short-lived in public education if your bigoted, ignorant ideas don't change."

Margaret turned on her heel and walked back to her classroom, stopping by the janitor's closet for two boxes as she made her way down the hall. She entered the classroom to find her students laughing and talking among themselves. Margaret never acknowledged that the students were not completing their assignment. She packed her personal items located in the desk within ten minutes. When the task was completed, Margaret turned to Carl Black, a student whom she had grown close to over the past school year.

"Could you help me take these boxes to my car?"

"Sure, Mrs. Montgomery."

They walked in silence out of the brick high school building.

When they reached the car, Margaret unlocked the trunk, and they placed the boxes inside. She closed the trunk and turned to Carl.

"Thank you for helping me."

"Are you leaving for good, Mrs. Montgomery?" the boy asked.

"Yes, Carl, I am."

"I know most of the parents called Mr. Howard last night. Everybody knows what those parents wanted. You sure are brave. You stood up for what you believed in. I hope I'll be able to do that someday. You know, I'm joining the army as soon as I graduate from high school. I'll always remember you."

Margaret sadly placed her hand against Carl's arm. Years later, she would discover that he had perished in the fields of Vietnam.

~ ~ ~ ~ ~ ~

Margaret and Anne sat together in the living room of Anne's lavish home. Margaret had driven directly to her sister's house upon leaving the Milner High School. They now sat sipping hot tea on that chilly February afternoon. The two sisters had spent long hours discussing Margaret's current situation. Margaret had been shaken and was in tears when she arrived at her sister's impressive home. Anne had proved to be a great comfort. The sibling conversation that day focused upon the transformations that had occurred in Margaret since her move away from Barnesville years earlier. They also talked about Henry's alcoholism. Margaret felt much better, much stronger following the conversation that had lasted for hours.

Margaret looked at her watch to realize it was after five o'clock. "I need to get home," she said to Anne. "I can't thank you enough for letting me pour out my troubles to you today."

"You know," Anne said, "I'll be there for you if you need anything. Do you need money? I can write you a check now, if you need it."

"No. We're not living high on the hog, but we're getting by. I've made a decision today, Anne. I simply have had enough. I know now that I can't live with Henry another day. I'm going to ask him to leave tonight."

The Locket

"What will you live on without a job?"

"I've got a little money saved up. That should carry me through for a few more months. We'll need to go on and put the house up for sale. The money I split with you from that sale will get me started again. Then, hopefully, I'll find a job outside of teaching. I doubt I'll stay here. I might go back to Virginia. If I could say I ever had a measure of happiness in my marriage after the war, it was during that time in Virginia." Then Margaret spoke her thoughts aloud in a whispered tone. "Maybe," she said, "that happiness stemmed from seeing James so often."

Anne wore a surprised look following Margaret's last comment. At that moment, the telephone rang. Anne left the room to answer the piercing ring. Margaret sat for long moments, waiting for her sister to return.

When Anne did return, it was with a concerned look on her face. "Margaret," she began, "that was a call from the head master at Gordon Military Academy. I'm sure you know him well. He and Daniel went to school together. He really wanted to talk to Daniel to explain to him why he wouldn't hire his brother-in-law. It appears that Henry showed up today wanting a job teaching at Gordon. The headmaster said Henry was so drunk his speech was affected, and he could hardly walk."

"I need to get home," Margaret stated with urgency.

Anne grabbed Margaret's arm before she raced out the door. "I'm so sorry all of these horrible things are happening to you. Please call me if you need anything, even if it's in the middle of the night."

Margaret nodded her agreement. She drove the fifteen-mile stretch of road between Griffin and Barnesville as fast as possible. The dinner hour had approached, and nightfall was upon Margaret as she turned the rickety Ford into her driveway. More lights than usual burned brightly in the two-story, white frame home.

When Margaret walked to the front door, she was met by Matthew. "It's not a good night, Mama," Matthew stated ominously. "I guess Aaron couldn't live another day without telling Dad he had no intention of going to West Point. He just told him about twenty minutes ago. Dad's pretty drunk. Looks like he's been drinking all day. Dad's been yelling a lot, and he's broken some things." Margaret saw shards of glass from her favorite vase lying on the living room floor. A figurine that had once belonged to Granny Harris had been reduced to a hundred or more assorted pieces. Matthew went on. "I made them leave the door to the study open. So I'll hear if he does anything to Aaron. I swear, I'll beat the shit out of him if he hurts Aaron."

Margaret could hear the yelling Matthew described. It was escalating. With an unusual calmness, Margaret walked past the staircase to turn right and enter Granny Harris's old bedroom, which was now Henry's study.

Henry was prowling around the room yelling out his consternation as Aaron sat with his head in his hands. Aaron looked up when his mother entered the room. His face was red, and his eyes were swollen from crying. Aaron looked very relieved to see Margaret.

"Aaron," she said in a calm tone, "go on up to your room now. Tell your brother to go to his room too. I want to talk to your father alone." Aaron looked uncertain, as if fearing for his mother's safety in the presence of the drunken man. "Go ahead. I'll be fine. All of this will be over soon." Aaron left the room.

Margaret turned to the man who was now a stranger in her eyes. His hair, it seemed, had gone gray overnight. He was at least thirty pounds underweight. Dark circles surrounded both eyes, giving them a sunken look. Deep wrinkles had surfaced throughout the face Margaret had once considered to be handsome. The healthy glow of his skin was long gone to be replaced with a sallow hue. Recently, Margaret had even noticed a small tremor causing his head to move ever so slightly during his waking hours. The fifty-one-year-old man before her could easily be seventy-one. Henry was a shell of his former self.

"I tell you, Margaret," Henry slurred. "That boy's going to West Point if I have to drag him there."

"I'm not discussing that right now," Margaret said in a dismissive tone. She took a deep breath and then continued. "I know you

The Locket

probably won't remember much of what I say tonight, but here it goes. When I married you, Henry, I loved you, or I thought I loved you very deeply. The first few years were good, very good. But we weren't together much because of the war. The war changed you. When you came home, you weren't the same Henry. The war was a thief. It stole you from me emotionally, mentally, and physically.

"I made excuses for you. I tried to blame your problems on a thousand different scapegoats. I attempted to change myself to suit your vision of the perfect officer's wife. I did everything I could to make this marriage work. But the war and the army took my marriage from me. We haven't made love in years. And that's because you're too much in love with this." She held up the liquor bottle that sat on Henry's desk.

"You're a drunk. I refuse to allow you to rip us all apart any longer. The voyage to wisdom for me was a long and difficult passage. At times, I thought the turbulent waters of our marriage would prevent me from ever reaching a land of inner peace. I'm there now. I don't love you anymore. Your self-destruction will have to take place elsewhere because you're never sleeping under my roof again. I want a divorce." A deep, satisfying serenity filled Margaret with each liberating word she had spoken.

Henry sat down, stunned at Margaret's words. "Can't we work this out, Margaret? I still love you. That should mean something."

"No. We can't work things out. You love yourself, Henry. And you love liquor. Me? You don't love me. I don't know if you ever loved me. I want you out of this house immediately. You can stay in the Barnesville Motel until you find your own place. I'll pack you a suitcase now."

She walked out of the room to march up the stairs into Henry's bedroom, which had belonged to Anne as a child. Margaret hoped she could erase the memory of Henry's presence in that room as soon as possible. She shoved socks, underwear, pants, and shirts into a solitary suitcase. A wizened, frail Henry entered the bedroom during the process. He said not a word but simply watched the beautiful woman pack his things. Henry's world was tumbling down around him. A choice he made in Jakarta long years ago had brought him to the dead end he faced that night.

The broken man followed his wife downstairs. Margaret placed the suitcase on the front porch. She gathered together her husband's coat and hat. One solitary tear streamed down the lines etched into Henry's cheek. Margaret handed him his coat and hat and said, "You can walk to the motel. It's only two blocks from here. You should have enough money in your wallet to pay for the room. Goodbye, Henry." Margaret watched the thin, weak shadow of a man make his way down the front steps. She sighed and then headed upstairs to tell the boys.

~ ~ ~ ~ ~ ~

Margaret was awakened at four in the morning, from the deepest sleep she had enjoyed in months, by an insistent ring of the doorbell. She arose to don her robe and slippers. She made it down the staircase to be confronted by two police officers. Margaret could see them through the glass in the front door. As they stood on the porch, Margaret opened the door.

"Are you Mrs. Henry Montgomery?" the officer on the right asked.

"Yes, I am. Come inside and get out of the cold." The officers walked into the foyer. Margaret slowly closed the door, dreading what she might be about to hear.

"Mrs. Montgomery," the tallest officer said. "I'm so sorry to have to tell you this." Margaret clutched the banister. Her knuckles were white. "Apparently, your husband stole a car earlier in the night. Mr. Montgomery was driving that car when he was involved in a terrible crash. Between Barnesville and Griffin, he ran off the road and hit a tree head-on." Margaret's face became pale. "He didn't make it, Mrs. Montgomery. We are so sorry for your loss."

Chapter 20

June 1962

Margaret was humming a popular show tune while she straightened the tie on Aaron's dress uniform. She even started singing when she clipped dainty pearls onto her earlobes.

"You know, Mama," Aaron commented, "I haven't heard you hum or sing around the house in years. You used to sing to us a lot when we were little. I remember it."

Margaret smiled at the memory. She had surprised herself with the spontaneous melody. "You're right, Aaron. I've had no desire to sing for many years, but things have changed. I'm happier now. I guess you need to be happy to just start singing like that. I must say, it is a nice feeling."

"It's great to hear you sing again," Aaron responded.

Matthew entered the room during Aaron's last comment. "Oh no," he said. "You mean we've got to listen to off-key singing all morning? I'd better go get some earplugs."

"You hush, young man." Margaret made a face at her feisty son. "This is a special day for the mother of two grown men. Just let me savor it. If I feel like singing, you'll just have to put up with it. Let me go get my camera. This is something else you'll both have to put up with today. I want loads of pictures." She located the camera and snapped several photographs of the two men standing before her.

It was high school graduation day at Gordon Military Academy.

Commencement was scheduled for eleven o'clock that Saturday morning. The Montgomery family, now minus one member, had special plans for later that day. James, Leonard and Maggie, and their daughter, Olivia, had arrived at the Griffin airport earlier that morning. Anne and Daniel were to meet the clan from Connecticut at the airport. Margaret expected them to enter the driveway of her Barnesville home at any time now.

Thoughts of James had burned within Margaret throughout the night. Sleep was elusive, so the proud mother spent most of the evening looking through photographs of her boys, remembering happy occasions, and writing thoughts in her journal. James's presence was felt throughout each of her happiest memories. The powerful man still crossed her mind each day, even though she had not seen him in many years. Margaret looked down at the mint-green summer suit she wore. The suit was an extravagance for which she had sacrificed financially. She wanted to look her best for this special day. She also wanted to look her best for James. Margaret surveyed her appearance in the mirror that was hanging on the wall of the foyer. She pulled the locket from below her collar to wear the sentimental piece of jewelry with joy and reflection upon what it meant to her.

Matthew noticed the action. "You've worn that locket as long as I can remember," he commented. "Did Dad give it to you?"

"No," she replied. "James gave it to me when you boys were babies. It has always meant a great deal to me."

Matthew and Aaron exchanged glances. It was as if their mother were a school girl again on that sunny Saturday morning. They attributed her starry-eyed expression to the upcoming vacation they would all soon enjoy. James had made plans to fly them up to his Connecticut estate following the commencement ceremony. They would be spending the next week in Connecticut, while Maggie, Leonard, and Olivia would take the rare occasion to spend the week in Barnesville, visiting Maggie's family.

Margaret heard the slamming of several car doors outside her home. She and the boys rushed out to greet their friends from up north. Margaret hugged Maggie and Leonard. Following the embraces, her eyes fell upon their daughter, Olivia. She had seen many pictures of Olivia over the years but had never met the young girl. Olivia had just turned twelve years old. She was tall and lanky. Her features reminded Margaret of Maggie at the same age. Olivia's large, dark eyes and the graceful lines of her body made Margaret think of a young doe lightly making her way through a sunny meadow.

"Olivia," Maggie said. "This is Margaret, the woman I've always told you about. Your grandmother worked for Margaret and Anne's family for many years. Mama loved the Harris family so much." Tears sparkled in Maggie's eyes while she looked at the Stafford Avenue home and felt the presence of her mother.

Margaret took Olivia's hand. "I am so happy to meet you, Olivia. You've grown to be so tall and so pretty." Margaret looked at Maggie and Leonard and said, "I hope all of you are still planning to attend the commencement ceremony with us."

A look of trepidation entered Maggie's face. "We would love to, Margaret. I just hope it won't stir up trouble."

"Don't worry about that," Margaret replied. "I've stirred up so much trouble in this county over the past few months, they have all come to expect it. Besides, we've got the house up for sale now, and we'll be moving to Virginia soon. Barnesville knows their little problem on Stafford Avenue will be taken care of soon." There was sadness in Margaret's eyes as she spoke those last words.

Margaret looked past Maggie and Leonard to allow her hungry eyes to rest upon James. His commanding presence was like a beacon to Margaret. He was dressed in a dark suit, as if he had just left the executive board room of his Connecticut-based conglomerate. James's business success had soared to phenomenal heights over the past ten years. Margaret had spied his name in business and financial articles from the *Atlanta Journal and Constitution*. As ever, he remained closely aligned with the March of Dimes as one of its largest contributors of funds and personal time.

Now at fifty years of age, James looked ten years younger. His skin enjoyed a warm, healthy glow. His piercing blue gaze was as sharp as ever. A few wrinkles now visible around his eyes gave him an even more distinguished look. James's wavy blond hair displayed a silvery hue near each temple, but this did not diminish his good looks and obvious strength and vitality. Margaret could see the powerful outline of rippling muscles beneath the jacket he now wore. Her heart fluttered.

"James," she murmured as she rushed up to the man who entered her thoughts each day. Margaret leaned down to hug James and place a small kiss upon his cheek. He held her hand to plant a tender kiss on the softness of her skin. "It's been so long since we've seen each other," Margaret said in a breathy voice. She felt a bit unsteady and weak.

"Way too long," James responded. "I'm so glad to be here for this special day." Margaret nodded, feeling overcome with emotion. The other adults exchanged surprised glances at the obvious intensity of emotion they now observed between the man and woman.

Margaret felt their gazes upon her, so she fought to hide the depth of her feelings for James. As Anne and Daniel walked up, she alerted everyone there was no time to spare. There were a few more greetings to be exchanged, and then everyone filed into automobiles for the short trip to Gordon Military Academy.

When they arrived a few minutes later, Margaret spied numerous old familiar faces from her youth. Parents and grandparents of young men and women graduates were walking out onto the football field for the Saturday-morning ceremony. When everyone got out of their vehicles and James was ensconced in his chair, the group traversed the parking lot to the field across the way. As they reached the gate to accept written programs handed out by various ushers, Margaret could feel the pointed stares delivered by local residents well known to her. The only dark-skinned faces there that day belonged to Maggie, Leonard, and Olivia. Even though Maggie was a native of this small southern town, the disapproval of her family's attendance at an all-white affair was clearly written upon face after face. Margaret would forever be astonished that hatred for another human being could be based solely upon skin color.

"Walk with pride, Maggie," Margaret whispered to her dear

The Locket

friend. "You have a right to be here just like everyone else." Maggie looked over at her friend with a nervous smile. Margaret squeezed her hand.

The group settled into their seats. Matthew and Aaron left the circle of family and friends to join their classmates inside the school before their processional. Maggie, Leonard, and Olivia sat sandwiched, in a protective manner, between Anne and Daniel on one side and Margaret and James on the opposite side. Margaret's eyes flashed in defiance at local folks who gawked at the mixed company. Then she realized she should not allow herself to feel resentment or hatred in her heart for those poor, unenlightened individuals. She looked beside her at James's handsome form. He made her feel secure and happy, feelings she had just started to enjoy once again.

"It's so fitting for you to be here today," she whispered to the man beside her. James gave her a warm smile.

The processional began, and they watched the proud graduates file out onto the field to take their rightful place. The male graduates were resplendent in their dress uniforms, and the female graduates wore the traditional black cap and gown. Margaret's heart fluttered to see her two boys, now men. She had to keep reminding herself that their boyhood was over. They would be entering the workforce soon.

With sadness, Margaret had informed the boys weeks ago that she would be unable to pay for college tuition right now but hoped to be in a position to help them out in that endeavor within a few more years. Matthew, who had never really wanted to attend college, was not disturbed by the announcement. Margaret read the disappointment in Aaron's eyes, even though he attempted to hide his feelings. She surmised that both boys could live at home and save their income until they were ready to live out on their own. Margaret was in no hurry to see them leave. They both helped chase away the loneliness that invaded her being.

They all listened to the valedictorian's moving speech. The speaker was Sadie Samuels's grandson, and Margaret knew the elderly woman, sitting somewhere among the crowd, must be filled with pride. Tears gleamed in Margaret's eyes as she watched each of her twin sons receive their high school diploma. It closed an era in their lives. The future was so uncertain, but Margaret knew it had to be brighter than her recent past.

As the commencement ceremony came to an end and the headmaster delivered his closing remarks, all of the graduates from the class of 1962 removed their caps to fling them high into the air. Shouts of joy were heard throughout the applause. The graduates scattered to be reunited with their proud families. Matthew and Aaron made it back to their family group with large, exhilarating smiles. They all chatted together for a few more minutes.

When they began to make their way back to the parking lot, Margaret saw a local man she had known to be a disgruntled customer of her father's in the past. The man walked near them with his wife on his arm. He then spoke in a tone meant for all nearby to hear. "I didn't know they let darkies come to graduation around here. What's the world comin' to?" A sneer was evident on the man's face. Leonard, Maggie, and Olivia had heard the man's stabbing words. Margaret saw Leonard clench his fists. Maggie quickly touched his arm to staunch any possible confrontation.

James wheeled his chair directly in front of the man who had spoken the offensive words. Margaret had never known James to use his disability as an advantage. On that day, he would. James looked at the man and said, "The world, my friend, is coming to a place where those that are different will be treated equally. There will be a day, not too far from now, when a person like me with a disability, and those who have become disabled by society, simply due to their skin color, will enjoy the same rights and privileges that you do. I hope you live to see that day. You had best be hoping that something will touch your heart to rid it of the hatred that fills it now."

A pinched expression entered the man's face. His wife looked frightened. They all knew the stranger would not raise his hand to a man living his life from the confines of a wheelchair. The irony of the situation stemmed from the knowledge that incredible strength

The Locket

and power emanated from this man who should have been weakened by the unfortunate physical limitations he experienced.

"Let's go home, Shirley," the stranger commanded his wife.

Their entire group laughed following the confrontation. Maggie reached down to hug the man who had taken care of her and her immediate family for years. A much older Sadie Samuels walked slowly up to Margaret. She limped and now relied upon a walker to aid her mobility.

Sadie winked at Margaret. "I've been hearing an awful lot about you lately. I admire a woman who stands by her beliefs. Just keep it up, honey pie. If I can help you in any way, let me know. I enjoy giving these ignorant asses around here something to chew on." They all giggled. Sadie moved along to be with her family.

James had witnessed the encounter. "Now that," James commented, "is a woman I sure would like to get to know."

~ ~ ~ ~ ~ ~

Margaret and James waved goodbye to Matthew and Aaron as they rode away from the Connecticut estate in a long, sleek limousine. James had engaged another domestic employee to take the young men to New York for the next three days. He had made arrangements for splendid accommodations, elaborate dining experiences, a Broadway show, and a Yankee's baseball game. Margaret knew her sons would have a wonderful time. A deep, satisfying feeling invaded Margaret when they entered James's lavish home. She looked at the opulence and splendor that surrounded her, a sharp contrast to the financial struggle she had experienced over the past year. Her road ahead would continue to be difficult.

James looked at Margaret. "I'm certain you're tired. Take some time to rest, and I'll meet you in the solarium for drinks before dinner at seven thirty."

Margaret nodded her agreement to the arrangement. As she walked up the grand staircase to her bedroom, she felt the weariness that James had described. The sleepless night before was catching up with her. Margaret entered the old, familiar guest bedroom to note that it had been redecorated in lavender and white. Each detail within the room had been chosen with care. Margaret decided she liked the change to lavender. It was a peaceful color.

Margaret slipped out of the mint-green suit and then settled her naked body between the sheets. She enjoyed the feel of the bed covers on her bare skin. Before too long, her eyelids drooped, and she entered into a deep sleep. Margaret dreamed of James when they were younger. She replayed events that had happened in her life prior to her marriage and other events that had occurred when the children were babies. James was ever present in each scene of her dreams. It had been that way for a long time. At one point in her sleepy musings, Margaret reached forward to be folded into the powerful man's embrace. He reached down to explore her mouth with his lips. Margaret then awoke with a start while beads of perspiration trickled down her graceful neck. Her heart raced, and her chest heaved as she took quick breaths.

She looked at the clock to discover that it was six thirty. There would be enough time to draw a bath and take a good soak. Margaret noticed that someone had placed a bottle of her favorite wine in a bucket of ice that stood on a stand. She knew James had taken care of every detail. He never forgot the importance of little things in life. Margaret remembered he had once told her that little things were the glue to keep healthy relationships together. As she touched the piece of jewelry that encircled her neck, Margaret realized that the words contained within that locket had proven to be true throughout her life, "Eyes Opened by Truth. Pain Healed by Love." James's wisdom was often astonishing.

An hour later, Margaret scrutinized her appearance in the bedroom mirror. She had chosen a beige sweater and skirt set. The sweater had three-quarter-length sleeves and a folded-down collar that was worn off the shoulders, necessitating that she don a lacy, strapless bra. The set hugged Margaret's figure provocatively. Margaret had chosen to grow her hair a bit longer over the past year. On that evening, she swept the dark tresses into a French twist in the

The Locket

back. A few stubborn, curly tendrils of hair graced the nape of her neck and the right side of her forehead. The loose bits of dark locks served to soften her hairstyle and made her appear much younger than her forty-one years.

When Margaret was satisfied with her reflection, she left the bedroom to walk down the stairs and meet James in the solarium. James had chosen a beige summer suit of linen for the intimate dinner that evening. As Margaret entered the room, they both smiled to notice they had selected matching colors for the occasion. James watched Margaret's graceful body that was accentuated by the clinging fabric of her sweater and skirt. He noticed the light glistening on the gold locket he had given her long years ago. The young woman who had accepted the locket so long ago was, most likely, gone for good, to be replaced with an older woman who now saw life through a new and different lens.

James poured two glasses of wine. He handed one to Margaret. She accepted the drink with a grateful smile.

"I'm certain you're very proud of your two sons," James commented. "They've grown into fine young men. Have they made specific plans yet for life beyond high school?"

Margaret released a long sigh before answering James's question. She had spent numerous sleepless nights fretting over her inability to fund a college education for each twin. The reality of college enrollment for her sons would remain elusive for some time to come. A seemingly endless chapter of her life had just concluded. She was starting over again with limited finances.

"Both of them have plans to start working this summer. They want to save some money before entering a university. I suppose it will be good for them. Gaining a little maturity before settling down to study never hurt anyone." Margaret attempted to sound flippant about the forced decision she and her sons had made regarding the delay in gaining a college degree. "Anyway," she added, "I don't really think Matthew is college material."

James smiled and nodded. "What about you?" he asked. "Have you made definitive plans for your future?"

"Anne and I have put the house up for sale. In fact, Anne informed me yesterday that she has located a very interested buyer. When the house sells, I'll be leaving Barnesville. I plan to move back to Alexandria, Virginia. I've told Aaron and Matthew that they can move with me or find themselves a place in Barnesville. They're both quite protective of me. So, I suppose they will move with me to Virginia. I've got to get away. I feel so smothered in that small town." James had never heard Margaret sound quite so decisive or determined.

"So, you've resigned from your teaching position?"

"Let's just say I was relieved of my position several months ago," Margaret said in an offhanded manner.

"What happened?" James was curious.

"It's a long story, so I'll just give you the major details. I was way too outspoken regarding my support of integrating the public school system. I discussed my feelings in various classrooms and within the community. Many parents complained, and I was fired—fired, I might add, due to excessive tardiness, which was a fabricated reason. Needless to say, I'm a social outcast in Barnesville now. That doesn't really bother me, but the town has left a bitter taste in my mouth. I need a bit more time to heal the wounds in my soul. I can't do that in Barnesville."

"I understand how you feel." James admired Margaret's spirit and the courage it must have taken to openly voice her beliefs regarding racial equality. He was certain the Barnesville community had not been ready to hear her words. Her decisions were good ones. It was time for her to move on.

They enjoyed a casual, intimate dinner served on the back patio. It was a warm summer evening. Small candles, placed on their table and in various locations around the patio, flickered in a light breeze that carried the scent of lilac. Margaret enjoyed the meal. She felt so at peace with herself now. She exuded a confidence that James had not seen before. Margaret's aura was attractive, and he found it difficult to tear his gaze from the lovely woman before him. Their dinner conversation had been light, and Margaret had a smile on her

The Locket

lips much of the time. They rounded off their meal with a delectable ice-cream confection.

When their dinner was concluded and a chill had entered the evening air, James suggested they return to the solarium to relax with some brandy. After handing Margaret her glass, he looked directly at the desirable woman in front of him with sadness in his eyes. "I was so sorry to hear of Henry's tragic death. I apologize for not coming down to Barnesville during that difficult time. It's just that Henry had grown to hate me over the years. He wouldn't have wanted me there."

Sadness also entered Margaret's gaze, but she would shed no more tears over Henry's self-destruction. "It's all been so hard, but Henry was determined to destroy himself. I've tried to remember the good in Henry and the good times in our marriage. His alcoholism ripped everything apart. I've searched my memories to decide when things began to go wrong. I first noticed it when he returned from the war. Over the years, things got worse and worse. It was clear that Henry loved the bottle much more than he ever loved me."

With an inner strength glowing in her gaze, Margaret went on. "The day I lost my job, I confronted him with my feelings. Henry had killed the love I once felt for him. I couldn't allow him to destroy me or my sons' lives any longer. I told him that I no longer loved him. Then I packed his bags and asked him to leave. I went on and told him I wanted a divorce. He was supposed to walk down to the Barnesville motel. That was two blocks away. But a neighbor of ours had left the keys in his car. Henry stole the car and drove off. Later that night, he died in a terrible car crash. The role I played to create his distraught state of mind that night will haunt me forever."

James's blue eyes flashed. "Don't take on that guilt to bear. Remember, Henry made his own choices. His weaknesses were his demise."

Margaret gazed at the handsome man sitting beside her. She remembered the lease agreement she had found beside Henry's drunken form in the backyard. "James, there is something I've wanted to ask you about since Henry's death. The night before he died, he passed out in a drunken stupor in the backyard. When we were getting him into the house, I found some papers on the ground. He had apparently retrieved them from the storage shed when he blacked out. He was way too drunk to explain them, so I didn't bother to ask. The papers were a lease agreement for an apartment located on Seventeenth Street in Atlanta. The papers were old. They were dated sometime in 1945, and they were signed by you. What did it mean?"

James knew this liberating moment would arrive. The time had come for Margaret to know the truth. James took a deep breath and said, "I'm going to answer that question, but I need to show you something. Wait here while I get it." He wheeled from the room toward his library and home office. Margaret was puzzled. She sensed that a shroud of secrecy had obliterated her vision of truth in the past.

James wheeled his chair back into the solarium. With ease, he transferred his muscular form onto the couch to again sit beside the captivating woman. He removed his jacket, loosened his tie, and retrieved some yellowed paper from his pocket. Margaret knew she needed all the strength she could find for what she was about to hear.

"Margaret," he began, "I hope you will find it in your heart to forgive me for my part in this deception. As you hear what I am saying to you, remember that I owed a debt of gratitude to Henry for the physical assistance he provided me over all of those long college years. In 1945, he asked me for a favor. It was a favor I could easily grant. So, I did. I did it primarily because an innocent victim was involved." James quickly swallowed the rest of his brandy. He handed Margaret the letter Henry had written to him many years ago explaining the situation with Ma Le and Susan.

James watched Margaret's face as she read each line of the letter. Her hands shook when she swallowed the bitter pill of Henry's deception. After the letter was finished, she sat there for long moments, mesmerized by the scrawling penmanship sending her, it seemed, a message from the grave.

She slowly looked up at the handsome, powerful man who sat beside her. Tears glimmered in his dark blue gaze. She touched his

The Locket

hand and said, "I forgive you, James. I admire your loyalty to a friend. I am forever amazed at your far-reaching concern for innocent and helpless individuals trapped in situations not of their own making. This letter explains the mysteries of my life with Henry. It's somehow strangely comforting to discover the cause behind the distance in our marriage. I never knew the real Henry. I never understood him. Now I do." Margaret touched James's strong hand. "What has become of Ma Le and Susan?"

James gazed at Margaret with more adoration and respect. It had taken great strength of character to forgive him for the role he had played during those years of deception. He would be forever amazed at the grace and poise Margaret now possessed. It made her utterly breathtaking. James tore his mind from passionate musings about the woman beside him to answer her question.

"It's quite a sad story, really. I received a frantic call from Susan right around the time of Henry's death. It seems that her mother, Ma Le, had suffered a terrible nervous breakdown requiring hospitalization. It's my impression that the woman had been behaving in an odd manner for some time. I think the physical part of her relationship with Henry had ended a long time ago."

"Is she fine now?"

"No. I don't think she ever will be fine again. She has been committed to a state psychiatric hospital in Decatur, Georgia. That's just outside of Atlanta, so Susan can visit her. From what I hear through Susan, she's shown little, if any, improvement. This is shocking to believe, but the doctors have discovered that Ma Le actually murdered her own mother back in Jakarta, Indonesia, to expedite their departure from that war-torn region to the promise of a better life here in America. It's ironic that this is the better life she inherited."

Margaret released a long, slow sigh at the numerous shocking revelations of the evening. It was a cleansing feeling.

"Tell me about Susan," she stated with interest.

A light came into James's gaze, and a slight smile touched his lips. "I was hoping you would want to know about her. She's an incredible young woman with wisdom beyond her years. Susan is articulate, intelligent, and strong. How she lived with a deranged mother like that for so many years, I'll never know. She now lives in the apartment on Seventeenth Street by herself and has just started a full-time job at the Atlanta Public Library. The scope of her intelligence is broad. She was the valedictorian of her senior class."

A small smile touched Margaret's mouth. "I suppose you've been supporting her financially over the last few months."

"I've only paid the rent. Now, I won't even be doing that. She is determined to make it on her own. Independence is very important to Susan. I would like you to meet her someday."

Margaret's eyes widened a bit at James's last comment. She knew him to be an excellent judge of character. She believed the wonderful things she had heard that evening regarding Susan. Still, Margaret felt a measure of trepidation at the thought of establishing a relationship with the young woman. "I just don't know about meeting her yet ..." The uncertainty in Margaret's tone was undeniable.

James reached over to pour them both more brandy. Margaret swallowed a large gulp of the spirits to calm the nervous jitters she had experienced since seeing James again for the first time in years. She thought back to the enchanted Christmas she had spent with James so long ago. The fire felt in the pit of her stomach on that winter's evening had not dimmed over time.

The same fire burned within James. He longed to hold this elusive woman, to taste her, to touch her soft skin, to murmur his deepest desires. James knew their evening of truth had brought them both to a fork in the road of life's journey. He could not remember a time when thoughts of Margaret were not part of each daily routine. James needed to possess this woman. He reached down to bring her soft hand to his lips. He pressed the softness of her palm against his cheek.

"It took great courage for you to speak out regarding your opposition to the injustices suffered by others based merely upon race. It took great strength to endure the injustices of your marriage.

The Locket

You've now reached a point where you can walk in wisdom with open eyes."

Tears fell from Margaret's dark eyes at the honesty of his words. James pulled Margaret into a fierce embrace. His head bent to rake his lips over hers in an exploring kiss. His tongue probed the sweetness of her mouth. He trailed kisses along the elegant column of her neck that caused waves of excitement to consume her. Margaret could not remember the last time she had been touched in such a manner.

"I want you, Margaret," James murmured in a hoarse voice. "I want to see you, to taste you, to touch you. I want to make love to you in every possible way. I love you. I had to know you could be mine completely with no thoughts of any other man. I know that now. Let me show you my love."

Margaret's heart raced at James's words. She now saw the love she held so close in her heart reflected in this man's eyes.

"Yes, James. Make love to me tonight. I want to feel you inside of me. You've always been in my heart. I love you."

They fell into each other's arms again and exchanged hungry kisses. Margaret's hands reached out to further loosen James's tie and to unbutton his shirt. Her hands explored the hardness of his expansive muscular chest while drinking in the sweet wine of his kiss.

In a moment, James raised his head to speak. His mouth remained close to Margaret's crimson lips. "I'll meet you in my room in a few moments," he murmured with uneven breaths. Margaret nodded her approval. She left the handsome man's warm embrace to walk from the room in an unsteady manner.

By the time she reached her bedroom, Margaret was weak with desire. She dropped her clothes onto the floor to don a deep red, satin night gown with delicate straps and a plunging neckline. Margaret covered the revealing gown with a robe of the same fabric and color. She then made her way out of her room and down to the end of the hall. She knocked on the door to James's room but received no answer. Thinking that he must still be downstairs, she entered the room.

James's bedroom was quite masculine. It was decorated with dark blue and burgundy accents. All of the wood furnishings were mahogany. A soft lamp glowed in one corner of the room. Candles flickered on both bedside tables and in various locations throughout the room. Margaret could hear water running in the bathroom sink, so she realized that James, the man who would forever fill her thoughts, was just beyond the dark wood of the door.

At that moment, James opened the door to gaze upon Margaret's lovely form. James wore dark blue silk pajama pants. His massive, muscled chest was tan and bare. The rippling muscles of his shoulders and washboard-like stomach made Margaret burn with desire. Neither of them spoke a word. On that night, they would speak with their bodies. Margaret dropped her robe to the floor. Her breasts, pressed together by the bodice of the provocative gown, moved sensuously up and down with each breath she took. She walked over to turn off the lamp, wanting to see their lovemaking in the soft glow of candlelight. She then slipped beneath the sheets of his bed. He, in turn, lithely transferred his body onto the large bed. They fell into an exploring embrace.

James kissed Margaret with the softness of his lips and tongue. His hands trailed over her shoulders to tug at the delicate straps. The straps gave way as she lifted her body for James to remove the barrier between them. He pulled the covers back to reveal her erotic nakedness. James then hesitated a moment to gaze, with adoration, at the delicate curves and lines of her body.

Margaret reached over to pull down the silk pants James now wore. In a moment, he was fully naked before her, his skin glistening in the flickering glow of the candlelight. His manhood was fully aroused. Margaret trembled with the intensity of her excitement.

She touched the hardness of his erection. "It's been so long, James," she murmured. Her pulse quickened.

"I know," he replied in a whispered tone. "It's just you and me now. I love you. I want to explore every inch of you." That is just what he did. His eyes, his hands, his velvet tongue raked over her body in erotic waves. James was an incredible lover who read every movement, every nuance to produce a roller-coaster ride of pleasure Margaret had never before experienced.

Three times that night, the couple submitted to their animalistic urges to become one flesh. Each climax became more intense, shocking Margaret with newer heights of ecstasy. The smell of James's nectar was intoxicating. She never wanted their erotic night of pleasure to end.

As small slivers of light streamed into the bedroom that next morning, Margaret opened her sleepy, satisfied eyes to find James giving her an adoring look. She smiled back into her lover's knowing gaze.

"I love you, Margaret." He again spoke the words he had held deep in his heart for years.

"I love you too. I must have loved you since the boys were babies. But my eyes were closed, and I didn't allow myself to recognize it." It gave Margaret an odd sense of freedom to voice her feelings.

James continued to gaze tenderly at Margaret. He hesitated not a moment before he presented her with an important query.

"Will you be my wife?"

"Yes, James," she replied with a slow, intimate smile. "I would be honored to become your wife."

Chapter 21

June 1966

Margaret gazed with fondness at the accomplished young woman sitting across from the luncheon table. It was difficult to imagine that Susan had only been a part of her life for about four years. Soon after Margaret's marriage to James, the persuasive man had broken through all of his wife's reservations regarding the young lady before her. From the moment the two women met, a deep and lasting bond was created. Margaret had slipped into the role of a substitute mother for Susan. To Margaret, it felt almost as if Susan were an extension of the fathomless love she held for James. It had been quite fitting and natural to bring Susan into their new family.

Ma Le's psychiatric condition had not improved. Most of the time, Susan's biological mother never displayed even a glimmer of recognition for her daughter during a visit. The frequency of Susan's visits had decreased to only two or three times a year. Margaret's presence was now a constant in Susan's life, filling a void for both women.

Susan's keen mind will take her far, thought Margaret. She had just completed her undergraduate degree in biology from Vassar. The decision to fund a college education for Susan had been an easy one for James and Margaret. Susan now had plans to enter medical school that fall. Margaret admired her drive, determination, and boundless energy.

The Locket

On this bright, sunny day, Margaret surmised that this would be Susan's last summer of fun and freedom before the pressures of postgraduate studies and professional life descended upon her. Margaret was certain Susan could face the challenges ahead.

The two women sat on the back patio of the Connecticut estate, enjoying a delectable lunch. They had been discussing their shared interest in reading. "Margaret," Susan began with a gleam in her eye, "you really should think about writing a book someday. You're always scribbling in those journals. Why not organize them into a novel?"

"I don't know if I've got what it takes to become a novelist." The idea was appealing and a little frightening.

"You would have no problem at all," Susan replied with confidence. "We could start on it together this summer. We may never have another vacation like this together again. I bet we would learn an awful lot about ourselves in the process." Margaret was intrigued.

"But what could I write about?"

"It needs to be about something you know intimately. Something you may have experienced throughout your life." There was a moment of silence, and then a broad smile crossed over Susan's face. "I've got it. You could write about other mothers."

"What do you mean by other mothers?"

"I mean women like Mattie and Miss Winnie in your life. You've told me so much about them. They were your other mothers. Don't get me wrong. It sounds as if you had a wonderful mother of your own and a terrific childhood. But Mattie and Miss Winnie in Barnesville also played key roles in your development as a woman. They were your other mothers." Susan paused a minute and then said with tears in her eyes, "And you're my other mother."

A tender look came over Margaret's face to hear the heartfelt emotion in her other child's voice. She stood to embrace the young woman. At that moment, Leonard walked out of the French doors onto the patio.

"Margaret," he called, "Aaron is on the telephone asking to speak with you."

Margaret turned back to Susan. "Excuse me just a minute."

She walked into the solarium and picked up the telephone. In a warm voice, she said, "Hello, dear. How are you?"

"I'm all right, Mama, I guess." Margaret could sense a nervous edge in the voice on the other end of the line.

"What's wrong?" She asked.

"I've been drafted, Mama." His voice quivered. "They will be sending me to Vietnam."